I0545859

Sweet Dreams

Book six in the McKenna Clan Series

Christine Young

Published by Rogue Phoenix Press, LLP
Copyright © 2020

ISBN: 978-1-62420-595-8

Credits
Cover Artist: Designs by Ms G
Editor: Sherry Derr-Wille

Published in the United States of America

Chapter One

Cactus Junction

Guy McKenna negligently leaned against the bar in the Red Neck Bar and Grill, a beer in hand, watching the line dancing. He was bored and tired of waiting for something he didn't think would ever come his way. In the pub the air was stagnant and the music boisterous. He relished the noise as well as the crowds that filled the small bar on Saturday nights. It took his mind away from the fact he was nearing twenty-seven and he still had not found his mate. His brothers and sisters were happy, content in their lives with children.

After returning from Iraq, he needed the familiar sights and sounds. So much that happened over there had been out of his control and the night visions terrified him, would cause him to wake in a cold sweat. They were nightmares that taunted him mocking his very existence.

Now his dreams and visions changed.

Needing to forget the dreams haunting him night after night for the last month, he stayed at the bar when he would have usually gone home. His soul mate permeated his thoughts but he'd never seen her, didn't know where to find her, certainly not in the Red Neck Saloon in Cactus Junction. He supposed stranger things could happen. When he closed his eyes at night, falling into a deep sleep, her face was central to the entire dream. The sight of her was etched in his head, seared through all eternity.

If he saw her, he would know her.

He watched a young couple kissing in the corner of the bar, the young man's hands roaming in too many places they shouldn't. He shrugged to himself, knowing if the opportunity with his soul mate presented itself, he'd be doing the same, but in private. Tempted to tell them to get a room, he kept his words behind his teeth. He wasn't about to share his mate with anyone. Second thoughts assailing him, he almost walked over to the couple to tell them there were rooms upstairs they could rent for the night or a few hours.

The McKennas were too well known in this state to let anyone see them share intimacies with a soul mate or any woman for the matter. The gossip would spread quicker than a man could blink. He had his share of women over his lifetime. He needed to move on and find meaning in this world. His siblings had found their mates. Now it was his turn, but where was she?

Well hell, if not in Cactus Junction, where then?

His beer glass drained he turned at the bar, taking his gaze from the doorway for only a moment to request a second beer. Dipping his hand in the bowl of peanuts, he was surprised by the sensation scurrying down his spine. The hair on the back of his neck prickled, stood on end. A fine sheen of sweat formed on his forehead. Unnerved, unsettled, excited for something. He knew not what.

The soft fresh scent of oranges waffled through the air. For a moment he couldn't think, couldn't breathe. When the moment finally passed, he sucked in a huge draft of air.

"What are you drinking, cowboy?"

Her body pressed against his, luscious curves that would fill his hands seemed to be the focus of all the sensations coursing through him, a primal heat filling his soul. He was afraid to look at her, terrified he might do something incredibly foolish. A one-night stand was not something he wanted.

This was different.

The lady's voice was a sultry purr sending his body quivering with need, titillating shock waves pulsing through him. A woman's body let alone the sound of her voice had never affected him like this. He paused a moment as tension mounted, radiated through him from toes to head, stopping momentarily in his groin. Slowly, he turned to look at the face possessing the amazing voice and the full curves he wanted to wrap his hands around. His breath stopped for a few seconds at the vision smiling at him. He was staring into the face he had dreamed of.

His mate.

His woman for life and into all eternity. His mouth went dry while his gut churned in anticipation.

He cleared his throat, but his words still came out in a feeble croak, nothing like his normal husky timber. "Beer." The bartender handed him the bottle he asked for earlier.

"Pinot Gris," she told the bartender, leaning casually on the bar. Half turned toward him, her body was as sultry as her voice. The blouse she wore was unbuttoned so far down he could see the lace of her bra. It was tucked into a tight-fitting pair of short shorts. She didn't seem to care she was half dressed while he was lusting after her. He could barely keep his tongue in his mouth as well as keep himself from drooling.

"Drinks on me," he told her then nodded to the bartender. "Keep them coming. I think we're going to be here for a little while."

Long enough so he could ask her to come home with him tonight or find out where she lived. He couldn't let this one go without getting vital information.

"Yes, sir, Mr. McKenna," the man said. "Let me know if you need anything else. Obviously, drinks are on the house."

She held the glass by the stem and leisurely sipped seeming to keep her gaze on him. "Thank you," she murmured, licking her lips while she slowly twirled the contents of the glass, her eyes seeming to be focused on the liquid, no longer on him. He meant to change that, needing her full attention. Nothing less would do.

"What brings you to Cactus Junction?" he asked politely, intending to know everything about this lady.

Besides the basics such as what's your name, this seemed the simplest place to start.

She looked at the bar, her long blond hair falling in front of her face. When she looked up, "Guess one could say I'm looking for something and I'm running from something."

She pushed the hair behind her ears, her blouse parting provocatively with the gesture. The soft swell of her breasts was oh so noticeable.

Unable to keep his eyes from the view she presented, he decided not to try. If she was showing, he was looking. He wanted to reach out and touch the strands just to see how soft they were.

"A riddle?" he asked, "Would you like to find a table?"

Preferably a table in a dark corner where no one would see them.

She was shaking her head, lips smushed together provocatively her soft lips parting slightly. "No riddle, just the truth." She offered a tiny smile and slight shrug of slim shoulders. "And yes, a table would be nice. I don't usually talk to strangers," she mumbled, staring into her glass before turning her attention to his mouth. "For some reason I find odd, you don't seem to be a stranger."

He wasn't a stranger. He needed to tell her the truth but understood she'd have to figure it all out for herself. "Follow me." He leaned forward then waved his hand at the bartender, "Have Jan bring us some fries."

To the lady who had yet to introduce herself, guess he hadn't introduced himself either, "You hungry."

"I could eat a few fries," she admitted as she followed him, her smile a bit hesitant. "As long as we've ketchup."

At the table, he held out his hand in greeting, "I'm Guy McKenna."

He paused waiting for her to reciprocate. He was acting like a love-struck fool, knew it. Didn't care.

"No names between us is so much easier. However, if you insist, I'm Cas Doyle."

"Irish, I see."

"Scottish?" she asked.

Her elbows rested on the table while her fists were under her chin seeming to hold it up.

The fries arrived while they stared at each other. Guy, for the first time since he could remember, was tongue-tied. He thought when he met his mate none of this first date stuff would be happening. *This wasn't even a first date.*

"Okay..." he paused, "Yes, Scottish once, now American. I could tell you the story of my clan, but it would probably bore you to tears."

"You really don't have to make idle conversation. I like you and if you must know, I think silence," she paused, staring at him with her summer sky blue eyes, "is refreshing."

Her glass of pinot was almost empty so he ordered a second. Sometimes silence was refreshing, but he needed to know more about her. Everything about her, he amended. If he had to close the bar with her tonight to learn a few things, he would. He wanted the answers to the riddle she inadvertently challenged him with. "Where do you live?"

She shrugged her delicately slim shoulders again before smiling at him. "Here and there. Mostly there. Never stayed in one place very long. I'd like that to change though."

"That's mighty vague," he told her, looking for something more relevant. If she was running from someone or something, the more he knew the easier it would be to find her if she left here without a word. That thought sent a cold chill down his spine in the heated atmosphere and called him back to the very reality they were just meeting. He had no hold over her.

"I'm guessing you live here, in Cactus Junction."

She reached out to touch his hand, effectively changing the subject from her to him.

The sensation sent a jolt of sexual longing straight to his groin. He wanted to pull that beautiful hand to his mouth and kiss her fingers, suck them into his mouth but realized prudently it was too soon. Scaring her away was not a good ploy, not when he had so much at stake. "Just down the road then off it to the right. Can't get to my house unless you walk or ride a horse. Well, a Harley would get you there too."

"See, you like your privacy and perhaps silence also. We are much the same in that," she told him while she held her glass of wine to her lips, her blue eyes shining provocatively above the rim. "I don't get along well with very many people. I'm a bit of a recluse I've been told, but I like you."

The second glass arrived. The waiter took the first away. Guy wondered how many he should let her drink or if she would stop herself. He did mean to take her home tonight if she was agreeable. He really wasn't a drink 'em up take 'em home kind of guy. Yet that was exactly what he was doing.

For the greater good, he told himself.

He had an excuse or better, a reason. She was, after all his soul mate. She would be willing without too much to drink. Maybe not tonight. He wanted her tonight.

"I like my privacy but I wouldn't call myself a recluse," he agreed, his voice soft. "Only because I haven't found anyone to share my home with. Perhaps if I do find someone, I'll build a road to my house. Wouldn't want my special person to get lost trying to find her way home."

"Me too," she said, moistening her lips, her small pink tongue sweeping erotically across her bottom lip, "like privacy and my laptop more than people."

He wondered if she knew how provocative that tiny gesture was. Anything she did would arouse him he admitted. Absolutely anything. "So, you come from here and there. Where was the last place you called home?" he asked, needing to back up to the first question which wasn't actually the first question. Eventually, he'd find out what she was running from.

"I was in graduate school. Stanford." She pursed her lips then finished the glass of wine. "So," she tapped her fingers on the base of the glass, "I guess you could call that the last place I called home."

He ordered both of them another. Clearly distraught, it seemed she didn't want to open up to him. Yet he craved knowledge about her.

"You left. Why?" He drummed his fingers on the table, waiting for a response, impatient yet trying to understand her hesitancy because they didn't know each other. "I guess that's none of my business."

"You're right, it's not but I don't think you'll hurt me. I feel safe with you and I don't understand the reasons. Don't feel that way around men very often. Don't talk to men." Another glass of wine was set in front of her. She stared at it for a moment before looking to him again. "Are you trying to get me drunk? I should slow down."

"No and whatever you want."

Her dark sooty lashes lowered making a perfect arch across her high delicate cheekbones then, "I guess it is up to me to say no."

Lord, but he didn't want her to say no to anything. "What were

6

you studying?"

Perhaps that would be an easier question and might give him some insight into his recalcitrant soul mate. She obviously felt some attraction for him. Unfortunately, she didn't appear to understand exactly just how potent and raw that magnetism was between them.

"Paranormal abnormalities in the southwest. There have been plausible sightings, you know, shapeshifters, mostly big cats but there was a wolf sighting a few years ago. I left my studies because something terrified me. I started running but whatever it was it followed me. For some reason I ended up here."

His heart caught in his throat. He wasn't sure where to go with this information but knew she wasn't telling him the entire story. "Do you think shapeshifters exist?"

Slowly, he sipped keeping his gaze focused on her over the rim of the glass.

She smiled at him again. This smile was somehow different. One perfect eyebrow rose a fraction. Then, "I know they exist. I know something else too."

He finished his beer before ordering another round for both of them. After minutes of thought, "How? How do you know something so strange or is it just speculation?"

She shrugged those delicate shoulders again, ones he wanted to kiss from one side to the other, "Just my gut. No, actually I've seen one, a coal black jaguar shapeshifter in my dreams. I've seen all of him except his face. I've seen him take his clothes off and shift then in another dream I've seen him change from the jaguar back to a human."

Cas had seen him... naked. Or had she seen one of his brothers or sisters? No, he was sure she was speaking about him.

She said him. "What do you mean?" he asked, suddenly feeling out of his element and a bit at a disadvantage.

She'd seen him naked and... strangely he didn't feel at all violated. He had this unthinkable need to ask her if she liked what she saw. He drew in a slow breath of air while he thought about all she told him.

"I think I've had a bit too much to drink." She finished the glass in front of her then changing the subject, "Should be getting back to my room before I fall asleep right here."

"At the hotel?" he asked, "I'll walk you back, unless you'd like to come home with me."

Where did that come from? He didn't want her to think all he wanted from her was a one nightstand when he craved a lifetime. If she was truly running from something dangerous though, he wasn't about to leave her alone and unprotected in the hotel. If she refused to come home with him, he'd stand guard outside her room.

Or inside, female permitting.

"You said," she paused, "a person had to walk. Don't know if I can make it that far in these shoes." Cas looked at her feet before she let him help her to stand then leaned on him. "I'm feeling a wee bit tipsy. I think I drank too much." Her words began to slur a bit.

She was adorable, endearing.

"You don't have to walk. I rode my horse." He chuckled thinking of holding his mate in his arms while riding the big stallion, taking her home, to what would be their home soon, he hoped.

"You're not going to walk." She wrapped an arm around him, steadying herself. "Should I tell you now or later that I don't know how to ride a horse? Terrified of them. I could fly..." she gasped, putting a hand over her mouth, her eyes wide as saucers.

He stared at her a moment trying to understand then chocked it up as too much wine. "Neither of us is going to walk. We're both riding my horse. Come on, I'll show you." His eagerness came through all too clear, but she didn't seem to notice.

A few minutes later they stood in front of his horse. "Name's Sam. He always sees me home even when I've had a few too many. Knows his way with his eyes closed. Don't even have to use the reins. He's as gentle as a kitten."

She stepped back a few feet, her hands outstretched as if she warded him off. Repeating an earlier statement, "Don't know how to ride a horse. Never been this close to one either. How the devil am I going to stay on? How am I going to get on?"

"Easy enough, I'll ride the horse and you can sit on my lap. I'll make sure nothing happens to you. I promise. You can trust me."

He almost said *and you can ride me* but stopped himself just in time. He might explore with his hands, just a little. The last thing he wanted was to send her running away from him before they even got to know each other. He didn't want to be the one she was running and hiding from.

"How do we accomplish this?" Her words slurred even more now. She wavered slightly, her hands reaching out to grab him for support. "I doubt if I can mount that thing."

"I'll mount Sam. You can give me your hand then I'll pull you onto my lap," he said as he proceeded to do just that.

"Don't know..." She was backing away from him, her head tilted slightly, her eyes squinting as if she tried to see what was in front of her.

"You can do it. Besides, I know you don't want to stay at the hotel by yourself. Whatever you're running from might find you there." He watched her face pale while she swallowed hard.

"I never thought of that."

A few minutes later, Cas sat on his lap, her body trembling as he slowly let Sam take the lead. He held onto her, praying something wouldn't spook her or his horse. He was sure he just died and was in heaven. Her feminine curves fit soundly against the hard planes of his body.

"You have to trust me," he told her, his whisper close to her ear. He lightly touched the lobe with his tongue, felt the tiny shiver of desire. "I'm not going to let anything happen to you. I've got you. All you have to do is relax."

"So you say," she murmured softly, leaning against him doing as he asked. "I wish..."

"Do you trust me?" he asked, hoping she'd say yes, his hands running up then down her arms.

"I want to," again a whisper.

He began to chant a song his great grandfather, an Apache medicine man, taught him when he was a child. The chant always soothed his nerves when he was upset or frightened as a child as well as during the skirmishes, the endless nightmare he lived in Iraq. He felt Cas slowly relax into his body. She could be falling asleep she had so much wine, but her body didn't relax totally. Her hand rested on his forearm. He felt the curve of one breast push against his chest.

This was good. It was all so very good. He would find out more about her when the time was right.

A full moon appeared in the sky just as he reached his home. A slight breeze cooled the hot summer air. His house was built in a small grove of trees, some he planted years ago, some more recently. In times of draught, he had to haul water yet they survived just as his clan survived, lived and prospered in these barren lands.

He bent close to her ear and whispered. For a moment he was tempted to touch the shell of her ear with his tongue but held back. He wanted her to be the aggressor this first time with her, "We're here."

She placed her hand on his chest, her fingers kneading his skin through his shirt. "I think we've stopped. Told you Sam knew his way home."

"Umm..."

"I'll let you down. All you have to do is land on your feet. Do you think you can do that?"

"Maybe. I'm like a cat. I always land on my feet."

Her words sent a shiver down his spine. *Like a cat.* "Here you go. There's a bale of hay beneath your feet so you don't have so far to go. Be careful. Don't fall."

She slid through his arms and while she didn't exactly land on her feet, she didn't fall either. Looking up at him, she sat on top the bale of hay, smiling. "I'm okay."

He dismounted. "I have to take care of Sam. You wait here and I'll be back in a few minutes then we can go to the house."

"I'll just lie down here. Wake me up when you're done." She curled into a ball, her hands beneath her cheeks.

Once again Guy felt as if he died and was in heaven. Her long blond hair splayed around her. Her breasts peeked out from the half-unbuttoned shirt she wore and the tiny short shorts barely covered her butt. He was tempted to trace the swell of her cheeks with a fingertip but shook the impulse away. If she agreed, there'd be plenty of time to explore her, when she wasn't drunk and asleep.

Later, "Cas, wake up. I'm done with Sam. I need to put you to bed where it's more comfortable."

"I have to pee," she said as she sat up and pulled straw from her hair, blinking.

"In the house. Can you walk?" he asked as she tried to push herself from the bale only to fall back down.

"Of course, I..."

He didn't wait for an answer but scooped her into his arms, striding to the house. Inside the bathroom he set her down before backing out and closing the door behind him. "Call me if you need me." He leaned against the wall by the bathroom door, his breathing strained as he thought about the woman he discovered this evening.

Seconds seemed to turn to minutes, "Guy?"

He peaked his head through the door. Cas was standing and she looked so damned adorable with her shorts around her hips and unzipped. "You need help."

She closed her eyes. "I need something to drink. Can't seem to swallow. Throat's so dry."

She didn't mention the fact she was half dressed. "I can do that. Water?"

"Yes."

"Would you like me to help you with your shorts?"

"Yes."

Never quite having been in a situation of this nature, he wasn't sure how to proceed. He'd removed clothing before but never fastened them. Right now, at this second, he had no idea...

With caution, he told himself as he slowly touched the zipper as well as the silken flesh of her lower abdomen. He held his breath as he zipped the shorts and snapped them shut.

"Would you like to go outside? I've a fireplace and we can watch the stars." He loved lying by the fireplace gazing skyward to star watch. It would be even better with Cas beside him, in his arms. He didn't care if they fell asleep without having sex. Knew he wanted her cradled next to him, needed to feel her warmth.

"I think so. My little nap on the hay bale woke me up." She pulled her bottom lip between her teeth, her grin hesitant but there nonetheless. "Another glass of wine maybe?"

He sighed softly, wondering just how much control he had but he couldn't deny her. "Anything you want."

Her long legs, naked legs, except for the tiny bit of fabric covering her butt called to him. He never thought of himself as a leg man, was always infatuated by a woman's eyes. This was his mate, perhaps that was why things seemed so different.

In the kitchen, he grabbed a bottle of white Bordeaux he had shipped over from France one year, as well as a couple of glasses. "Do you want any food? If you do, grab a bag of chips over there, he nodded.

"Chips and fries," she murmured seeming to wake up a tiny bit more. "Great diet."

Outside he lit the fire, setting the glasses and wine on a nearby table. She sat down on a huge lounging couch and poured the wine. The bag of chips she pulled onto her lap while she made herself comfortable. "Junk food, my favorite kind."

They settled on the couch, watching the fire then the sky. Her body next to his was an aphrodisiac calling to him. These sensations were new to him and he wanted to savor every moment.

"How did you end up in Cactus Junction? I'm just curious. You told me you were running and hiding from something or someone."

If she would let him, he would protect her.

"Besides the ones about the shifter I also had dreams that seemed to lead me here," she said, closing her eyes. "I don't know why but I'm sure it was you I saw..." She stopped abruptly, her hand covering her mouth.

Once again, he wanted to ask if she liked what she saw but didn't want to embarrass her further. He ignored her statement. "I'd like to learn more about your dreams and the shifter you saw."

"What about you? You've lived here all your life. Why would your family settle in this desolate country?"

"It was the only place my family could live where they felt comfortable to be themselves. Once you get used to it, the land is beautiful, doesn't seem desolate at all," he told her honestly. "They tried to settle other places but they couldn't do what they wanted. We came from Scotland a long time ago for that very reason. We craved freedom and land to roam."

"My family was Irish. My name is more than Cas."

"Oh?" He was intrigued, fascinated. His siblings had names that were Celtic and apache with meanings and they were all shortened but his name was just Guy, nothing more. "What is it?"

"Casidhe Doyle." She turned to him, "I'm a wee bit chilly. Do you have a blanket?"

"There's only a huge sleeping bag. We would have to share it."

"That would be nice," she murmured as she placed a chip on his lips.

He took it from her, tasting her fingers combined with the salt from the chip. "Do you want to sleep outside?" he asked wondering if she even wanted to sleep with him.

"Right here? Don't think I've ever slept outside under the stars. Is it safe?"

"Yes." During his stint in the future with his brother in law and his sister, he learned how to say the words that would make a protective barrier around them. He silently said a few words then chanting to words in his great grandfather's language, a barrier was formed.

"That's it?" she sounded skeptical. "I don't see anything different."

"Don't try to leave without telling me. That barrier you can't see will stop anything from coming in and from going out. If you need to leave, I'll get rid of it."

Her eyes grew wide, "I don't understand."

"I promise I won't hurt you and I'll let you out whenever you want. I don't know how to explain the barrier. Just trust me. It's magical, just like tonight, just like you." He moved a strand of her long hair away from her face tucking it behind the ear he wanted to kiss.

"I trust you a whole lot more than I've ever trusted anyone even though I've only known you a few short hours. I fear what's chasing me enough to accept whatever you do."

"You've handed me a whole lot of power where you're

concerned."

Overwhelmed by all she said with no reason except her instincts, he kissed her forehead, unwilling to test their fledgling relationship further. When they made love for the first time, he wanted her sober and able to say yes or no.

~ * ~

When Cas opened her eyes the next morning, she stared into the steel blue eyes of the man she went home with the night before. She never did anything like that. He was grinning at her and brushing flyaway hair from her face. Last night she told him far too many things about herself.

"Good morning, Cas." He brushed a light kiss on her forehead. "Did you sleep well?"

"You didn't touch me? We didn't have..."

She wanted that, sex with this man but he'd been honorable. Practically throwing herself at him, he still didn't take advantage of her. Now she could feel the heat of his breath and the tender stroke of his fingers across her shoulder. She could also feel the length of his body, hard and hot, pressed so very close to her. Heat slowly rose to her cheeks.

"Sex?" he asked, rolling from the bed to stare down at her. She wanted to see the rest of him. "When we make love, you're going to be sober. I want you to remember what we do."

"Oh..." she murmured turning away for a moment, unable to think of a smart comeback. Naked from the waist up, he was exquisite. Her drunkenness came about because she didn't think she could have let him make love to her if she was sober but now, she knew better. He could do anything he wanted with her, too her. She would never complain or say no.

"If you want to stay here today, you're welcome. Don't know what you planned. I've a few errands to run in town, so I'll have one of my siblings bring your things from the hotel."

"How will I know...?" She was still thinking of her people who chased her. The thoughts of the swarms bearing down on this small area were terrifying. He would run in the opposite direction if that happened, if he knew the extent of the plague following her. She had to find a way to bind him to her, a way that would hold him close for the rest of her life, a way that would dissuade her pursuer.

"My brothers look just like me only a tiny bit smaller and my sisters, well, Kimi and Lynn, they're twins and if they come, I'll make sure they come together. In any case if you're outside, they'll just leave your things inside the front door. You can retrieve them anytime you want."

"What about the barrier? I need it to stay in place." She couldn't stop the trembling despite her best efforts and truly she didn't want him to see her terror.

"I can leave it up and give you the words to take it down if you need to go to the house. My family all know the words to put it up and take it down. No one else in this area can do that."

"Good then I'm sure I'll find plenty to do. I've my research, so as long as I have my laptop, I'll stay busy. It'll be nice to have a few hours of perfect quiet."

She was actually looking forward to the day and perhaps something different tonight. Tonight, she wouldn't drink so much, maybe just a glass or two. He had to make love to her. It was imperative.

"Hope it's not too much more time. I'm going to take a shower. Help yourself to anything in the house."

Cas rolled onto her back, staring at the sky above and pulling the huge sleeping bag up to her chin. She knew she was in the right place. If he'd been naked, if the line of his jeans was just an inch lower, she could have confirmed her guess that this was the man she'd seen shifting into the most beautiful sleek black panther then back to human form.

The position of the scar would tell all.

Last night she'd been mesmerized by his eyes and the way his mouth turned up slightly when he smiled. She'd been surprised when he didn't take advantage of her drunken state. She'd had too much wine, hoping he would do just that. Protection from this family of shapeshifters was necessary to her survival as well as her well-being. If he cared enough to bed her, well, perhaps he would protect her. She would have to find some way to bind him to her. Sex seemed to be the only way. A pregnancy would be even better.

If she carried another man's child...

Not much time passed before a man resembling Guy left her baggage inside the house just as Guy told her would happen. She waited until his brother left before she emerged from her hiding place behind the fireplace. When she watched his brother, she couldn't help the fine trembling sweeping within.

Tip-toeing across the grass, she entered Guy's home, showered then changed her clothing before she settled down cross-legged near the fireplace with her laptop open and a cup of coffee. A shamrock she'd kept perfectly preserved since childhood rested inside. Picking it up she closed her eyes thinking of her people then quickly realizing if she did think about them, they would find her. She opened her eyes, thoughts going quickly to Guy.

Hours ticked by slower than ever before. She ate then napped. She decided she would need to find some way to seduce Guy when he returned from work or his errands or whatever he was doing. She didn't have any idea how to coax a man to have sex with her. Her dreams led her to this man for a reason, and she meant to succeed with her plans.

She wandered to the pool. The sunrays hitting the ground told her it must be near four o'clock. By her calculations he would be home soon. After all, at four yesterday he'd been finished with work and tucking away a few beers. Inside the saloon she'd watched him, even studied him, needing to put aside any fears she might have. It took all the courage she possessed to confront him. She remembered how her feet lagged.

She slipped from her cover up, lying on the huge couch they'd slept on the night before. Now she wore only her thong bikini. Resting her head on her hands, she closed her eyes and waited for him, hoping this ploy might prove more profitable than last night. For her there was so much to lose. She caught his scent before she heard his footsteps. He was light on his feet, just like a cat, just like the sleek black panther he could change into.

"Cas, you out here?" he called out, walking toward her. "Sunbathing I see. Hope you used a lot of sunscreen."

"I did," she murmured without turning over to look at him, "Pretty hot though. You don't have much shade." She inhaled a deep long breath of air she'd sucked into her lungs for courage to go through with this.

He sat down beside her, running a calloused fingertip down her spine, hesitating but not moving lower. The sensation sent little spirals of heat swirling in the pit of her stomach. She felt as if butterflies invaded her. Perhaps she wouldn't have to coax him at all. Maybe just lying here mostly naked would do the trick.

"Should you do that?" she asked, starting to sit up, but he gently pushed her down, kissing the back of her neck, stroking her shoulders before grazing his teeth across her sensitive skin.

"Only if you like it." He slowly began to massage her shoulders and down her back, following the soft caresses with his lips. "You have the most beautiful back, long and sleek, silken flesh, so hot..."

He was leaving her spineless and when his hand closed around her butt and squeezed gently, she felt her body tense with need she never felt before. This was uncharted territory. Not only spineless but mindless, even though she planned the seduction, it didn't seem she could end it if she wanted to which she didn't.

"I think I like it too much." She started to turn over then realized the little triangles covering her breasts would no longer do their job. Unsure if she was ready to show almost all of her body, she stopped.

"It's hot. Would you like to skinny dip with me?" he asked shedding his shirt as he spoke and tossing it to the ground, his hands resting on the fastenings of his jeans, waiting for her to answer.

"Would love to but I don't know how to swim." Actually, water except coming from a shower or inside a tub, terrified her. "I'll watch, thank you."

"I'll teach you," he said softly, trailing kisses down her spine and lower to her rear.

His fingers stroked a fantastic dance upon the bare flesh of her thigh and formed over the curve of her derrière. She murmured and would have turned to him to throw her arms around him, but he held her still. "I like this swimsuit. Doesn't leave much to the imagination."

He nibbled kisses everywhere, grazing with his teeth. She moaned softly, tiny sounds she had no control over rippling from her throat. God, but this was amazing. She found she was unable to stop herself from responding to his tender seduction and the gentle slow rise of heat filling her.

Her body reacted to his mercuric attentions as he turned her over and pulled her to him. Sometime during the massage, he'd untied the string behind her neck. The suit fell from her and her breasts were bared to his gaze. The subtle caress of his fingers across her body left her trembling with need the sensations delicious. He was staring at her and she was nearly naked.

She stared back, focusing on his mouth then higher. His eyes were warm with passion and the steel blue softened to almost silver. With the back of his hand he grazed her nipples, watching them as they hardened into tight buds.

"You're beautiful." He slipped from his clothes then sweeping her into his arms, he walked into the pool. "Too beautiful for the likes of me, but I'm not going to say no if you're willing and sober. You are sober, aren't you?"

She was in his arms before she could see the scar yet she found time to nod. "I told you. I don't know how to swim. I'm not sure what you have planned." She looked skeptically at the water shimmering in the full sunlight. Now ripples spread out around them as he walked with her, the liquid swirling around her bottom.

His lips met hers briefly, sweeping his tongue along the seam of her mouth and when she opened for him, raking her teeth and tongue. "Never expected to find you nearly naked waiting for me. Kind of expected you to turn tail and run this morning. If you did that, I would have had to chase you down. It seems I can't stop thinking about you."

The water reached her neck. "Guy, I can't swim." Moments of panic swept through her as she struggled in his arms. "Hold me tight."

He chuckled softly, nipping at her ear, swirling his tongue inside the shell. "For what I've planned for us, you don't need to swim. All you need to do is hold me tight." She felt his fingers hook the top of her suit bottom and slide it down her legs. "Now wrap those beautiful long legs around me and hold on fast. I won't let anything happen to you. We're going for a ride I know I'll never forget."

18

"Guy," she began but his hands roamed and explored all of her.

His lips possessing hers, he created sensations within that were primal and hot, the magic between them undeniable. Without conscious thoughts her hips moved in a rhythm it seemed he set, yet she didn't understand how.

Again, he bent his head to kiss her, very slowly rubbing his lips on hers, letting his hand drift down her throat to her breasts. She leaned closer to kiss him back. She placed her hand on his chest. His heavily muscled broad shoulders as well as his wide chest fascinated Cas. His lips molded to hers. He opened her mouth with his, moving his lips back and forth almost roughly. His tongue drove between her parted lips in a fiercely erotic kiss, retreating, plunging again, and again, until desire was streaking through her. Pulling her closer, he kissed her until she heard herself moaning softly. Now, his lips were at her aching breasts. His hand was sliding downward over her stomach, reaching lower, covering the soft mound between her legs. His fingers teased and tormented her. Cas was clinging to him, her legs around him holding tight to him and giving him access.

He kissed her again then, "Tell me if I do something you don't like." He pulled away from her mouth long enough to speak those few words. "My god, but I can't think of anything but you."

"Guy."

Once again his lips were upon hers, his hands cupping her breasts, tweaking the hard buds until she moaned softly in the back of her throat. He kissed and explored, leisurely taking his time to arouse and entice. Tiny sounds emanated from her as he possessed all of her, leaving no place untouched, unloved. He savored and cherished every part of her. His fingers explored the most intimate parts of her, seducing her, bringing her ever closer to something she never experienced before.

"Cas, you okay?" he asked, his voice soft yet deep as if he was overcome with emotions. "I'm going to come inside you now. Tell me no if that's not what you want." He paused, seeming to wait for a response.

"Guy, I need..." It seemed that was enough.

In one quick move he possessed her, claimed her as his. She cried out. Pain washed through her as he broke through the small barrier proclaiming her innocence. "Guy..." She let her head fall on his shoulder, moisture pooling in her eyes. "I didn't know it would hurt."

"Cas." He froze. "Why didn't you tell me?"

Abruptly the pain seemed to vanish as quickly as it came upon her. Her hips began to move, urging him to finish what they started. He drove inside her even as he massaged the small, silken knot that seemed to give her the greatest pleasure. Suddenly, intense spasms one right after another washed through her. "Guy!" she cried out as she climaxed, the water a thin barrier between them, yet it seemed magical and enchanting, no barrier at all.

As they calmed, she rested her head on his shoulder. "I tried to tell you but..." She licked her lips. "You kept kissing me. I couldn't talk. I couldn't think. Now I can't move."

He laughed then, his voice gruff. "I'm sorry. I didn't know you were a virgin. I might have done things differently, but I would have still caused you some pain."

"It's alright," she told him as he pulled her closer. "I'm glad you were my first lover." *My last, I hope.*

"I promise you, I'll never hurt you again." Once more his lips met hers in a long drugging kiss, one that continued to heat and arouse, seducing her magically to his will. When he looked at her, his eyes shimmered with a steel gray passion and molten heat.

"I know. I wanted you to make love to me last night. I thought about it all day and I was going to seduce you, but I didn't know how." For a brief time, she looked away. She met his gaze again. "I suppose you took the task away from me."

"That bathing suit worked wonders. Now you've nothing on and we can make love as much as you'd like, but first I think I'm going to teach you how to float on your back."

"No, let's get out. I also didn't tell you I'm terrified of water. I think I must have drowned in another life." Her murmured words sent a strange look to Guy's face, one that she meant to ask about.

"Don't say things like that," he said his voice husky. "Before you leave here, I'm going to teach you how to swim. I promise you you'll never drown."

He touched her in ways she could have never imagined. She shivered thinking about his words as well as what they did, sealing her fate for the better she hoped and prayed. "That will be a daunting task."

"Why is that?" he laughed accidentally touching her nipple and finding it hard and ready for his attentions. Before she could answer, he sucked the bud into his mouth, grazing the hard tip with his teeth then circling it with his tongue.

"I can't float," she said, resting her hand on his chest. "Never have been able to."

"All women can float," he said, laughing. "It's getting to the bottom that is difficult."

"I'm an unwilling participant," she countered.

Truly, now that her virginity was gone, she wanted out of the pool. She needed dry land to touch her feet and she wanted to see if he possessed that scar. Yet he didn't seem willing to move in that direction. She was his prisoner until he decided to walk from the pool or allow her feet to touch bottom.

Without her realizing what he was doing, Guy turned her onto her back, her legs splashing as if that would help her gain more balance while she tried to sit. "Guy, no!"

"Now, just you relax. I'll do everything and I won't let anything happen to you, ever. I promise. We're only in four feet of water, and last time I looked you were over five feet tall."

"Don't let go of me."

She realized the words were true, her fingernails biting into his flesh. She couldn't help the panic rising from the pit of her stomach. Couldn't help the deep-seated fear securely ensconced in her head.

"I won't ever let you go." One hand was behind her back and the other behind her head. "Take a deep breath. See how you just float with the movement of the water?"

"No, you're holding me. I don't want to learn."

She did feel some buoyancy but didn't want to put anything to the test. Once again, she tried to sit. He would have nothing to do with her efforts.

"Relax, Cas."

He slowly withdrew the hand on her back. Immediately, she kicked her feet and tried to stand on the bottom of the pool. "You lied." She brushed water from her face and eyes sputtering all the while.

He was laughing, the sound almost infectious. "No, I didn't. I was still touching you, still am." He pulled her close, kissing her, sweeping his tongue across her lips. "Hell, I don't want to stop touching you, ever."

"It's not funny." She hit him on the chest, pounded a second time for good measure.

"I'm sorry." He looked contrite but she wasn't at all sure he would let her touch dry land again. "I don't want to be in this water." She felt like a petulant child but her words were the truth.

"You're going to have to learn to swim sometime. It's fun and you'll like it." He carried her in his arms up the steps and out of the pool. Close to her ear he whispered, "Trust me."

"I won't." She felt argumentative since he kept insisting.

"There you go. You're in control on dry land." He set her on the lounge and stepped back as if to admire her.

"Good lord, you're beautiful," she whispered in a long sigh, her gaze riveted on his scar, knowing he was the man in her dreams. "You are the man I saw shifting in my dreams."

"How do you know?" He sat down beside her, towel drying his hair.

She reached out and gently touched him, "This scar. How did you get it?"

"It was a long time ago. Do you want me to retrieve your bikini bottom?" he asked seeming to ignore her question or in any case not wanting to answer her.

She nodded, her eyes wide with the realization there were things he didn't want to tell her, at least not yet. Naked, he strode down the steps of the pool then dove, coming up with the missing part of her suit. "Is this what you want?" His grin was infectious. "You'll have to come and get it."

"Guy, no..."

She laughed feeling totally at ease with this man she barely knew. In truth she felt as if she'd known him from the beginning of time, longer if that were possible. Perhaps she'd even been in love with him that long, known him in another lifetime. She had no memories of him though, just this gut feeling she couldn't shake nor did she want to. He was the man who would protect her, the only man who could.

He strode from the pool, her tiny swimsuit in hand, chuckling then settled down beside her, pulling her close. "It seems I just can't get enough of you. You're becoming a part of me."

She hoped he was becoming a part of her. "You're all wet, dripping," she said attempting to push him away but only succeeding in drawing him closer.

Somehow, he made her laugh and stop looking so deeply into herself. He helped her forget her fears.

"Water is wet."

His lips melded across hers, he kissed her lightly then deepened the caress until she joined in, her tongue exploring the deepest part of his mouth. His hands ran up and down her back even as she wound her fingers into his hair, tugging them closer.

Once again molten fire swept through her, rampaged within as if one of the summer storms that thundered down the mountains and into the valleys during the summers possessed her soul. Her fingers bit into his shoulders, pulling him closer craving him more as her body became alive with vibrancy and a sweet fury to match him. She had never felt this all-consuming desperate need.

He created within her an enchanting magic, an aching pleasure that was indescribably delicious, raw and savage. Blood pulsing within as he pressed kisses and his lover's fingers softly caressed her breasts, held them reverently in his hands, cherishing her.

"Guy..." She tried to speak but the words wouldn't form.

"Shh..." his whisper floated close to her ear and he came to her again with more whispers and secret caresses. "Just let your body feel the mercuric heat simmering between us. I don't think I will ever get enough of you nor do I want to. You are part of my heart, Casidhe. I will never let you go."

"How do you do this to me?" Her hips rose to meet him, needing him deep inside her while she cried out softly, reaching for the sunlight, for the soft breeze filtering through the leaves. Reaching for the release only he could give her.

"No, how do you do this to me?"

The ensuing tempest swept into her and around her in an enchanting fury that could not be denied, at least not by her. His fascination with her exploded inside her as sweet as silken teardrops, filling her limbs, her body, the center of her with hot liquid delight. She trembled against his large frame, feeling him as he moved in rhythm, groaning, shuddering, holding her fast one last moment as his body surged into hers, seeming to touch the length and breadth of her in one stroke of pleasure. Shock waves spilled through her, testing her, tempting her and teasing her.

He fell still for a moment then caressed her, touched her gently again. "Are you alright? I didn't hurt you this time?" It was a question and a statement all in one breath.

She tenderly placed her hand on his cheek felt the subtle growth of beard, smiling. "Never been better."

Rolling off her, he stood then and brought her a glass of water and a tube of sunscreen. Handing her the water, "Drink some, don't want you to get dehydrated. The desert air can have that effect on newcomers. Now turnover, you need more protection." He paused a moment, his smile vanishing then it seemed he thought more on what he said. "Turn over."

She did as he bade, felt the cool slide of the cream across her back and shoulders, hot where he touched her cool when his fingers glided away. His touch was slow and smooth, erotic in and of itself. Falling under his spell again would not be difficult. A soft sleepiness invaded her. When he finished with the sunscreen, he stretched out beside her, holding her in his gentle embrace.

Sleep was elusive with his body pressed against hers. She came here with one purpose in mind. Now that she met him, knew him intimately, she didn't like herself very much. Still she would have done the same, had no choice if she were to escape those who chased her. Guy's home was an oasis in heaven, a place where she could forget her past, perhaps forge a brand-new future.

"Guy."

She ran a fingertip across his shoulder, and for the first time noticed the tiny tattoos covering his body, the shifter in her dreams, but he'd been black. She inhaled sharply not understanding.

"What is it?" He pulled slightly away, his gaze on her, his eyes seeming to smolder and invite more lovemaking if she was willing.

"I don't know."

She closed her eyes for a moment, needing to divert his attention from her thoughts. If he could read her mind it wouldn't surprise her simply because he seemed so in tune to her every emotion.

"Are you hiding something from me?" he queried, kissing the tip of her nose, a playful gesture telling her clearly, he wasn't in the mood to make love but to talk. "If you're afraid of something or someone, I can help. Talk to me."

"No more than what you're hiding from me," she whispered, smiling and pulling her bottom lip between her teeth. "It seems we both have secrets."

"Let's see, we should begin with something simple," he paused. "You know I have two brothers and a pair of twin sisters."

"I have no siblings."

"An only child, how intriguing. You know I'm a shifter and you saw me naked before we even met. Now I've seen you with nothing on." Tenderly he caressed her. "I guess everything on that level is fair now."

"You were just as beautiful then as you are now."

She stroked his chest, letting her fingernail skim over his tiny male nipple. His swift intake of breath told her she could seduce him if she wanted to avoid his questions. She smiled at the soft rise of color to his cheeks.

"Men aren't beautiful. I've scars and hairy legs. And... well my feet could use an overhaul."

"I wouldn't want you any other way, but..." she paused grinning at him, allowing her gaze to smolder down the length of his legs, "let me see your feet. I haven't had the chance to look as closely at them as other parts of you," She tried to pull away to do just that. He held her fast.

"What if I'm suddenly bashful? I've never had a woman say anything like that before. I'm not too sure I want my feet examined."

His hands cupped her butt as he pulled her against his arousal.

"Not already?" she asked. "I..."

She didn't know how to deal with this all-consuming passion yet with a stroke of his hand he could bring her to that point where she would never tell him no.

"Not again, not yet. It seems our attempt at conversation was easily sidetracked. I'm a starved man where you're concerned. I crave knowledge about you, perhaps as much as I need to bind you to me. I find I cannot keep my hands to myself."

"Through sex?"

If they continued on this path a child would bind them. Only that fact would keep her safe. Would he resent her then? When he discovered everything about her, he would think she plotted that very thing. Yet she was using no magic.

Refused to do so.

"No, not sex but through knowledge and love," he told her, bringing her so her head rested on his chest. He stroked her hair, playing with the strands, letting them fall against her.

She felt the slow rise of his chest with every breath inhaled and heard the easy cadence of his heartbeat. "Are all your siblings shifters?"

"They are and they are also all married."

For a few minutes silence and the sound of their breathing was all that stirred the air. "Are all their wives and husbands shifters?"

"No."

It seemed he didn't want to elaborate, "Do I have to pry it out of you?"

His long breath of air dampened the spirit of the conversation, but she needed to understand more about his family before she would feel comfortable telling him more about herself and her family if she had one. He was beginning to think she might not.

"Brody, the oldest, is wed to Sadie. She's one hundred percent human, no powers remarkable or otherwise except her extreme intelligence. Carr to Margo and of all things she's a firestarter."

"Really? You're joking. Firestarters are a myth. There is no proof..."

26

"I'm sure she would take objection to that." He chuckled gently brushing the curve of her breast, seeming to enjoy her reaction.

"I suppose so. Perhaps I should add firestarters to the list of anomalies I'm studying. What else does Cactus Junction have in anomalies?"

"Just a witch and whatever you are."

He spoke so quietly for a moment she wasn't sure she heard him then she chose to ignore the words, unwilling to give herself up just yet.

It wasn't time to tell him about herself. While she was sure she could trust him, she didn't know about those around him. He would tell them about her and the more who knew, the easier it would be for those who sought her to find her. She couldn't be found until there was no going back.

"Hmm... a witch, a firestarter and shifters. Together you must be a formidable group."

He let out a roar of laughter seeming to enjoy her as well as the plethora of questions. "We've been known to win a battle or two. Enough about me, tell me something about you. I know you are not one hundred percent human. What are you?"

She lifted her shoulders, still unwilling to divulge her deepest and darkest secrets. Perhaps she could tell him something. Not why she was running but something that would appease him for the time being.

"Promise not to laugh."

She hoped a ray of humor would make it easier. By nature, she was shy and talking about herself didn't come easy.

"Why would I laugh at you? You didn't laugh at me. Perhaps because you haven't seen me shift."

"I have watched you change both ways. I was in awe of your prowess as a cat as well as a man. That is one of the reasons that brought me here."

"You sought me out," he said, his body stiffening beneath hers.

His hand tightened around her arm then quickly loosened.

"I did. Is that so bad?" She suddenly had second thoughts about telling him more. Her privacy was important. Knowledge in the wrong hand could result in her death.

"No, I wanted you to look for me and find me because I had no idea where you were or how to find you. What is it you wanted to tell me that would have me roaring with laughter?"

"I never said roaring," she protested, feeling a bit put out with his comments and ready to change the subject once again.

"I concede. What was it you were going to say? And," he bent to nibble her lips before stroking them gently with his tongue, "I promise not to laugh."

She moistened her lips then pushing away from him, she placed a fingertip on his lips. After a long deep breath of air and a moment of quiet meant for courage, "I'm a fairy."

~ * ~

"Caucus." Brody McKenna the oldest of the McKenna Clan called his siblings together in his living room, concern for his little brother at the forefront of his mind. Guy was in deep, deeper than he'd ever been before. This female was cunning, far from innocent. The family would have to come together to protect Guy from himself.

The siblings and their spouses gathered around him, chatting and eating just as they always did when they were together. An easy camaraderie existed between them. Now they were all worried about the youngest brother in the McKenna Clan. This was about Guy as well as the rumors simmering in and around Cactus Junction.

Sadie stood beside Brody, her husband of several years, one hand resting on his shoulder. "We're all worried about Guy. We've good reason to believe the girl he has staying at his home is using him. She has powers of some sort. Just don't know what they are."

"And," Brody continued for her, "he believes she is his soul mate which gives us even more reasons to be concerned about his mental stability as well as his ability to think logically. I have reason to believe she sought him out for her own purposes. I've heard things from some of the others."

"Why can't she be his mate? You all have one," Margo asked. "Don't you all think he has one? If I need to remind you all, no one was sure about me in the beginning."

"That's not the reason. We all have a mate somewhere. Eventually, he'll find her, but this lady is not what she's pretending to be," Brody said matter of factly. "Until she is upfront and honest with Guy, we have to watch out for him. That's what family is for."

"Just what would that be?" Carr asked. "She hasn't walked up to him and said hey, Guy, I'm the mate you've been looking for. Just how will we know when she tells him what we want her to tell him? He certainly isn't going to come running to us with that information. If I'm guessing correctly, he's already feeling defensive."

"No, but she's studying paranormal anomalies in the world and she suddenly turns up in Cactus Junction?" Lynn asked seeming just as skeptical of this situation as the rest of the family. "It doesn't take a genius to put that knowledge in its proper perspective. We don't want to lose what we have here. Our family has been at peace for so long. No one wants to be uprooted. Here we have room to roam and be ourselves."

"How did you figure that out? That paranormal studies thing?" Deacon asked his wife. "Don't think she told anyone, certainly not any of us. When did you speak with her?"

"And that's exactly my point," Lynn told him indignantly, "Anyway, I googled her name. It wasn't hard to find. She's some professor's assistant at Stanford. Wrote a paper on shifters. One of the points she makes is that she's seen one. Now you tell me if we have something to worry about and if we should tell Guy."

"He's a big boy," Maska said. "Guy can take care of himself. He won't like any of us meddling in his affairs or his love life. If she's the one or he thinks she's the one, he's not going to listen to us anyway."

"Maska's right, we need to stand back and be ready to jump in to help if he asks for our input," Kimi said supporting her husband. "Otherwise, mums the word."

"We need to be there for encouragement," Margo said agreeing, holding on to Carr's hand as if it was her lifeline. "None of you were around when I met Carr. I'm sure if you were you would have been having this same conversation, which you actually did once you met me. I didn't know how to use my skills so..."

"Margo has just made her point. None of us are so naïve or weak that someone can take advantage of us. Guy will see through her if she's lying to him. I'm guessing he is already using his suave social skills to get her to talk. Give him a chance."

"What do you suggest we do?" Brody asked, grinning with the realization his siblings would protect Guy while giving him room to discover the truth about his mate because he didn't doubt for one second Guy was wrong about the female in question.

"We should go visit them," Carr said, gazing at his wife as if she was the one speaking. "We do need to get to know this girl if we intend to pass judgment."

"When?"

"Right now," Brody said.

Chapter Two

"Hush, I think I hear something."

Guy's body tensed more alert than he'd been in a very long time. He stood and tossed her the cover up lying nearby. "Get dressed. We're about to have unwanted company."

He watched the color on her face turn to a chalky white.

For a moment she clung to her skimpy covering as if she didn't know what to do with it. As if regaining her sense, she quickly slipped it over her body. Guy grabbed his jeans where he'd dropped them earlier and pulled them up just as his siblings rounded the corner, proceeding to the pool.

"Good God, no. They're all in and there's nothing to do to dissuade them."

He buttoned his fly. What had he done to deserve the entire clan of McKenna's invading his private space? His property? He wanted time alone with Cas so he could learn more, get to know her on a different more intimate level. The tiny bit of information he gave her was not nearly enough. If she needed his protection, he had to understand what he was up against.

She reached for the bottom of her bikini but stopped, "I don't have time, do I?" she crossed her legs instead, the cover up barely covering her. "Can't you get rid of them? I don't have anything on under this thing." Her face now turned a bright red.

"You don't know my siblings, stubborn to the core. Only a natural disaster would dissuade them from whatever their purpose is here. I'm sure they are in the vicinity because they want to learn about you."

They would think she wasn't good enough for him or had some

nefarious purpose, but she didn't. He would know if she did.

Having his siblings seeing them this way, vulnerable, irritated him. They had no right to barge into his life. Even on the pretense that it was for his own good. "I'll get rid of them." He started forward but she reached out, touching his hand.

"You just said you couldn't."

He raked his hands through his hair, leaving it a disheveled mess and wishing there was something, anything he could do to change the course of the next few hours. "I'm sorry," he whispered. "We're going to have to put up with them, probably for the entire evening."

She was shaking her head, smiling at him as if she tried to reassure but knew it wasn't working, "They have every right to care about you. In any case, I need to meet them and prove myself to your family. I'm sure the doubts outnumber the positive thoughts. Haven't you ever felt the same way about one of their mates?"

Thoughts of that day when Maska disappeared with Kimi from Infinity Cliff in a cloud of dust at Lynn's wedding bolted into his mind. Not one of his siblings trusted that man, not one agreed with what he did. Yet eventually and with a great deal of determination, Maska O'Keefe won everyone to his side. He was Kimi's mate. So, he was accepted.

Eventually, the same would be true with Cas.

Stepping back, he settled his hands on his hips, Guy spoke, "Everyone but Sadie, we questioned all of the sibling's mates. We probably put them through this same kind of hell. Sadie was different though. She seemed to belong from the first moment we all met her. Hell, Carr was half in love with her too."

"Guess you had to make sure no one was taking advantage of any of you. Problem is, Guy, I am taking advantage of you in more ways than I care to admit. I'll tell you more later then you can decide for yourself. I'm guessing they've discovered some things about me and have questions. They only want to make sure we're on an even playing field." She pulled a towel over her legs and the gesture made him grin.

"So, you're taking advantage of me? What was it I just did with you in the pool, also on this very lounge chair?"

"You know that's not the same," Cas said, her smile only half of

32

what it should be. "I was very willing."

"Knowing my siblings, they haven't learned anything, they're just curious about you, us and they are nosier than hell."

He wanted to pull her into his arms and reassure. There wasn't time to make his point and convince her.

At the moment, Maska seemed to be chanting and Guy watched as the feeble barrier he'd built around their sanctuary was quickly vanishing. He needed to work on his spells or there would be no protection for her.

He waved his hand at the entourage, "You all are not invited to our afternoon of leisure and privacy. You should all go home. I want to be alone with my new friend."

"You have to eat," Lynn said a grin spreading across her face. "We've just come to feed both of you."

"Interrogate," Guy murmured.

"Potluck," Sadie called out stepping on to the tile surrounding the pool. "We all brought something to eat, our specialties, and Maska's going to barbecue the hamburgers."

"Do you like hamburgers?" Margo looked to Cas then, holding out her hand. "I'm Margo and this big brute is my husband Carr. The men are all little pussycats once you get to know them. If I were you, I'd be more afraid of the twins." She set what appeared to be a bowl of noodle salad and a tub of wings on the table near the barbecue.

"I'm Cas, Cas Doyle. Glad to meet you."

She tugged on Guy's hand, whispering, "I'd like to get dressed."

Her face was back to white. He understood the distress. She was naked under that skimpy covering.

"I'll walk with you."

Then to his siblings, "Cas would like to get dressed in something other than her swimsuit. You should know upfront that none of you are welcome even though you say it's just for dinner."

He turned, not wanting to hear the ribald rebuffs to his statement and escorted Cas to the house. He understood what his sibling were thinking beneath their all-knowing grins.

Once inside he pulled her into his arms and kissed her long and deep, pulling away from her, "You okay? I can get my shotgun."

She inhaled deeply, her beautiful breasts rising beneath the clothing that barely covered, "I will be when I'm a little closer to equal footing, when I'm not half naked." She touched his chin with a fingertip, her smile wavering with what he could only suppose was uneasiness. "Thank you for protecting me. If you hadn't heard them, they would have walked in on us. I'm embarrassed enough as it is."

"Naked, both of us stark naked," he finished for her. "I'm sorry but they do take a bit, no, a lot of getting used to. They were actually making enough noise to raise the dead, for our benefit. I'm sure they would not have wanted to walk in on us in a compromising situation."

"Are you sure about that? They are a confusing bunch of people, and I've only been around them a few minutes." She pushed away from him, studying him closely. "They seem awfully brazen and uncompromising."

"For us it's family above everything else then the clan. Outsiders are kept at arm's length until they've proven themselves."

"And I'm not part of that family."

She inhaled sharply, sucking in the air as if it was her last breath.

"Not yet." He wanted to promise her she would be but it was way too soon. Winning her over needed to come first.

"Perhaps never," she whispered, softly lowering her lashes.

Hell, the fear in her summer sky blue eyes had his stomach somersaulting. He needed to get her to trust him as well as his family. Whatever bothered her was not something little.

"They are not callous or impolite. They are curious and very protective. We've been through a lot shielding our mates from those who would do harm. Get dressed and join us whenever you're ready. If you don't want to get to know my siblings, I'll understand. You can stay in the house until they leave."

"Thank you for understanding. Of course I'll join you. I just need to get put some clothes on and calm my nerves. A few minutes alone as well as several deep breaths should do the trick."

"Good." He backed away, grinning at her, so glad she was willing to at least talk to his incorrigible siblings. "I'll see you soon then. Take as much time as you need."

Exiting the house, he whistled, his lighthearted mood filling him with a happiness he never felt before. Cas was everything he ever dreamed of. She would fill his heart as well as his hearth. He was crazy in love. Guy could hardly wait to have little shifters and fairy's running around his home. He paused a moment, once more thinking of the protection he always used. Remembering with Cas in his arms was impossible.

"What did we interrupt, lil bro," Carr asked, laughing as guy stepped onto the patio. "You look awfully serious all of a sudden."

Guy wasn't sure if he should shoot back an answer or ignore his older brother. "None of your business, big bro." He decided conversation was better than silence.

"That's the way it is then?" Brody asked as he seemed to make himself comfortable at Guy's expense, leaning back in a well-cushioned pool side chair, his long legs stretched out in front of him, beer in hand. "Are you using protection?"

The question was innocuous but it stopped him midstride, once again trying to recall the moments before he made love to her. He coughed to cover up his hesitancy before clearing his throat. "Of course," but he didn't want to admit to forgetting, realizing what they did here this afternoon in the pool would change his life. He wanted Cas to change his life, but he didn't want to do things too fast or too soon.

"You got enough beer and wine, or should I run to the bar? What else do we need?" Lynn asked as she set serving spoons in the dishes and Maska, Kimi's husband fired up the barbecue.

"Don't know if I've got enough. Why don't you send Brody or Carr? One less brother to contend with for a few minutes would be heaven."

"Send Deacon instead," Carr said seemingly unwilling to leave. "Got a lot of questions for you."

"I'll be back in a jiffy," Deacon said as he started out at an easy jog. Over his shoulder, "Don't want to be part of this interrogation. Been on the other side and it's nasty."

Guy sat down, staring at the house and wondering if Cas was even now in his shower naked and if he dared skip out of this crowded venue to join her. He inhaled long and deep, knowing if he did something like that his clan would follow him. Maybe not into the shower but close enough to make life uncomfortable for them.

"What do you know about Cas Doyle?" Lynn set a plate of appetizers in front of him before handing him a cold beer and finding a place to sit across from him. "It seems you might be rushing this relationship," she paused appearing thoughtful, "Unless it's just a one-night-stand."

She appeared concerned not nosy. "What do you know about her?" he challenged back. Believing she wouldn't know any more than he did and hopefully less.

"We know about her stint at Stanford studying anomalies such as us," Lynn said, her gaze riveted on him, he knew looking for a reaction. "We know from reading her paper she's seen a shifter. Was that you?"

"Is that all?" he asked lifting his shoulder in an attempt to appear unconcerned, wondering how much more they knew and if she'd seen more than him.

"She says she's seen one shifter." Lynn repeated seeming to be holding her breath while she waited for his reaction.

"You've been too nosy. She's exactly what she appears to be, a young lady who is in Cactus Junction for purposes that are not nefarious. She is studying shifters and other unusual forms of human life. She is probably interested in Margo, our firestarter too." He questioned his words as soon as he spoke them. "And there is Maska, the witch."

"You know that how?" Lynn shot back unhesitatingly. "Has she been telling you the truth?"

"I trust Cas. She's my mate. I knew that fact the moment I saw her. Just as the rest of you knew the truth when your partner for life stared you in the face."

Trust was an elusive commodity and had to be earned even by mates, but he wasn't going to admit the lack of it to his siblings. They would have to wait.

"Your unfailing trust could be your downfall." Kimi slid onto a nearby chair. Leaning back, she sipped her glass of wine. "You've always worn your heart on your sleeve, even before you knew we each had a mate. Remember your first sweetheart back in fourth grade?"

No, he didn't need to be reminded of that fiasco. "I trust Cas to tell me everything as soon as she's more comfortable with me and can trust me. Trust goes both ways you know." For a second time he looked to the house and wondered this time if she chose to stay in hiding.

"Do you have so much confidence in her that you're willing to trust your life as well as ours on her honesty?" Lynn asked, her face a mask to her true feelings.

He placed Lynn's hands in his. After a few seconds of silence, "I have to rely on her judgment and wait for the truth. You on the other hand do not. The clan will never stop questioning. Neither will I but I refuse to push her too quickly. I'm not unaware of the fact she hasn't told me everything. Neither have I been completely transparent with her. Trust and truth cannot be forced, little sister. You should comprehend that fact better than anyone."

Lynn pulled her hands away then nodding quickly, "I do understand. And you're right, no one will stop searching for answers."

"Ah, Cas, you're back."

Guy pushed Lynn's words aside while he met Cas between the house and the pool. He was relieved to be out of the hot seat even if it was only for a few minutes.

"Did you doubt me?"

Her smile was forced. It seemed this was the last place she wanted to be. The fact shouldn't surprise him. It was the last place he wanted to be also.

"I promise you I won't let you down. Will tell them all I dare. Regardless, there are things I need to reveal to you before the rest of your family is told."

"Not for a minute, little imp. You will never let me down." He kissed her forehead pulling her closer, his hands cupping her bottom as her belly flattened against his sex. "What didn't you put on under this dress? Are you naked or did you put on some skimpy little thong panties with lace?"

"I guess it's for you to find out," she whispered, sounding very nearly breathless at the thought of him discovering what wasn't beneath her dress. "Later."

"I will. Right now. Don't want to wait."

He drew her behind a tree, effectively hiding her from the view of his family. Tugging at her dress, winding it through his hands, he touched her rear. "Thong panties," he murmured, kissing her while he pushed the underwear down her legs. "Now step out of them," she made little noises in the back of her throat but she complied.

She didn't seem to have any objections. Picking the tiny lacy covering from the ground he stuffed the panties into the pocket of his jeans. "Now we'll both know you're ready for me."

"Arrogant." She ran her fingers across his shoulders, her passionate eyes sending heat pumping through his veins.

"Confident."

He touched the tiny shell of her ear with his lips, twirled his tongue inside, felt her shudder against him in response. God, he needed to be alone with her. Damn his siblings. He wanted to delve beneath her dress again to see if her soft feminine folds were wet and swollen, impatient for his touch.

"Please..." she murmured as he pulled away and placed her hand in his.

"Please you until you cry out in pleasure?" he asked wickedly but didn't delay for an answer, understanding his family waited for him. If they didn't show up in a timely manner, they would surround them.

Sauntering, uplifted just by Cas' presence he did feel more confident in confronting his family. "Are you hungry? As usual there is enough food here to feed the population of Cactus Junction three times over."

"No, not hungry. My stomach is turning somersaults and my nerves seemed to be frayed," Cas said as they approached the pool, seeming to hold back.

"Maybe later." He squeezed her shoulder, guiding her to a spot next to Kimi who he hoped would understand her better than the others.

"Can I talk to you?" Kimi asked, handing her a glass of wine.

It seemed Cas could do little but nod as she walked to the opposite end of the pool with Kimi. The color still had not returned to her face.

Guy wanted to go with them, step between Cas and his sister, but Brody held him back with a fierce glare.

"We should talk," Brody said, his voice holding no room for argument. "In private."

"I suppose I can't change your mind. Let me get a beer first." Guy walked with his oldest sibling to a shaded area away from everyone else.

"What do you know about Cas Doyle? Hopefully more than she studies us." Brody asked the one question Guy had few answers to.

Guy rocked on his heels for a moment before he sat down, resting his forearms on his thighs and studying the expression on his brother's face. "Not much. Lynn asked me the same question a few minutes ago."

He wasn't sure he was willing to share what he did know. What he knew was how her soft pliant body fit perfectly against his, how her hips flared from a narrow waist and her passion, hell her passion inflamed him.

"Why are you falling into her web with such little thought? You need to proceed with caution."

Silence hung heavy over Guy. He didn't have a rational answer to the question. "I trust her. In my gut, I trust her and I think she trusts me."

"She's tossed fairy dust into your eyes and now you can't see anything except her or what she wants you to see."

Guy inhaled a deep sharp breath of air as his heart seemed to stop. There were things he couldn't remember where Cas was concerned. Things such as protection, but he was pretty sure his family didn't know about her one confession to him. They wouldn't know she admitted to being a fairy and that the possibility Brody just tossed out could be true. Yet it didn't make sense to him. Why would Cas want unprotected sex?

"She couldn't do something like that," he bit out eager now to confront Cas on this issue.

"Why not? Because she's not a fairy? You don't know that."

Unable to meet Brody's gaze, Guy looked away for a few seconds. Rubbing his chin, "I don't want to talk about things that are private between the two of us, at least not until we are surer of our relationship."

"You believe she's your mate then," Brody said, his eyes boring into his.

"With all my heart and soul."

"I suppose there is nothing left to say. I would act and do the same thing if I were you. I would defend and protect her with all my strength. Take care of your heart, little brother. She already has you tied in knots and unable to think of anything rational where she is concerned. I remember those days when all I could think of was possessing Sadie and claiming her as my mate. I was never in control when I was around her. With Sadie there was never a threat of fairy dust."

"Everything you say is true. Cas is my mate. I can feel the truth of that fact in my bones and in the farthest recesses of my mind."

Guy looked to the end of the pool where he watched Cas' back stiffen even more. Kimi had put her on the defensive. He needed to fix that. She had been grilled long enough.

"That fact doesn't mean she won't hurt you. I know from experience when Sadie left me while she was carrying my…our child. I was devastated and felt as if my life had come to an abrupt end. She ripped my heart out. Lucky for me she came back."

All Guy could do at the moment was to nod, his rebuttal caught in his throat.

"I don't want that to happen to you but I'm sure I can't protect you from everything. That's just the way of the world. I have to concentrate on my children now."

"No, you can't protect me from my feelings and emotions. When I close my eyes, her face haunts me. I can't get the image of her in my arms out of my mind nor do I want to. Thoughts of her have eased the horrific memories of my tour in Iraq, and for that I'm forever grateful." He rose then and walked toward her before turning around.

"Kimi won't hurt Cas if that's what you're afraid of. She will only ask what she feels is necessary."

"That's what I'm afraid of," Guy murmured thoughtfully. "If she asks if we love each other, I know love will come. I know it's in my heart as well as hers. How much time it will take is what I don't know."

"She may not be there yet, in love. How long have you known each other, a little over twenty-four hours I presume?"

"Going on twenty-five," Guy spoke defensively. Yet he grinned thinking about those nearly twenty-five hours.

Brody let his head back and roared with laughter, collecting the gazes of their family. "I understand. If I think back, I fell in love with Sadie the moment I saw her bending over her dehydrated mustang. No one could have dissuaded me from pursuing her. Nobody."

"No one stopped you or held up roadblocks if I recall correctly. Indeed, your relationship was applauded and encouraged."

Now he heard bitterness in his tone even though he had some of the same reservations Brody voiced.

"Perhaps we should leave the two of you alone. After all, we've said our peace. We will be here for you if anything goes wrong or if you want advice. After we eat, I'll make sure everyone leaves."

"Thank you, I appreciate that sentiment. Cas and I will figure this out by ourselves, I'm sure. However, I need Maska's help in conjuring a better barrier. She is afraid and she is running from something or someone."

"You should take her into the mountains. The peace and quiet will give the two of you insight into yourselves. Take her to meet great grandfather and tell her about your heritage, the history of the McKenna clan. Perhaps when you share your ancestry, she will open up about herself."

"It will give us time alone where we won't have anyone intruding on our privacy. I do need to learn more about her, I know that. She's afraid to bare her heart to me."

Despite what I've told my family, how I've defended her to them, I'm also afraid of baring too much of my soul.

"I wouldn't go so far as to believe you would be alone." Brody laughed seeming to enjoy the strained look on his face.

"You and Carr wouldn't."

"I seem to remember another time when Carr shifted and followed me into the mountains, but I was never sure if you were with him. The panther scream in the middle of the night terrified Sadie."

He felt heat rise to his face. "What comes around goes around I suppose. If I recall though, there was more than one reason to follow the two of you."

41

He did remember that adventure with his brother. While Carr followed Sadie and Brody all the way to grandfather's, he'd returned home after two nights.

"You should show her Infinity Cliff. That spot has a lot of history to our family," he sighed softly running his hand across his face. "I almost lost Sadie there. You must be careful if you take Cas to the cliff. Tell her of the danger."

A ripple of fear swept down Guy's spine, suddenly terrified of losing Cas. It wasn't the cliff that threatened her, it was something else, some entity he couldn't define or see clearly. Once again nothing rational filled his thoughts.

"Look," Brody pointed to the barbecue, "Maska is taking the burgers off. You hungry for food or just Cas?"

"Both," Guy said laughing slightly and trying to find some humor in this home invasion, still thinking about what wasn't beneath her dress. "I can appease both appetites after all of you leave."

"Ask her to go with you into the mountains," Brody said again, "Take her to the cave and the hot springs. See if she really is your mate, and mark her as soon as she is agreeable. That gesture might save her life."

A shiver of fear at his brother's words settled in his gut. What did Brody know that he didn't? Guy watched his brother stride back to the main group. It seemed Kimi was now finished grilling Cas. She didn't appear any more relaxed now than when she left with his sister.

Cas walked straight to him and into his arms. Her body molded familiarly into his, her face on his chest. He wanted to give her her smile back. The trembling of her body sent tremors into his soul. Trying to make sense of his family's need to protect him against this tiny woman held no logic in his eyes. He was a grown man and could take care of himself.

"You going to be alright?" Guy asked, tenderly lifting her chin so he could look into her eyes.

"I'm stronger than I look. Just needed a moment to collect my thoughts and banish the emotions your sister instilled in me."

"That wouldn't be too hard. You're not very big."

"Come, let's present a united front. I'm sure your interview went better than mine. You were smiling when I saw you."

"At first no, but Brody recalled his time with Sadie when he first met her. He realized we treated the situation so differently. She came with baggage that eventually threatened all of our lives as did the rest of the siblings. It would help if I knew your secrets, if they knew your secrets but I'm not pressing you."

"Thank you, it's hard for me to open up and tell a stranger things about me I don't even want to admit to myself, things I yearn to banish from my thoughts as well as my life."

"For all practical purposes, we are strangers yet I know you more intimately than anyone else. You will tell me all of your mysteries when you're ready."

"What about your secrets?" she asked her eyes hopeful.

"You know more than anyone but our immediate family. There are some in town who guess about the McKenna's ability to shift, but no one knows except our spouses."

"So, your secrets are...?"

~ * ~

"In the scope of things my secrets are not very important. Would you like to go on an adventure with me? I've a need to show you this land where I grew up, the countryside that formed me into the man I am now."

"Where exactly?"

She didn't know whether to be excited or apprehensive then she followed his gaze towards the mountains. A shiver of apprehension swept through her. They would be alone and vulnerable, something she avoided at all cost.

His eyes were focused on the south. "To the mountains. A place where I feel as if I've gone back to my roots. When we're alone I'll tell you some stories about my family and how they came here. Clan Chattan has been around for centuries." She'd been his mate for centuries.

"Remember I can't ride and it sounds as if it's too far to walk. Probably can't sit on your lap all that distance either." She swallowed hard, wishing there was some other truth to be told here.

"Is that a yes, no or perhaps a maybe?" His voice sounded apprehensive, questioning.

"An adventure waiting to happen."

She'd hoped all her escapades were over when she finally located Cactus Junction and Guy McKenna. Apparently, Guy had something else in mind. He wanted her to know him better. Something she wanted too but...

"You can meet my great-great grandfather. He lives high in the mountains and is a bit of a recluse. He is Apache. He knows things. Listens to the wind as well as the earth. They talk to him."

"High in the mountains." She accepted the fear growing inside, understanding this quest was inevitable. "What else will we be seeing, wild animals? Snakes, I don't like snakes or bugs of any sort and I really hate spiders."

"Just my brothers. I know them and while they will leave us alone, they'll never be far away."

"No privacy."

"More than if we stayed here. They will give us our space." He grinned then, his even white teeth showing behind his lips, "We won't even know they are out there somewhere."

She felt her maybe swaying to a yes. "I'd love for you to show me the places you call home. Maybe my home too, someday."

"There is a beautiful cave with sparkling lights and a hot spring."

By the look in his eyes, she was sure his mind drifted to lovemaking. Yet that one word, cave, sent chills shivering down her spine. "Cave?"

She tried to keep her voice steady, but the waver in it couldn't be avoided. He would start to think she was afraid of everything.

"Are you afraid of caves?" His broad smile vanished.

"It's about time the two of you joined us," Lynn said handing out plates filled with burgers and buns. "Condiments are over there. Deacon returned with more beer and wine. Just help yourselves and join us. You don't have to separate from us even though I can't promise there won't be more questions."

"Thank you," she said, feeling no more at ease now than she did when they showed up. A trip to the mountains would be nice just to get away from the questions. "Wine please," she told Guy who'd set his plate on the table and was now rummaging in the wine fridge. He poured her a glass before grabbing a beer.

"What were you talking so intently about a few minutes ago?" Carr asked while he chewed a huge bite of food.

She needed to laugh when Margo elbowed him as if he was a little child. He didn't mind and drew her into his arms, his steel blue eyes seeming to shimmer with passion for his wife. She realized she wanted that from Guy, needed to see him look at her in just that way. Perhaps he was coming to mean more to her than she'd ever expected or even hoped.

"Guy is going to take me into the mountains," she paused, "to meet the great grandfather." Directing her attention to Margo, "I don't know if I want to travel into the mountains. It all seems so uncivilized. I can't ride and that seems to be the means of travel."

"Actually, he's our great-great grandfather but everyone has stopped saying so many greats." Carr told her as he seemed to study her impassively. "It's not so uncivilized. Our grandfather lives in a very modern home, seemingly on the top of the world. One can see in a three hundred sixty-degree circle."

"Then he's very old." She didn't know whether to ask questions about his home or him.

"Older than time," Guy handed her the drink chuckling. "He knows things, can call up the elements; fire, wind, water, as well as the earth."

"That old, you say," She inhaled a breath thinking of the fairy king who was probably older than their great-great grandfather and his son. She closed her mind to the thought, focusing instead on Guy and the location of his hand, which now rested on her upper thigh. She knew what he was about, feeling a rush of heat rise to her face.

"Do we have a horse that is gentle enough for a beginner," Guy looked to Brody for an answer.

"Sheba's still in the stable. She can handle that ride. I'm sure Cas will be able to control the old girl. After all you won't be traveling fast, and she was great with Sadie when we rode to grandfather's." Brody told them. "Sadie couldn't ride when we started out on our journey."

"Then it's settled. We'll leave tomorrow at the break of dawn."

Guy seemed eager to set out.

The stress she'd seen on his face vanished, replaced by the look of a much younger man, one who had no worries.

"So soon?"

The farther away they were from Cactus Junction the longer it would take for them to find her. So why did she want to stall? She hesitated because she was terrified of the unknown.

"I'll teach you everything you need to know. Let's get back to the house and see what additional clothing you're going to need." Guy grabbed her hand and nearly dragged her off her chair.

"But..."

"But?" he repeated grinning as if he knew exactly what she was going to ask. "Trust me," he told her, repeating the words that seemed to be the very essence of their relationship. Guy seemed way to eager.

"Your family is still here, at your place. It's not polite." She looked from sibling to sibling realizing not one of them would rescue her from this trip she had conflicting emotions about.

"They know their way home. They can swim or stay here and eat all the food they brought. As long as they are gone by the time we want to come back out here to sleep under the stars, I'm fine with that. Come on, I've got other plans too." He pulled out an inch of her panties for her to see. "Maybe you'd like to earn these back."

She tilted her head a bit sideways, smiling despite the fact she didn't want to encourage him. "A gentleman would just give them back to the lady."

"It's more fun the other way, and the blush on your cheeks give me reason to keep teasing. I promise you'll like what I've planned. Race you." He ran at an easy clip while she stayed in the same spot watching the play of muscles across his back, the ease with which he ran.

She was half tempted to unfold her wings and fly. Instead she followed him at an easy pace, not running but walking, enjoying the view of his backside until he disappeared into the house.

"Oh!" she cried out startled when she entered the room and Guy stepped in front of her. His arms spread wide in invitation.

"I thought about shifting, but if you were any louder the rest of the family would be at your side trying to revive you. I don't want to terrify you before we've even begun our adventure."

He drew her into his arms twirling her around in circles until they collapsed together on the couch, giggling. She lay on top of him, her hair falling softly around his face. He was hard everywhere she was soft. She traced the line of his jaw as she peered into his steel blue eyes, *McKenna eyes,* she thought.

She moistened her lips thinking of kissing him. Suddenly, his hands were beneath her skirt, skimming her legs until they rested on her butt.

"Guy, you shouldn't. Your brothers... they could come in here at any minute."

"Of course I should. I've been waiting all afternoon for a chance to do this very thing and my brothers would never invade my home. They know what they might interrupt."

"Your brothers," she repeated breathless from his advances and tender exploration of intimate places.

"My sisters would be the most likely to invade my space." With a heavy sigh, he removed his hands and smoothed her skirts. "Suppose this will have to wait until later."

"You said we need to make sure I've appropriate clothing for the trip. I've no idea what appropriate clothing is. You're going to have to help me with everything."

Good lord, she didn't want to disappoint but she had no idea what was expected of her.

He pulled out his phone and began to punch in some numbers, "Margo is closest to your size."

"What are you doing?" She pushed away from him, gazing at him. "You're not inviting anyone into your home, are you?"

"Texting Carr to ask him to help Margo look through her things. You'll need a warm coat and some sweaters. You didn't have a very big bag so..." He kissed her lips, a quick kiss but it enticed despite the fact she tried to think of anything but Guys hands on her. "They'll have to go home," he grinned.

"I don't have any of those things," she protested, trying to sit but he held her down.

They spent the rest of the afternoon and early evening assembling the equipment and packing their bags for the trip into the mountains.

Cas rode Sheba long enough for the two to get acquainted with each other. Still, Cas couldn't imagine spending an hour riding her let alone several hours.

Clothes were borrowed. Their bags were packed. "Are you as excited as I am?" Guy asked, his hands on her hips, his grin wide. "I can't wait to have you all to myself. Make love in the hot springs."

She laughed at him, tenderly stroking his jaw as they lay on the couch near the pool, the protective shield up for the night. They were nestled inside the sleeping bag. "No one could be as eager as you. From what you've told me we'll hardly be alone."

He was on his side, gazing at her, smoothing her hair behind her ears. "You shouldn't have your pjs on. They are absolutely no protection to what I've planned."

"What should I be wearing?"

She stroked his chest, enjoying the play of muscles beneath her fingers. His nipples were hard. He groaned when she touched them with the palm of her hand followed by her lips and teeth.

"Nothing," he murmured tenderly caressing the curve of her breast. "You should be wearing absolutely nothing at all."

"You're the one who told me to wear pajamas," she told him, indignant now that he was acting perverse. "You can't keep changing your mind. Only a woman can do that."

"I don't know why. It doesn't seem to matter what you have on. I want you. I need to be inside you. I crave to hear the tiny sounds of pleasure you make while I kiss and explore every luscious inch that is Cas Doyle. I crave the sweet tempest that brews between us when you touch me."

"I would happily give in to the temptation, but you told me we have to get up before the sun rises. You told me we should not make love tonight because we need to sleep. It's almost that time now, the sky grows lighter with each passing second. You don't want me falling off Sheba because I'm so exhausted, I can't stay on the saddle."

She rolled over putting her back to him, believing that would stall his passions.

Before she could blink, his hands were beneath the skimpy top she wore and the bottoms of her pajamas settled on the ground. He was inside her and his fingers were working their magic creating the mercuric heat and the sweetest tempest. His lips kissed and stroked across her back. He bit tenderly. She moaned softly responding to his affectionate caresses.

"Guy..." she whispered as she felt her body reach the most amazing pleasure while he talked softly to her, murmuring the gentlest words to her, promising more delight when they made camp this evening. In his arms she seemed to dose, her eyes closing, the feel of his heartbeat close to her.

He rose from her then and shifted in front of her, becoming the sleek black cat she dreamt of before. In her dreams when he ran, he was wild and free. She felt energy flow from him into her. She wanted him to need her, to crave her enough to protect her from the fairy king and his son, the plans they wove for her.

If she kept lying to him, he would turn her over to the old man without blinking. She couldn't let that happen. She had to tell him the truth, all of it. She couldn't leave out one minute detail. The fairy dust had worked so far, except for last night when she'd had no idea he would make love to her. He forgot though or no longer cared if he used protection. Three times, even now they could be pregnant. If that were true, she would have no more worries. Just the fact she was no longer a virgin might dissuade the old man's son from claiming her as his own. She didn't want to risk her life and her dreams that way.

Now the king stood in front of her. Evil and anger emanated from him. She felt the icy fingers of death wind around her heart. Guy knocked him over, springing on him, his claws bared. Blood flowed from the wounds but the king rose from the ground sending Guy into the air with a powerful blow.

"No," she sat up with a start breathing heavily, unable to think. Her eyes wide open. The dream finished.

"What is it?" Guy held her and she couldn't stop her body from shaking. She closed her eyes trying desperately to absorb his strength into her.

"No, Guy, it can't be."

She pushed her hair from her face starting to tell him everything before he stopped her with a kiss. A long drugging kiss that sent her mind spinning to more pleasant thoughts than her nightmare.

"You'll have the chance later. We have so much time on the trail as well as several nights alone together. I'll listen to everything you need to say. I promise I won't judge." It seemed he understood she was ready to confide in him. "It's time to get started. We've a long day ahead of us. The sun will be shining down and heating the earth. We need to make camp before it gets too hot."

Once again, she found herself nodding in agreement as if she had a say or understood anything he told her about the trip. "It's still dark outside. The sun isn't shining yet."

It wasn't really an argument. She was just trying to make conversation and figure out why exactly they had to leave so early.

"By the time we get the horses loaded on the trailer and drive to our starting spot, the sun will be up, shining in all its wonderful glory." He was out of bed and playfully pulling the covers from her. "On the other hand, perhaps we could have a quickie before we start."

"Guy McKenna, get your mind out of the gutter. You know if you start something you'll have to finish and we won't get started until tomorrow."

She sat up knowing his gaze was riveted on her breasts and enjoying that small power she had over him.

"My mind is exactly where I need it, on the trip and you as well."

Yet he sat down and once more pulled her into his arms for a long deep kiss that left her needing more.

When he pulled away, "My mind is in the same place as yours. What should I wear today?"

"Jeans, boots and a lightweight shirt covered by a lightweight jacket. Don't waste any time. Shower because it's going to be a few days before we get to great grandfather's home."

She suddenly had another wave of second thoughts about leaving all this behind. A shower every day was a necessity to her. She liked modern convenience and hated dirt.

It seemed he read her thoughts, "Remember the hot springs. You can wash the trail dust off there. The water comes from somewhere deep in the mountain and is nice and warm then there is a creek that winds down the mountain." He paused, watching her. "It's not warm though. Well it's usually ice cold. Still one can bathe if they choose to do so."

She felt a tad bit better. She could handle cold water if that was all she had. When she finished the shower and dressed in the borrowed clothing, Guy was ready, his hair damp from his shower at the pool house she supposed. He held out his hand, his smile infectious enough to reach her heart and give her confidence she'd been lacking.

"Our adventure awaits."

"That's what I'm afraid of," she murmured softly hoping he didn't hear her but she was sure he did.

Guy drove the truck, hauling the horses and she rode shotgun watching the changing scenery that seemed to go from barren to nothing at all. Yet when Guy stopped, mountains rose above them, a few gnarled trees dotted the scenery, as did some sparse greenery close to the ground.

"It's only semi-green right now because we had a storm a few days back," Guy told her. "Have to be careful of thunder storms. They usually come with flash floods, washing down the gullies."

"It's not really green though is it?" Then it seemed she realized his ending sentence, "Flash flood?"

"No, it's not really green and everywhere we camp is on high ground. No fear of rampaging rivers of water. I know the land. Have lived here my entire life. Are you ready?"

She chocked back her ensuing emotions. At each turn he terrified her with some new danger. "As I'll ever be."

She wasn't too eager to spend the day on a horse, but it seemed better than being on high ground with water racing on either side of her. "I'm afraid that after hours in that saddle I won't be able to walk."

That wasn't the worst of her fears. Being found out was.

"If that happens, I can carry you." Guy waggled his eyes brows at her, grinning and seeming more than eager to set the pace for the day. "Today's ride is shorter than the ensuing ones. Each day the ride is a tad longer. We don't have to travel every day. We can take as much time between rides as we want. We've plenty of food. This should be a leisurely trip."

"So, I can get used to the saddle?" she asked looking at the horse as if Sheba was a monster.

"So, both of us can. I haven't ridden this far since the last time I rode to great grandfather's home which was a couple of year ago."

"You're just placating me. So, how far?" She needed to hear the bad news up front.

"Two hours until lunch then another two hours and we'll make camp for the night."

"On high ground? Will my cell phone work?" She wanted to be able to call 911 if something happened.

"No towers where we're going," he told her, "Don't worry, we're just roughing it for a few days not for the rest of our lives."

"Could I let lose my wings and meet you there? It wouldn't take me that long. Just point me in the right direction," she asked tilting her head a little sideways and trying to smile flirtatiously at him. She thought of how quickly the flight from Stanford to Cactus Junction went.

"I won't stop you, if that's what you're asking." His harsh voice surprised Cas, giving her reason to pause.

She needed to know what he was thinking. "Don't worry. I'll do this the hard way." She held on to his arm as they walked to the horses. "You're changing my life in so many ways I don't understand."

He gave her a quick boost up. "I hope this is not too hard for you." Sheba nickered and sidestepped a couple of times, but when Guy started out Cas' little mare fell in line behind him.

"Nothing is too hard for me when I want to accomplish the feat put in front of me," she told him with a tiny irreverent sigh.

As predicted, they ate a meal after a two-hour ride. Cas stretched her legs and tried to look forward to the next two hours but found it incredibly difficult. She was determined, however, to make the trip without a single complaint.

The groan that rumbled from her lungs when Guy finally helped her down at the camping spot that night couldn't be stopped. She wanted to apologize but knew that would be a form of complaint.

"Let me help you," Guy said, his arm wrapped around her waist, seeming concerned about her.

She straightened, determined to prove herself to Guy. "I can do this, all of this. I'm not some simpering damsel." She waved her arm around. "I can help out, start the fire, whatever else needs to be done..." Her breath seemed ragged to her but she meant to do her part despite his idea she was helpless.

"There's no need." He squeezed her waist as if saying she was too delicate to do her part. "I can do everything."

Cas moved away trying to push home her point. Yet when she bent over, another groan followed. It seemed her knees gave out. She wanted to yell out at him that he wasn't supposed to do everything. She was a big girl and she could do her part.

"I promise you that when your legs stop cramping you can do whatever you want. Haul all the water, stoke the fire all night long, anything but right now you need to rest. I'll massage your muscles so they'll work in a few minutes. I'm not trying to be domineering or to belittle your abilities which are all amazing."

"Why aren't your legs cramping?" she asked indignant that she was the only one susceptible to this kind of pain. "You told me it had been a couple of years since you rode this far."

"While I don't normally ride this long or this far, I've experience. To my knowledge, you've never done anything like this. Just relax right now."

She sat down stretching out her legs.

"You're amazing. I don't know another woman who's never ridden a horse could have done what you just did."

"You're just trying to make me feel better."

"That's not true. I'm telling the truth as I see it. You're as stiff as one those tree branches." He methodically rubbed her muscles from her calves to her thighs then once more as the massage seemed to be easing her pain.

She sighed in pure bliss and his hands worked their magic. "Thank you, they feel so much better."

She knew she could have used some of her magic to ease the pain but she didn't want to get used to magic now that she meant to become human.

"Later tonight when I can massage the liniment into your muscles, they'll feel even better. Can you walk now?"

She nodded, standing on her own. "Should I get the firewood then, you know help out?" Still she didn't think she was ready to do anything strenuous.

He laughed again. "In case you didn't notice there is no need. We keep this campsite stocked so no one has to ride up here at the end of the day and gather wood for the fire."

She blushed, heat rising to her face and all the other parts of her. "I just want you to know I can hold my own. That you don't have to pamper me."

"What if I want to pamper you?" he asked as he started the fire, flames licking the tinder making the base of the fire. He seemed to be ignoring her, even while responding to her queries.

"I don't like sitting around doing nothing." She didn't want to talk about his irrational need to do everything for her.

"If your legs are working now, you can take any of the packs from the horses that you can lift. We don't have to cook dinner tonight, we've a basket of food and beverages somewhere in all the gear."

"I think I can do that, unload packs. Good thing I don't have to cook on an open fire."

She set about the chores he gave her, feeling as if she was contributing even though Guy didn't appear to care. He seemed content to let her watch him.

Together they worked until the camp was livable for the evening. A tent was set up near the fire and a sleeping bag laid out inside.

Cas sat cross-legged at the opening of the tent watching Guy as he seemed to study the perimeter of the campsite.

"Are you always so attentive when you're camping? What are you looking for?"

She smiled at him, sipping the glass of wine he handed her a few minutes earlier and nibbling on the tiny appetizers leftover from the evening before.

"Yes, I'm always attentive when we're outside in the wild. Also I'm looking for any signs of my brothers. Actually, I'll probably hear them before I see them, if I see them."

"You'll hear them?"

She moved away from the tent then leaned against a log that seemed to have been set up for that express purpose.

"Sounds like a woman screaming in pain." He told her, crouching down beside her. "Don't let it scare you." He reached out and replaced a stray lock of hair behind her ear.

"Scare me?"

"Can be terrifying if you've never heard it before. You know we're all shifters and when we're in our cat form we make sure we mark our territory. Carr and Brody will be doing that tonight just to protect us from anything or anyone who might mean us harm."

"All right then, I'm forewarned. Is it my imagination or is the weather changing?" Staring at the darkening sky, she noticed the wind picking up, blowing various plants along the barren ground. The change had been subtle at first but now it seemed to intensify.

Guy looked to the horizon, "Looks like a thunderstorm is brewing." His voice held a hint of anxiety. "Don't like the look of it. Wish we were at the cave."

She didn't know what that meant. Guy seemed concerned. She wasn't too sure she wanted to spend the night in a tent when lightning flashed around them recalling his comments about flash floods.

"Are you afraid of storms?" Guy asked when she didn't say anything. "There is no way to avoid this one. We'll be right in the middle of the thunder and lightning."

"Not when I'm in a house, protected. Out here I feel as if..." she didn't know what to say. "I feel vulnerable."

"You'll be safe. Let's get the food items inside the tents. The horses are sheltered and we'll be fine."

"They have more protection than we do." Her voice quivered,

"Don't you think we should move the tent to their shelter?"

"If you want to smell horse all night."

The screech penetrating the night sent her into Guy's arms.

~ * ~

Cedric paced the opulent throne room, swearing with each step as frustration with the seers simmered in his gut and out of control. "Where the hell is she?" Casidhe was a slip of a girl, one who shouldn't be able to disappear for so long. He had to acknowledge she was cleverer than he thought but he would find her. She didn't stand a chance against his superior network of spies.

"Sir." A young woman approached, a servant who would see to his physical needs until he found Casidhe. "What would you like?"

He growled the question still put out by the aggravation Casidhe was putting him through. He didn't want this lady. He wanted his woman. "Nothing for now. You can remain in my chambers until I'm ready for you." He sat down at the conference table, waiting for the prophets to assemble and the news if any they would bring. His father was already irritated with him and his unreasonable desire for Cas.

Another servant appeared with a decanter of wine and a few dishes for the clairvoyants to eat while they conversed and made promises they likely couldn't keep.

Six men and three women marched into the throne room, finding a place at the table before settling their focus on the king's son. Except for a single light on the table, darkness pervaded the room. An eerie silence descended around the table as they seemed to hold their breath waiting for the explosion of wrath that was sure to follow.

Cedric took a perverse enjoyment at their discomfort. They should feel that way, should be ashamed of what they failed to discover. Casidhe was just a fairy, nothing more, no hidden magic or talents. He had never thought she had enough friends to protect her this way. She should be in his arms and his bed. His people failed him.

"Well?" he asked, drumming his fingers on the table and praying some level of competence had pervaded their last meeting. His irritation

56

grew exponentially during the last two weeks since she went missing. "What have you found out about my soon to be wife and her disappearance? You should know something by now."

One man cleared his throat, daring to speak. "She flew south, perhaps LA maybe farther. As of this moment we can't be positive. It seems she's found some way to cloak her GPS signals."

"So, you still don't know anything. Incompetent fools." He stood, his hands planted firmly on the table, staring hard at each member of the assembly. "You will find her or pay for your mistakes."

Another person, a woman, spoke, "she was studying shifters and our research has discovered a clan of shifters who live in the Sierra Madre Mountains. We've good reason to believe she's gone there to study or for protection. We are not sure which scenario fits as of yet." At her last words and what they insinuated, she seemed to study her hands.

"You think your informants are right?" His voice resonated loudly through the chamber. "I don't want to waste time searching for her somewhere she isn't. The wedding was to take place in five days. I don't see how that can happen now."

She looked up then, crease lines marring her face, "I believe so." Her voice wavered slightly then, clearing her throat, "I've done extensive investigation into this. I wouldn't bring this to you if I wasn't sure. I understand how much you want to find her."

"Thank you for your diligence and hard work. You'll be rewarded when I bring Casidhe home and successfully wed her."

Cedric was rubbing his chin, thinking. Perhaps he would reward this young fairy now, in his bed.

"I don't need a reward, my Lord. Making you happy is all the recompense I need," she murmured softly, turning her head slightly.

He'd like to know exactly what she thought but that was for another time, perhaps a private session would prove enlightening. "Would you come to my chamber tonight? I'd like to learn more about your techniques. How you discovered your information about Cas."

He watched her shoulders slump a bit and the tiny shudder of revulsion sweep through her body. She would regret that. Everyone beneath him should bow down to his power and prowess. He was after all the king's son, soon to be king. His father was failing. Kings could have anything they wanted and tonight he wanted her. He chose her and she should be ecstatic, just as Casidhe should be thrilled to become his wife. That she wasn't infuriated him.

"As you wish." She didn't look at him, keeping her gaze riveted on the floor and he smiled. She would look tonight at all of him.

"What is your name?"

"Oriana," she told him,

"I like that name. Tonight, you will come my bed willingly."

Chapter Three

Cas was suddenly in Guy's arms. Silently he cursed his brothers, realizing the screech was calculated to put fear into her. Even though he warned her, the sound was still terrifying to those who never heard it before. Although he wanted her in his arms, holding her while she was terrified was not what he planned.

"It's just Brody and Carr playing games with you and me."

He swore beneath his breath, trying to search out their location. Thoughts of heading their way and telling his brothers what he thought of their antics was front and foremost in his mind.

"What kind of game is it to put terror in my heart? They should be whipped within an inch of their lives." She told him, pushing away from him, her beautiful blue eyes blazing. She still held her hand against her heart.

A fat raindrop hit him then another as the sky let loose with a torrent of water. Lightening flashed searing the earth as thunder rolled across the crackling sky. "The tent, now."

His hand on her back they raced to the meager shelter as lightning flashed again and again in the darkened night sky and thunder continued to roll down the valley. The light and the thunder were too close together to count the seconds between. Sheets of water hit the earth.

"I hope they get wet, soaked to their skin," Guy muttered laughing as he tenderly brushed dripping hair from her eyes. He thought about the sleeping bag and cuddling next to her. "I don't usually seek out revenge but this time it's warranted."

"We're not in danger of getting hit, are we? We are on top of the world right here," she asked as she tried to shake the water from her shirt to no avail. "I wasn't planning on a drenching. It feels as if I jumped into a pool with all my clothes on."

"You need to get out of your wet clothing before you take a chill," he told her grinning smugly.

Naked in his arms was the ensuing path. Nothing better than a storm to get what he wanted.

"Wouldn't you just like that?" she told him, punching him on the shoulder as she began to unbutton her shirt. "You're all wet too and what about the lightning? Is it going to hit us?"

"I would say I planned the storm for just this purpose, but I can't control Mother Nature. As to your question, you know I always like to see you naked. We could cuddle in the sleeping bag until the storm passes. Share our warmth. They usually move to the east. Just enough time to..." He let his thoughts wander, watching as her eyes seemed to narrow. He was glad he put a few things to eat and drink in the tent. Their dinner would have to wait until after the storm.

"And the lightning? Do I have to be afraid of getting hit?" she repeated again.

It seemed she didn't want to let go of that thought. Her wet shirt plopped to the ground. He groaned, couldn't keep his hands from the fastenings of her jeans.

"There's a lightning rod by the shed where we've tethered the horses. If anything comes close, we'll be safe because we aren't the highest spot on the mountain."

She let out a long breath of air in seeming relief. "I'm going to change into something dry and watch the storm. We can sit in the opening and enjoy the light show." She gently touched him on the chin with a fingertip. "We can cuddle later. I promise."

"Whatever you say or want. I'm yours for the night," he said softly, thinking her idea had its merits. "Perhaps we can talk about a few things before we curl up together in that sleeping bag where there's no chance in hell we'll talk."

She looked away, her body stiffening when he implied he wanted to know everything she was loathe to tell. He regretted the words almost immediately reminding himself he told her she could have as much time as she needed. Patience was not his strong suit.

"I'll try." She swallowed as she turned and on hands and knees crawled to the back of the tent where he stashed their bags.

He watched as she kept her back to him, shimmying out of her jeans and shirt with only her lacy underwear covering her. The need to trace the line of her spine swept through him. He pushed sexual thoughts to the back of his head, turning away to give her the privacy she seemed to be asking for tonight. The sudden need for privacy from her was something he didn't understand after what they'd already shared.

Cross legged, he sat at the opening of their tent, watching mesmerized as the lights flashed to the earth as well as from cloud to cloud. Only in the desert could one witness such amazing splendor.

"Your turn." She sat beside him covered in one of his shirts. Resting her hands on his shoulders, "I'm sorry. I think I gave you the wrong impression. I do agree we need to talk. It's just I don't know how to say what needs to be said. I'm terrified of what you're going to think and say."

"Cas, take as much time as you need." He meant the words, determined that he would take up the evening with his clan's history. She didn't have to say a word, "You don't have to defend yourself or your actions. You've given me no reason not to believe in you."

"No, you're right but they will find me. It might be later but he won't give up. It's just that all of the truth will change what you think of me." She looked up from beneath her long dark lashes. "I like what we have between us." She gazed at him wide-eyed and sincere even as she tugged her bottom lip beneath her teeth, a gesture that was beginning to drive him wild with desire.

"I doubt that."

Yet her words settled in his gut along with everything his siblings told him, churning his insides. She was his mate, he reminded himself. As soon as she acknowledged the fact the sooner, he could claim her as his and the easier it would be to protect her. "Nothing she told him could change his mind."

"I don't. In time you'll come to resent me and what I'm doing to you, how I'm using you. No man would like that or accept it, especially

61

from their mate if that's what I truly am."

She turned her attention to the sky, her chin lifted proudly as if that was a part of who she was. He understood there were doubts in her mind as well.

He studied her for a few more seconds. To Guy, she appeared regal and reminded him of queen sitting upon her throne. Yet she was in the mountains with him, wearing an oversized shirt, her gorgeous hair in disarray around her shoulders. It was how she conducted herself and held her head that reminded him of royalty probably too good for the likes of him.

Shrugging his shoulders then turning, he too crawled to the back of the tent and dressed in dry clothing, choosing a lose pair of jeans and no shirt. When he joined her, he wrapped an arm around her, a reassuring gesture in the midst of the mercuric discontent between them. He was pleased when she rested her head against his shoulder.

Slowly, choosing his words carefully, he began a short version of his family history. "The McKenna's lived in Scotland hundreds maybe thousands of years ago."

"My family is from Ireland," she smiled at him, snuggling into his shoulder while he ran his hand along the length of her arm. "I've never been able to visit there. Would like to someday."

He squeezed her shoulder, understanding commitment and revealing secrets were still a long way away. "I suppose that's a start. Our heritage then is not so far apart; Ireland, Scotland. We are neighbors."

"My mother was a fairy and my father was human. The ancestors didn't like that fact. He came to resent her and never knew if she used her fairy dust to change his mind or bring him to her will. My father, over time, became a very insecure man. He never knew if his decisions were of his own making or if magic created them. My father didn't trust my mother. If I am your mate, I don't want that to happen to you, to us."

Guy paused in thought realizing he wondered something similar after Brody put it in his mind. "Fairy dust to change a person's mind or to keep them from remembering?"

At this moment he didn't want to pursue the issue of her fairy dust and protection. The thought didn't make sense. He needed to trust her or they would have nothing.

"It's been done. The fairy dust to bend a person's will." She looked away from him, sipping from the glass of wine he poured her earlier and nibbling on some beef jerky. "I didn't."

The denial struck him, a surge of hope where for a moment he doubted. "I'm sure it has been used in that way by both genders. Do you want to talk more about you?"

He touched her chin with a finger and gently turned her to look at him. Slowly, and gazing into his eyes he kissed her, their lips meeting in a soft and tender caress before she pulled away, running her tiny pink tongue along her bottom lip further tantalizing him.

"No," She caught her bottom lip between her teeth. "I want to hear about your family. It's got to be far more interesting than mine."

"Feel free to butt in anytime you want."

He laughed, drawing her close to him, her back to his chest so they could both watch the storm before it passed them by. His hands settled just beneath her breasts, He felt the sure, steady beat of her heart, felt the movement each time she inhaled.

"Butt in?" She laughed sounding skeptical.

"Yes, interject questions or statements anytime you like. It won't bother me. I've two sisters and two brothers. I'm used to interruptions. We are of the Clan Chattan, which of course means clan of cats."

He let his chin rest on top of her head, enjoying the subtle scent of vanilla that seemed to follow her everywhere. "It was the early nineteenth century and it seemed the land the McKenna's possessed had become crowded, overcrowded to some. Many felt as if there was no room to roam and keep their secrets. Just as we are here, a jaguar being spotted would be a surprise and questionable if seen. Some might think we escaped from a zoo or a circus."

"So different from the fairies," she whispered. "There are folks who want to lure us to their gardens. They build houses for us to live in but most of us are too afraid to venture into a human's garden to live. We're afraid of capture and the loss of freedom."

"But you're not afraid to search for a man you don't know and have sex with him within twenty-four hours of meeting him." He tossed out the bait and wondered if she would take it.

"I was terrified," she whispered. "It wasn't like me. It was the only way I could think of to protect myself from Cedric."

"No, you were a virgin and I'm honored you wanted to gift me with that. Who is Cedric?"

"The gift was necessary."

He waited but she didn't elaborate further so he continued. "1831, I suppose it was a good year for some of the clan Chattan. It certainly was for my family. We came to the United States and made new lives for ourselves."

"How so?" She pointed to a huge flash of light followed by another then another, pressing closer to him. He felt her fear, deep and raw. It wasn't the lightening she was afraid of.

"Almost looks like time lapse photography doesn't it?" he murmured.

"There is so much power and energy. Sometimes I wish I had that kind of strength."

He didn't know how to respond to her. So, he continued with his story, "Eight members of the McKenna clan emigrated to the United States. Some settled in Texas. When their families grew, the McKenna's traveled farther west, setting down their roots here in the Sierra Madres."

"My family spread out too, but I don't know where any of them are. I was separated from my mother when I was ten and brought to a man who was supposed to by my husband when I grew into a woman. I do remember her though. She told me so many stories and warned me against certain things—of the fairy King—his power as well as his son."

Guy's breath caught in his throat at her sudden admission. "Is that who you're running from? This man who is supposed to become your husband? He's the fairy king?"

She nodded, a strange look of resolution on her face, "His son. It's not possible any longer. He can't marry me now. That's how I used you. I'm not proud of that fact."

"Not following. You used me how?" If she was referring to their lovemaking, he was a more than willing participant.

"It doesn't matter any longer." With a slight shrug she stood as if she meant to walk down the mountain and leave him behind. "I won't bother you any longer. The deed has been done so you don't have to put up with me."

"Cas, stop!" Water suddenly rushed down the mountain, not too far from them but far enough away to be safe until she left the tent's sheltering embrace. He reached her in time to pull her back. They tumbled to the slick ground, sliding toward the floods.

"Guy." Her legs were in the rushing water now. She desperately reached out to him, clinging with one hand to his arm.

His heart pounding in his chest, fear racing through him, "Hang on to me, Cas. Just hang on. I'll pull you out." He fought the power and the force of the river with all his strength. Second by second, she inched away from the danger.

His breath came in short gasps. Slowly he was able to win this war he fought with the tempest and Mother Nature. On solid ground now, she clung to him, sobbing. He needed to enclose her in his arms, keep her safe from whatever terrified, whatever elements threatened to rip her from his arms, be it the raging tempest or the fairy King's son.

"Let's get you dry." He whispered against her ear. "You're going to be fine, Cas. I won't ever let anything happen to you." However, knowing part of her story, he needed to understand what drove her away from him when she went through so much to find him.

"I'm sorry. I just keep messing things up. Didn't think you would want me anymore." Her sobs erupted into ragged gulps of air and tears.

"Never messed anything up as much as I have. I shouldn't have brought you out here so unprepared."

She nodded again and again as she gulped air, but didn't say anything, letting him help her into the tent. He found dry underwear for her after he slipped the shirt she wore from her shoulders.

"Do you need help?" he asked needing to see her smile, wishing the color would come back to her face.

"No, I'm a big girl. I can dress myself."

She turned from him, unclasping her bra then slipping on the dry one before she replaced the damp panties with new ones. "At this rate I'm going to be out of clean clothes before we get wherever it is we're going."

"The top of the mountain." He unzipped the sleeping bag and opened a flap for her to climb inside. "You need to get warm."

"You too?" she asked an expression he'd never seen before painted on her beautiful face.

"You need warmth, not sex," he said wishing he could trust her again.

Between what she just told him and his brother's nonchalant suggestion of fairy dust he didn't much feel like sex with her. Finding out her secrets along with her intentions about him seemed paramount before he succumbed to sweet bliss in her arms again. He could certainly understand how a man would lose confidence in his decisions. The very thought was unsettling.

"I see. It's starting. I don't blame you for the mistrust. I knew it would happen, but please don't give me to him when he comes for me. Despite what you feel about me, please, I beg of you. He'll seek revenge for what I've done. After all I was promised to him. When I ran from him, I dealt him a huge blow to his ego. He will be angry when he doesn't get what he purchased. Cedric is not a nice man."

Her body shook with either cold or fear, either way he didn't want her to freeze or to be so afraid of something she couldn't count on him. Every instinct he possessed cried out to him that Cas was his mate. Still he questioned everything she'd said everything she pretended to be. Thoughts of magic guiding his actions infuriated him. She knew more about shifters than she let on. She would know they mated for life, for an eternity.

"I'm cold too." He shucked off his jeans before slipping inside the sleeping bag and drawing her close. His hand rested on her head, holding it gently against his chest while he listened to the beating of her heart and each breath she inhaled until she fell to sleep.

He would let her sleep but when he tried to move away, she stirred and reached out for him, "Guy, don't leave me, please. I can't sleep without you beside me. Don't want to."

Her sirens call lured every part of him. Magic? He didn't want to question her actions for the rest of their lives. "Is there fairy dust involved?" His voice was too gruff. He meant to keep her from using the sweet temptation.

"Yes," she told him, "I can't help myself. When there is something, I want... Habits die hard. I guess you'll go sit by yourself and watch the raging waters until they too die down."

One could wish for less. He was pleased she wanted him, but had she convinced him she was his mate with the silver enchantment he'd never seen?

"I'm glad you want me," he whispered as he drew her closer again.

He needed to talk to his brothers, ask their advice but for some reason he didn't fathom, he held back feeling this was between them, private.

"I'm supposed to become Cedric's wife. It's supposed to happen in five days. That's why I ran away. The thought of lying with him makes me gag."

His gut tightened, his nerves splintering. "That might not be so bad married to a prince, except I'm assuming that you don't love him."

"He must be two hundred years old," she grit out before looking into his eyes. "I loathe him."

"I'm glad I'm not two hundred." He tried not to laugh. "Just say no. Tell him you don't want him."

Gently Cas touched her finger to his lips. "No one says no to Cedric or his father," she whispered softly. "We should sleep now. I can already hear you telling me it's going to be a long day tomorrow and that we have to get up at the crack of dawn."

"That's where you're wrong. None of that is true for tomorrow. We can stay here if you like or we can ride to our next destination." He kissed her finger then her nose.

"The cave?" she asked, her voice a bit of a tremble.

"Yes, that place will provide more protection. I don't understand how this Cedric could find you way out here, but if he has his ways..."

"Fairies can travel quickly, covering hundreds of miles in a very short time. They thrive on gossip and innuendos. Cedric has seers to uncover secrets. If he wants to find me, he will. Cedric has helpers who can see things, into the future, where a person is, and so much more."

"I take it he does want to find you." Guy suddenly needed

distance, some way to collect his thoughts but if he left her, he might not see her again.

"That's an understatement. He handpicked me twenty years ago to fulfill his purposes. I hate him and his frigid touch."

"What aren't you telling me?"

"Cedric is the fairy King's son. I'm supposed to be his queen or princess or whatever."

She blurted out the words so quickly he had to repeat what she told him in his head.

"This puts a new slant on everything you've told me. You could have just come to me, asked me for my protection. You didn't need to sleep with me. I would have helped you."

"He won't want used goods," she told him, closing her eyes. "I'm used now, no longer a virgin."

"By me." He stopped running his hands through his hair. "Can't say I'm disappointed in that fact."

"Yes, by you. I was a virgin," she repeated

"There's more to this than what you're saying."

She was shaking her head as if to deny his claim even while her fingers were digging into his skin. Cas looked away then back to him, nervously licking her lips "I can't be positive if he would denounce me for that reason. I suspect but don't have proof. He might not want to wed me. He would seek revenge though."

Could she drag this out any longer? He felt as if he ripped her soul from her body. He knew the answer to all his questions. All she had to do was confirm his suspicions.

"Cas? It seems I've lost the patience I pride myself with. What are you trying to tell me?"

"I think I'm pregnant. I know I'm pregnant," she amended.

A black hole seemed to open up in his head. He started falling, falling into the abyss of a nightmare he needed to escape. For a few seconds he couldn't breathe then he realized it was far too soon for anyone to know, anyone except perhaps a magical creature.

He inhaled a long deep breath of air and held onto it for what seemed like a century. "Cas, what are you trying to tell me? It's only been a few days since we first made love. How could you possibly know?"

"It only takes one time." Her voice was whisper thin, seeming ready to crack. "I've been praying for it to happen and now I think it has."

"True but it does take a few weeks before you would even think to use a pregnancy test to find out the truth." He held his breath as he waited for her answer.

"At the moment, I'm just guessing," she admitted to him. "Other ways besides pregnancy tests exist." She looked away from him as her face flushed. "If it's true, I'll know soon enough."

"Tell me how. I've the right to know since I'm directly involved."

A father, he could be a father in nine months. A few days ago, he would have laughed at the thought but now, today, he didn't know how he felt.

"How I'm pregnant or how I got that way or how I know?" she asked, her body stiff.

He understood a lot but not her anger or why she picked him. He should hold the anger.

His fury grew and simmered deep inside despite his desire to keep it in check. "Don't try to be funny or talk your way out of this. I need to know everything. Don't keep anything back."

"I'm not trying to talk my way out of this situation." Her voice wobbled. "It's what I wanted. You don't have any obligations to me or this child."

"The hell I don't!"

"No, no, you don't, not if you don't want any."

"Don't you think you should have asked me if I wanted to be a father before you sprinkled your little silver sparkles and made me forget about protection?"

He wanted to lash out and hit something. Needed to shift and run for as far and as long as he could.

"Only once."

"What did you say?" He inhaled again, realizing now how hopeless this was. They were on the way to his great grandfather's and he was going to introduce her to the family patriarch as his mate, a mate who was having his child out of wedlock. It was not well done of him.

Gazing at him beneath her lashes, "Only once. I only used it once and that was the first time when we were in the pool. It all happened so fast, I just reacted."

"You're sure. Just the first time. No other time," he repeated hoping she spoke the truth.

When she tilted her head slightly. "It doesn't work in water," she said shrugging her slim shoulders. Shoulders that shouldn't carry the burden she did. "Washes off. So technically nothing made you forget except maybe..."

He didn't know what to say then, "No fairy dust." His heart felt lighter.

"No silver sprinkles of enchantment. Still, you did what I needed you to do. I would have never protested. In the end I couldn't make you do something that didn't come from the heart."

"Even to save yourself."

"I planned it, every second, every minute. You were so sweet to me. I'd seen you naked. Some of what you told me had to be true. I wanted you more than I understood, still do."

"Is there fairy dust this time, because I believe you even when I know I shouldn't."

"No fairy dust."

"Enough." He waved his hands in the air. "Time will tell. If you carry my child, don't ever think to leave me. Because unlike this Cedric of yours, I'll find you."

~ * ~

With a heavy sigh Cas watched as Guy unpeeled himself from the sleeping bag. Not bothering to say goodbye or good morning, he shifted. For a few seconds he stared at her, his tail twitching then he vanished.

Sitting up she pushed hair from her face before dressing in jeans and a t-shirt. Accepting the fact he was angry with her, she prayed he didn't mean to leave her here alone with the daunting task of finding her way down the mountain. She reminded herself Carr and Brody should still be nearby unless he could communicate with them when he was in his cat form. Unless he told his brothers what happened and not to help.

Truly, she didn't blame him for any of this or the way he obviously felt about her. She set her hand on her lower abdomen, feeling the warm glow of life beneath her fingers. Even if he didn't want to believe her, she was pregnant. She felt the essence of their child inside her womb. For her there was no doubt.

Cedric would not want another man's child, but at this stage abortion was too easy. If he found her and still wanted her, he could make her get rid of this child. Guy just didn't understand how much she needed him.

She brushed tears from her face, determined not to cry or show weakness. It was damn hard when she couldn't stop shaking. Outside, she sat down by the fire and discovered a pot of what seemed to be freshly made coffee sitting on a rock while a pan of bacon simmered on the fire.

"You hungry?"

Whirling at the sound of a voice, she stared into the face of Brody McKenna. His eyes were angry, questioning as well. She didn't have answers though even as his focus remained on her.

Startled by his sudden entrance, her hand at her throat, "I thought you were..." Cas looked into the distance where she believed Guy must have fled. "He's beautiful and angry," she paused, "and hurt. Sincerely I didn't mean..." She lowered her lashes unable to meet the heat of Brody's gaze, "I didn't mean to make him run."

"You didn't think of anyone but yourself," Brody accused her, his voice harsh while concentrating on the task in front of him as he'd taken over the cooking.

She was nodding her head, understanding everything Guy's brother said, held more merit than she wanted to admit. "If I was thinking of myself, it was the first time in years." She tried to defend her actions but couldn't find the words. "I wanted to live. I needed to get away from the man who held me prisoner. There were no other viable choices."

"So, you say." Brody sat on his haunches, turning the bacon over again. "Help yourself to the coffee. Breakfast will be ready in a few minutes."

"I don't lie," she told him while she poured both of them a cup and sat down on a boulder, her back stiff. "Where's Carr?"

"With Guy. Didn't know what happened here last night so we both agreed someone needed to run with him. Keep him from hurting himself." He dished bacon on to plates and poured eggs into the pan. "Perhaps you don't lie, but I'll bet you didn't tell him everything either."

"Guy knows everything now. Why are you babysitting?"

"I drew the short straw." He smiled at her. "Besides Carr is too soft hearted, more like Guy than myself."

"I told Guy everything," she repeated for his benefit and with the hope he would believe her. "He's just trying to understand the fear I've lived with for the last ten years of my life. I never thought I would get away."

"But you did."

"It wasn't easy."

"Mind sharing with me?" Brody asked. "It might be prudent to have someone on your side when he comes back."

"If I do that, you won't be on my side any more than Guy is."

Nervously she made patterns in the dirt with her foot. Her gaze swept the area around the fire. She jumped when an ember popped out.

"That bad? I've always prided myself in having an open mind and the ability to listen." He finished the eggs and dished them up. "Suppose Guy and Carr will have to eat cold food."

"I doubt that. Don't think any McKenna has an open mind when it comes to someone who's hurt a family member."

She ate but her stomach churned, wishing she would leave it empty. Guy needed to come back. He couldn't just leave her this way, without a word. She wanted to shrink down to fairy size and fly as far away as possible, but Cedric would find her the moment she revealed herself. She remembered the last encounter. He pulled her into his bedroom, intent on having her. She fought him. He laughed almost hysterically. All that saved her that day was the fact his father needed to see him. That was when she bolted. Didn't think of anything except getting away.

"Won't know if that's true unless you try me." Brody walked around the fire, his plate in his hand while he ate. "Tell me something, anything and I'll tell you if you're lying."

"It's private, between Guy and myself. If he wanted to share, I wouldn't have any objections, but I won't break a confidence."

She shivered remembering the day not long ago when he swept her into his arms. She'd lain with him beneath the twinkling stars. When she felt the tender caress of his fingers against her flesh along with the searing touch of his breath as he whispered to her. It was all so easy to recall. It was all so easy to fall in love. She couldn't give him those words.

Not yet.

So easy to reminisce the first time, the moment she lost the precious gift she had intended to give him from the first time she saw him shift in her dreams. He had made love to her willingly... Had forgotten the protection with no help from her. She had not used magic. She didn't intend to do so.

No one believed her.

She walked into his arms, giving herself to him. There were no false pretenses in this. He knew how babies were made. Had made his decisions with full knowledge of what could happen. This pregnancy was not her fault even though it was what she wanted from the start.

"I have the distinct feeling time will tell the tale. The question in my mind is of the magic and the enchantment. What hold do have on my brother? How did you sway him to your will?"

"None. I used no magic or enchantment. Indeed, it was the man who seduced and explored and yes, took what I was willing to give. What we did together is not something you need concern yourself with. We were both willing with full knowledge of any consequences."

But he wasn't aware of Cedric at the time and the hold the man had over her. He might well have been blindsided. She didn't want to think about that.

"I'll wait then. You haven't lied but you haven't told me anything either." He sat down, stretching his long legs out in front of him before tipping his hat down to cover his eyes.

"Are you taking a nap?"

She watched him and saw so much of Guy in him but there was something more, perhaps his age jaded him, maybe it was his responsibility as the oldest of his family. She couldn't be sure yet there was something about him that terrified her.

"If you're not going to talk to me, suppose so. Didn't get much sleep last night, the storm and all."

"I didn't sleep either," she mumbled thinking about last night. It had not turned out as she suspected, "Almost got swept into the flood. Your brother was chivalrous and rescued me."

"Should have stayed inside the tent like a sensible woman then you wouldn't have gotten yourself into trouble." His hands were folded on his stomach, and he didn't move except for the slight rise and fall of his chest.

"We were watching the lightening and talking," she said defensively remembering the night and the tempest, his anger when she told him she was pregnant, her sense of complete isolation and depression.

Brody swatted at something and she heard, "Pesky fly."

"No." Quickly, she retreated inside the tent, her heart pounding. What he hit wasn't a fly but a fairy. Cedric had found her, had sent someone to make sure he would keep track of her. She inhaled quickly understanding she only had a short time to find that cave.

"Casidhe." Her whispered name on the lips of her friend sent a shiver down her spine. She would recognize that voice anywhere, trusted her with her life.

Cas trembled, recognizing her friend. "Why are you here? Just by being here bedside me you're jeopardize everything."

"He is going to find you." She sat down crossing her legs. "It's only a matter of time before he sends the advance guards. He won't be gentle with you either. I've never seen him so angry."

"Don't you think I know that? I'm doing things." She stopped for a moment to pull her hair into a ponytail. "Cedric won't want me as his queen when he discovers the truth."

"No Cas, he's obsessed with you. He will take everything from you then make you his whether you're willing or not. These people can't protect you against his magic and the hoard of fighters he will send after you. You have to leave here now. The more you keep on the move the harder it will be for him. He's already used every tool available to him, and the seers are closing in on your whereabouts even as we speak."

"As soon as Guy returns from his run, we'll leave." She could barely speak, fear taking over all emotions. Her only hope was Brody, but he wasn't going to take her anywhere without Guy's approval.

"You could explain why you're running away from him. I'm sure that man out there will help. He's brought you this far," her friend told her.

"That man is the brother and he's more unmovable than a huge boulder. He won't do anything until Guy returns."

Cas didn't dare make herself small and fly. Yet every part of her wanted to shrink, needed to make herself inconspicuous. If she gave in to that need, there would be no hope for her. Her life would be a living hell.

"Tell him why. You don't have a choice."

"Thank you, I'll give it a try or I'll go by myself." Cas left the tent, walking to Brody and sitting down beside him. She watched as her friend flew away and quickly disappeared from view.

"You decide to talk?" Brody still didn't move, seeming to take that nap he told her about.

"I have to leave now. Will you take me to the cave? It's imperative, a matter of life and death." Her voice shook with emotion.

"That's a bit dramatic don't you think?"

"If you won't take me then point me in the right direction."

"Why should I do that, point you in the right direction? If you tried to go by yourself, you'd die." He did sit up though, his lips thinning as his brows drew together. "There are all kinds of wild animals in those hills, little things like rattlers and tarantulas that can kill you too. You wouldn't even see it before it bites. Might hear the rattler though."

Snakes and spiders, she inhaled swiftly, two things she hated. "Guy would want you to keep me safe. Isn't that why you stayed here? In case I needed help. Well, I need help now not tomorrow, not when Guy decides he doesn't want to run anymore, not in an hour or a minute but now."

"Still haven't answered my question. What's the hurry?" He was leaning on one elbow, a toothpick in his mouth acting as if she didn't have a care in the world simply because he didn't. "Why should I interrupt my nap just to take you to the cave when Guy can do that very thing in an hour or so?"

She swallowed hard, looking to the horizon, half expecting to see a swarm of fairies on the skyline coming her way. "You won't believe me even though I'm not going to lie to you and even though Guy doesn't trust me."

"Just give me one valid reason. I'm not a monster. If you need to flee this campsite right now without Guy, then I'll oblige you. I know a thing or two about magical creatures. I'm not a disbeliever." He grinned, and in the process challenged her.

"You were partially right the other day. I am capable of using magic to get my way. I never used it on Guy though, and I'm not going to use it on you. If you help me, it will happen because that's your choice."

"What kind of enchanting creature are you?" He suddenly appeared interested in the conversation.

Irritated, she waved her hand in the air. "Why does that matter to you? There is an evil man who wants to make me his wife. I can't just say no. He will force me. I thought Guy understood, but now I'm not so sure."

"Knowledge will help keep you safe. Tell me more."

His voice was matter of fact and it seemed he wouldn't do anything until she barred her soul to him. She wasn't going to do that. She barred her soul to Guy and he ran out on her. "I'm a fairy. I was pledged to Cedric the King's son when I was born. I don't want to marry the odious man and Guy knows all about him." She crossed her arms over her chest.

"He can't find you out here." Brody still rested on his arm, not appearing as if he meant to take her anywhere.

"You're so wrong. That pesky fly you swatted off your face was a friend of mine. She found me. He can find me. They'll be here any minute, so I've got to keep moving."

"So, you're telling me he'll find you anywhere you go. Why not just stand and fight?" he asked suddenly a bit more alert. "McKennas like a good fight. We always win."

"I don't have the means to fight that man." She breathed in deeply.

"Besides, Guy said we were going to a cave. Fairies are afraid of caves. He won't follow me inside. No one will defy him to come in and get me." She prayed that was true but wouldn't swear by it.

"Then you're afraid of caves also."

He was watching her now, studying her it seemed from the top of her head to the tips of her toes.

She wanted to turn away, hide from his probing gaze but she couldn't, not now when she felt as if she almost had him convinced. "Terrified, but I'm willing to face that fear in order to save myself from marriage to him."

"Saddle up," he said, striding toward the shelter that housed the horses. "Should I leave a note for Guy and Carr?"

"Guy will want to know even though he's furious with me. I think he cares for me a little. He'll want to know where I am." If nothing else he'll want to know where the baby is.

Brody let out a deep roar of laughter. "More than a little, you've got him knotted up so tight he can't get free, at least not in this lifetime. Hope he understands when he catches up to us that you have this way of talking a man into doing what he knows he shouldn't. Good thing I'm married or he'd probably kill me."

Cas stepped back startled by his words. "This morning he didn't act like he cared for me at all. Couldn't get away fast enough."

"Just had to think things out and decide on a course of action. I'll leave a note. He and Carr can pack up and meet us at the cave."

At the stables, Brody helped her onto the horse and taking Guy's he set out. Seconds turned to minutes then it seemed as if hours had passed. The sun was hanging near the horizon when they finally stopped in front of what appeared to be a solid cliff.

"Here we are," Brody said, leaning on the saddle horn. "I'm going to take you all the way inside. Too bad Guy isn't with you he would have liked to show you the beauty of this place. I remember when I brought Sadie here for the first time. That's why I suggested Guy bring you."

"That's okay, I can already feel the speeding of my heart. Just thinking about walking inside leaves my legs weak. Probably be so dizzy I wouldn't notice the beauty anyway."

Dismounting they led the horses to the mouth of the cave, tethering them. "You good to do this?" he asked, looking her over again. "You look a little ashen."

She gave a quick nod of her head as she inched forward one slow step at a time. "I'm going to make every effort to put aside any terror I'm feeling and forge ahead. This isn't going to stop me."

"Good girl." With a long drawn out sigh, Brody took her hand in his. "Don't think my brother would mind if it helps you conquer the terror as well as the inner battles waging inside you."

"Don't much care right now if he minds. I feel as if you're my anchor." She muttered, her hands sweaty, her heart skipping beats. "Is it normal to feel as if the walls are closing in on me?

"Only normal if you're terrified of caves. I've heard other people have felt the same."

When they stepped inside the cavern with the hot springs, light filtered in through several openings. Cas sat down near the heated water, wrapping her arms around herself. She closed her eyes thinking if she couldn't see anything, she wouldn't feel panicky.

"Where do you think he is?"

She needed to see Guy, feel his arms around her for reassurance. She needed to know he would return to her.

"On his way. Thing about jaguars is that they are fast but don't have much endurance. Not believing anything was wrong, he might have taken a nap, but he's bound to be headed this way as we speak."

"He doesn't have a horse." She looked to Brody for an answer she didn't believe he had.

"Together Carr and Guy can double up some of the load on the pack horses so they each have a mount. Don't have to take the tent with them since you don't need one in here."

A shadow flitted across the cavern walls. Her breath rushed out as the terror she'd been dreading seemed to be upon her. He stepped into the light, broad shoulders and narrow hips intimidating, daunting.

"Guy." Forgetting herself and relieved he was back, Cas rushed into his arms throwing herself at him and wrapping her arms and legs around him. "I'm sorry, so very sorry. Never meant to make you angry."

When he didn't respond, she backed off, taking in a deep breath for courage and letting her feet hit the ground. "I suppose you're still furious with me."

Walking away from him, she found a spot in the back of the cave to sit, her body shaking with humiliation and fear. She didn't know what to do or say. He came. That was enough for now.

Following her he sat down beside her then picked up her hand, "Not angry, just confused."

"I don't have any intention of leaving you and taking our child away from you. You could have asked before you jumped to a conclusion so ludicrous it doesn't bare repeating." Leaving him had never crossed her mind.

"What did you tell Brody?" he asked, seeming to keep an emotional distance from her. "To convince him to take you here without my permission?"

"Just enough to persuade him this was the only place I'd be safe."

She couldn't even remember all that she told him. She looked up just in time to see Brody's departing back.

"Did you tell him you were pregnant? He would have laughed and probably would have walked away." His brows narrowed.

"Like you ran away? No, I told him I was a fairy. He'd already guessed as much. In any case he was pretty sure I'm some type of magical creature and I influenced you against your will. Which I didn't."

"What else? That wouldn't have swayed him to your will." His words resonated inside her.

"Just about Cedric and that he wouldn't let me go easily."

"That's all?"

"I think so. It's hard to remember with you interrogating me."

"This isn't an interrogation," he insisted.

His harsh voice frightened her. The darkening of his eyes as well as the cold set to his mouth, terrified her. This wasn't the man she met a few days ago in the Red Neck Bar and Grill. He glanced her way with a certain disdain as well as distrust and rose, walking the length of the cavern then back. When he stopped his eyes closed warily then shot open. He glared at her with immense displeasure. He pointed a finger at her.

"What haven't you told me?"

She stared at him her eyes wide, confused. "There is nothing left to say. You know me inside and out."

His lashes fell briefly over his eyes. When he looked up, "So true," he agreed with her a half smile on his face. "We need to get to the ranch where grandfather can help protect you. I don't know if Cedric is known for cruelty, but everything you've told me about him points in that direction."

She didn't reply but lowered her head, swallowing tightly against the tears that burned hotly behind her eyes. She didn't know what mood he would show next. The cavern room was sparse, but they did have enough food to last a few days. She didn't eat much. "How can your grandfather protect me?"

"He has his ways, knows things no one else does." He arched both brows the stress seeming to dissipate as they sat alone and contemplated a confusing and puzzling future.

"That doesn't tell me much."

She wanted to lash out at him, craved the man she had come to know, not this elusive angry man who arrogantly stood in front of her and changed moods every other second.

"He's an Apache shaman. The future is his to see." Guy seemed to change before her eyes. "What shall we do, little imp? Should we stay here or should we make a mad dash for the ranch?" His voice gentled baffling her even more. He sank down, reaching out to touch her cheek with the back of his hand.

She lifted her shoulders before looking away from him. "Really, I've no idea. I've been running for so long my natural inclination is to do that very thing but..." she paused watching him.

"But..."

"I'm exhausted. I don't think I can sit on a horse right now. So, leaving this very moment is out of the equation."

"Even to save your life?" he questioned softly.

She felt as if he must know something she didn't. "What did you see on your run?" she whispered, her breath catching in her throat. "What has you needing to leave this minute?"

"Many things and perhaps nothing."

She wanted to hit him, pummel him until he stopped speaking in riddles. "What does that mean?"

"Thought you'd never ask."

She let a huge breath of air rush out of her lungs, perverse man. "I'm terrified and you play with my emotions. I've done nothing wrong and have not hurt you in any way."

"You used me and made sure you became pregnant without even discussing your plan with me. I find that quite distasteful. What do you expect me to feel? Pleased?"

"You chose not to use protection," she shot back at him. "Even though you want to, you cannot blame that on me." She turned from him unable to look him in the eye and see his disdain.

"No, I suppose I can't but you should have told me about your situation before we made love."

"Had sex," she corrected him even though she didn't feel that way. "I couldn't lay my heart on the line to someone I didn't know. I had too much at stake."

"But you wanted a child, needed one to the extent you lied to me."

"Stop it!" she cried out frustrated and irritated as well, but she still didn't turn around.

"Come here," he told her.

She didn't move, refused to do his bidding despite the softening of his voice. At this moment she didn't trust him. She was angry with him, furiously so.

"Cas, come here," he repeated. She didn't know what drew her around to face him, but she did turn. She walked toward him, too, standing before him, not touching him, but looking up into his eyes. She didn't know what emotion was betrayed in her, but he reached out and touched her shoulders and bent to touch her lips very lightly. He kissed her forehead drew her against him. For a moment she felt cherished.

"I don't hold you solely responsible for the child," he assured her. "After all..."

She pressed her palm against his chest, pushing him from her and looked at him seriously. "That's very noble of you, Guy, since we both understand sex and that it takes two people to accomplish the feat."

He threaded his fingers through her hair. "We must protect the baby at all cost. Everything we do must be for the child's sake. What would Cedric do with the baby if he managed to abduct you back into his stronghold?"

"If he let him live, he would become a slave."

"Him?" he queried, one brow slanting upward.

"It's a boy, trust me in this."

"Then we cannot let Cedric find you, can we? I can call in reinforcements. The others will come if summoned."

"They might not be able to reach us in time." She knew how quickly fairies could move when they wanted too. They would be in grave danger. "Cedric's power is strong, his magic... well," she swallowed, "His magic has grown with time and he is very old."

He kissed her tenderly once more, his hands holding her still. "We've a helicopter to use when we need it."

Her eyes widened, "We're riding horses."

"It's the ambiance. I wanted you to see this cave, needed to make love to you in the hot springs. Perhaps there is still time if we can trust my brothers not to intrude."

His touch was not so tender or gentle as he reached out, sweeping her hard and full into his arms. He kissed her again, and this caress of his lips was sweet and tender turning fierce and demanding but gentle in its own way. His lips melded upon hers with an all-consuming desire, his tongue teased her mouth, grazed her teeth, sought deep, honeyed recesses. He held her with tenderness too. His arms were ever ardent but gentle. His hand cupped her cheek, and his fingers trailed her throat as he held her to his kiss. His hands molded her breast and her waist then he broke away, gasping for breath, still holding her close as if he never wanted to let her go.

He pushed her t-shirt over her head while her fingers fumbled with the fastening on his jeans. Only seconds passed before they were naked and he was striding into the hot springs holding her in his arms.

He tested the water, "No hotter than bath water. You and the babe should be fine."

"Do we have a do not disturb sign to put outside."

~ * ~

Brody fed the blazing fire at the entrance of the cave. "She's got so many secrets she could dig herself a grave trying not to tell them. Her eyes spoke of fear and hatred when she talked about the man who wanted her. Truly, I don't know what to make of her."

"But you don't know what those secrets are. She's not so different from Margo and Sadie. They both ran from a man who wanted them at any cost," Carr laughed as he tossed branches into the flames then looking up, "You couldn't use that McKenna charm to worm the words from her."

"I understand just by looking at Cas she's terrified. She also used Guy to her purposes to save herself. Neither one it seems will admit that fact."

For lack of nothing better to do, Brody tossed more twigs on the fire.

"That about sums it up then? I thought you would have found out more. She's running from a man. We as a clan will come together to protect Guy's mate."

"We need to speak with Guy. She's not going to tell us anything more. It has to come from Guy."

Carr rose to do just that, heading for the hot springs.

"Wouldn't do that if I were you," Brody said a bit of laughter in his voice. "Shouldn't have to tell you why."

Carr stopped midstride, turning to confront him, "You think they're having a little fun."

"I'm guessing they've made up by now and are in the water sealing the deal. What should we fix for dinner?"

"What kind of instant food do we have in the packs?"

Chapter Four

Guy held Cas in his arms through the night, his emotions still in turmoil. This father business had come as an unexpected surprise as well as a shock. He'd always thought he'd be married for a while then the children would follow. Stroking her hair, he thought about his son, a son. She seemed so sure. Not that he cared if they were going to have a little girl. Either would be just fine.

He wanted children, he realized, always enjoyed his nieces and nephews.

He heard the soft tread of footsteps before he saw Brody at the entrance to the cave. Wiggling out of the sleeping bag, he pulled on his jeans. The night passed far too quickly. Now, when they traveled the rest of the way, they'd be in the open and vulnerable. All senses needed to be on high alert as soon as they stepped outside the cave.

"Time to leave," Brody said chuckling. "Oatmeal is cooked and waiting then we best get on the trail. No time like the present to start out on a new adventure. You guys have a good night?"

"If everything Cas told me yesterday pans out, we're going to need the open space at the ranch. If she can't dissuade Cedric, there is bound to be a fight. Sent my thoughts to the twins as well as Maska. The helicopter with them in it should be there before we are," Brody said while he looked to the sky as if he would see the vehicle bringing the others.

"It might be a good idea to see if Kimi can listen to Cedric' thoughts," Carr said. "Would be nice to understand what they intend. We can proceed one step ahead of the fairies."

"Right, I'll send her those thoughts."

At Guy's nod, Brody turned to leave, sauntering from the cave.

84

Guy would have liked to stay here a while longer. While all their differences had not been resolved, they now understood each other a little bit better. Her fear for the cave seemed to dissipate with time. Perhaps when all this ended, they could make a return visit. He wanted the cave to be a special place for them just as it was for Sadie and Brody.

Kneeling beside Cas, he ran a fingertip across her cheek, wishing the beginning of their relationship wasn't fraught with danger and lies of omission. "Wake up, little imp. Once we get to grandfather's you can sleep as much as you like."

Cas opened her eyes, her warm gaze meeting his, her hair a tousled mess tangling around her face until she pushed it back. "Won't be able to do that until Cedric is convinced he can't have me. Don't have any idea how to do that. Do you?"

"What would happen if he died?" Guy asked watching for a reaction that might give him another clue about everything she told him.

"The kingdom would be in chaos. The king would want his revenge. As far as I know Cedric is his only legitimate son. We have to find some way out of this besides risking anyone's life."

Cas sat up then, naked and Guy could barely repress the groan of desire rumbling belly deep. Her rosy tipped breasts against the alabaster skin beckoned his touch. He groaned deep in his throat.

She seemed to sense his need, dressing quickly. "Now don't be getting any ideas, Guy McKenna." She waggled a slim finger at him, along with her precious smile, "We've got a long ride ahead of us and neither one of us want your brothers in here asking what is keeping us."

With a heavy sigh along with a grin which promised he would find a way to make love to her as soon as possible, "You're right, of course. They have little patience but they're right that we need to get on the trail. It's a long way to the ranch. I planned to take two days. We're going to have to try to reach it by tonight."

A cup of coffee and a bowl of oatmeal then they were headed to the top of the mountain. Brody and Carr shifted, but this time they stayed close. She watched them as they loped nearby, their muscles bulging as they trotted.

"Do you see anything?" Guy asked when Cas looked behind her

for what must be the hundredth time.

She slanted him a half smile, "No, everything inside me is telling me they are close, but I don't see anything. My friend came to warn me yesterday. Don't think I told you that but it was the reason Brody decided to take me to the cave."

"A friend?" Guy pushed his hat back, looking to the skies. "What do they look like? You know, when you're a fairy what would you like? You've seen me as a shifter. It's only fair."

He liked the way she lifted her shoulders as if she was thinking or she really didn't want to tell him. "If there are a lot of them, a swarm of insects. Brody thought my friend was a fly and tried to bat her away. Good thing she was quick or he would have hurt her. When this is over, I'll show you my fairy form. Now, if I made myself small, Cedric would know where I am. He would sense me."

"You are small," Guy told her with a laugh. "You're just a little bit of a thing but so beautiful you steal my breath."

"You should concentrate on something else." She stiffened her back as she heard him chuckle behind her.

"Alright then, don't see anything like a swarm. Means we're safe?" he asked. Now she had him looking over his shoulder.

"For the time being. Cedric has people or fairies looking for me. That's what Destiny told me. She was afraid and well... if she can find me the others won't be far behind."

"So, what kind of fairies are searching you out? Ones with special powers?" He was hoping she would tell him her special magic. It would be nice if her magical abilities complimented the rest of the families.

"Ones who can see into the future. They are called seers."

"Do you have special magic? Is that why Cedric wanted you?"

"Nothing special, nothing at all. At least nothing I know of." She looked away from him, seemingly unable to meet his gaze.

He craved her honesty, all of the truth, not just bits and pieces. He needed to be able to see into her soul, read all the things she was afraid to say out loud. Needed to understand so he could protect her. "You're very special to me."

"As are you to me but that isn't all you wanted to know and I'm not at all sure you believe me. I suppose I should say I don't know if I have special powers. My mother was never around to help me discover them. I don't know what hers were. Powers do tend to be genetic especially among the women."

"It's the same for us. The twins have more powers than the rest of us. They will come in handy once we are all together."

This time he didn't think she held anything back. She would learn when the time was right. Until then, he needed to be patient.

"How far?" she asked.

It seemed she deflected so he would go along with the ploy for now. "An hour more. Why?"

"My butt hurts."

"And you're terrified." He added to her statement understanding if they'd been able to make this trip the way he planned they would be making camp again before reaching Niagel's house at the top of the mountain. They also would have taken a more circuitous route.

"I have you and your brothers. The rest of your clan we'll join in an hour. Maska can build a protective shield around the house." She spoke quickly her hand holding the reins shaking.

He rode close, touching her hand. "We aren't going to run."

"What? No one can defeat him and his warriors." Her words were a terrified whisper.

"We will stand and fight, like we always do. We've defeated demons before. We will again. It would be nice to know what magic you possess, but of course it's not necessary."

"You can't reason with Cedric and you won't beat him in a fight. He doesn't fight fair. He'll use your powers against you."

Perhaps I should tell you some of the stories, not lore passed down from one generation to the next, but the truth as the McKennas know right now and the recent past."

She waved her hand in the air, spooking Sheba who snorted and sidestepped. "It doesn't matter."

"You doubt our prowess? Together we win battles against great odds."

"Cedric never loses."

"He will this time. We are fighting for you, my mate."

The more she spoke of this arrogant man the more cautious Guy became. Cedric would be formidable, but together with his family he felt renewed confidence.

They rode in silence. The discussion or argument was best put on hold until she could meet his great grandfather and learn about all the different powers they possessed.

"We should arrive before the evening meal. You've done well. You can rest then the family can plan strategies." Guy broke the silence, watching her look over her shoulder again.

"I am hungry. I need to sleep and a shower more than anything else," she told him with a long soft sigh. "Every time I look..."

"You believe you're going to see Cedric," he finished for her as well as his army of fairies. "Tell me about your friend and why she was able to find you before anyone else? What was her name?"

"Destiny..." the pause was long before Cas inhaled a deep breath of air letting it out slowly. "She's been my friend since I was taken from my mother. She's my first real memory of the king's palace and the grounds. I don't know how she was able to find me, but we've always had a special connection, a bond that has never been broken."

"A special connection," Guy repeated trying to figure out what exactly that meant. He needed to sit down and talk with Destiny, perhaps she knew of Cas' powers. "Do you think she's one of these seers that Cedric employs to find you? She might have been looking for you to tell him."

Cas sucked in a sharp breath, seeming surprised or perhaps bothered by his accusation, but he had to pursue every angle. Anger, fear perhaps even confusion laced her voice. "She would never give me away to that man. Destiny understands exactly who he is and how much he will hurt me when he finally gets a hold of me."

"He won't."

"I pray you are right."

"In truth I didn't mean to imply that she might divulge your secrets. I've no idea how the two of you feel about each other. The way you speak of her, you hold her in high regards but you came to me for protection. Besides, if she gave your whereabouts away wouldn't Cedric be here now?"

"I suppose." Seemingly startled. "Destiny!"

"Well, I should be angry with the pair of you for not trusting me." Destiny seemed to be in a tiny pout. Her arms crossed defensively in front of her while she sported a deep scowl.

Guy couldn't help the laughter bubbling up inside. In too many ways to count that expression reminded him of Cas. "In my defense I don't know you and my first concern will always be for Cas as I hope yours is."

He leaned forward trying to see her closer before he focused his gaze on Cas. "Is this what you look like when you're small?"

"I'm much bigger," Cas said, stiffening as if she was offended by his question.

"Gigantic," Destiny told him.

This time Guy's laughter was a roar. "My petite Cas could never be gigantic. Compared to me she is tiny and beautiful."

He watched Cas shoot her friend a look he didn't quite understand before he slanted another watchful look over his shoulder. The hordes of fairies Cas spoke of could be anywhere.

Cedric could be anywhere for that matter. If the fairy was as tiny as Destiny, he'd never see him.

"You know what it's like to always be called gigantic, the largest of all the other female fairies?" Cas asked. "It's nice to be considered petite."

"I'm the largest of my family and many times I've been called gigantic or huge. In my feline form I also stand noticeably taller than the others. Suppose for a man it's a bit different, though," he said as he pushed his hat back a smidge and grinned.

"It's because my father was or is human. I don't know where he is or even if he is alive," she said sounding defensive then she waved a hand in the air. "Doesn't matter anyway."

He didn't want to make her feel self-conscious. "I would like to see you as a fairy. As soon as all this is over..."

"Of course I will show you."

She seemed to turn her attention back to Destiny with a thoughtful expression. "Are you a seer and do you have any idea if I have a special power?"

"I do confess," Destiny said, settling back on Sheba's head, trying to get comfortable. "I am a seer. Cedric was sure I knew where you were a few weeks ago, but I told him as little as possible. The last thing I needed was to find myself on his bad side. His revenge is not palatable."

"How much did you tell him?"

Guy's voice was rougher than he intended, but the truth was too important to overlook or waste time trying to figure out. He had little patience for this type of intrigue and Cas had used up every iota of patience he possessed.

"Yes, I saw you in a dream. You were in a saloon and I saw Guy as well. At the time I didn't know his name."

"But you didn't tell Cedric," Cas said.

"Of course not. I know how much you detest that man. While he is not as horrid as his father, a marriage to him would he terrible. He only wanted you because you are the most unattainable, and you made it clear you despised him."

"She's not marrying anyone but me." Once again Guy's voice came out gruff but he was angry now, angrier than he'd ever been.

"Do you know my special power?" Cas asked again.

Destiny was shaking her head. "No, even though I've tried to see into the future but to no avail where Cas is concerned. If she has one, it will be revealed when she needs to use it."

"You're sure about that?" Cas asked, adjusting herself on the saddle then looking to Guy. "How much longer?"

"Fifteen to twenty minutes. We can stop and take a break if you need it." Guy glanced behind them again. The relief he felt was tangible. They still had minutes to go before they could feel safe. Maska would build that magic wall he was so capable of doing as soon as they reached the ranch.

"No, it would not be good to stop." She picked up the pace a bit, seeming to realize the sooner they reached Guy's great grandfather's home, the better. "Hang on."

Destiny gripped the horse's hair. She was bouncing up and down. "Think I'll fly."

"No you don't. If you do..."

"He'll be able to find me and in doing so find you." Destiny repeated what Guy was sure was in Cas' head. "It makes little difference. Cedric will find you."

"Later would be much better," Guy murmured.

"Never would be more acceptable," Cas shot back his way.

Silence roared through Guy's head even as he watched the sky slowly darkening. Thunder echoed through his lungs until they burned. The air seemed to vibrate with hatred.

"Is that what I think it is?"

Cas' expression turned fierce. She nodded swallowing hard. "It is."

"How much time do we have?" Guy asked as he kneed his horse to ride abreast Cas, knowing Sheba would keep pace with the stallion. The biggest question was whether or not Cas could hang on and stay in the saddle.

"Probably about the same amount of time it will take us to reach the ranch house." Cas said in a breathless whisper.

"Can you go faster? Sheba will follow me."

"Yes."

The yes was far from strong and confident but she understood the urgency. "Good girl." He pushed ahead of her keeping his stallion at a gallop but not so fast Sheba would be unable to keep up with him.

He kept the sound of Sheba's hoof beats close. As he neared the ranch, he saw Maska and Kimi waiting for them and watching the sky behind. Lyn was striding toward the pair. Suddenly, he passed them by. He felt the closing off of their tiny part of the world. The barrier shut behind them with a resounding bang.

He pulled his horse to a quick stop, whirling to see his family standing tall to protect his mate. "What can I do?"

"Nothing for now," Maska said. "This barrier will hold. Go on to the stables and take care of Cas. She appears near to exhaustion."

He pulled his horse next to Cas' before drawing her onto his lap.

"Remember the first night I met you?" he asked as he nuzzled her ear in a feeble attempt to erase some of her fear he felt vibrating from her thin body. "You rode with me just like you are doing now."

"You don't have to do this," she told him, touching the side of his face with her hand and running her tongue across her lips, wishing they weren't surrounded by his family.

That was enough invitation for him. He didn't like going all day without a kiss. Gently he molded his lips to hers, tracing the line until she opened for him. The contact was short. He wanted to deepen the intimate connection between them but understood there were more pressing obligations to take care of.

When he drew away and gazed into her smoky blue eyes, he witnessed the raw passion but he also read the fear. "Everything will be fine, I promise. Cedric will not be able to get to you at our compound. We will meet him on our terms not his."

"That's a really big promise," she told him, her voice soft yet holding a wealth of doubt.

"Hush, when I get some time alone with you, we're going to discuss a few things we can do that will help keep him away." He understood his craving to claim her as his, but first she needed to comprehend the significance of his mark. She needed to understand they'd been together before, in a past life.

If Cedric felt the loss of her virginity as well as the child growing inside her, married her then his mark on her would serve to dissuade him even more. No matter what the fairy did, the mark would never vanish. It would stay with her for as long as she breathed and her heart beat.

"We've had miles to talk and you've said nothing." It seemed she complained a bit. "We could have spoken of all these secrets you want to tell me. I remember a few days ago you were angry with me for keeping things from you."

His jaw clenched understanding the truth of her words. "Have you forgotten? Brody and Carr are traveling shotgun and your friend has been riding on your horse." He wanted to laugh at her look of chagrin as she slowly realized the truth of his words. "This journey has been far from private and these are private talks meant only for your ears."

"What do you want to talk about?"

He looked around him, "The scenery doesn't seem to have changed. Everything appears just as it did the last time I was here." When he pulled up in front of the house, he set her on the ground before dismounting. Wrapping an arm around her they walked up the steps. Someone came around the corner to take the stallion.

The housekeeper greeted them with a warm smile. "Welcome, Guy."

"Where is Niagel?"

The lady looked to a barren spot outside. A blanket had been spread on the earth and his great grandfather sat cross-legged, chanting. "He is speaking to the elements of the earth; earth, wind, fire and water, praying for guidance as well as help. You must take care of your woman, see to her needs then you speak with Niagel. Everything will be fine."

Guy strode down the hall to his room, his arm still wrapped tightly around Cas. "Shower first. Eat second. Make love third." In his room, he pulled two terry cloth robes from the closet as well as two large bath towels.

"You have this all planned out? Are we going to sleep any time in this scenario?" she asked, skepticism in her voice. "Shouldn't we be doing something to help the others?"

"What can you do save fall prey to that man?"

"When you put it that way."

"By taking care of our needs first, we are doing just that, helping the others. We must be rested and relaxed before the final battle. We will sleep after all the plans are made and we have resolved our issues."

"Battle? Issues?"

"Doubt if it will come down to a fight but again, there are things you will have to decide before we confront Cedric."

He was terrified she wouldn't agree to wed him or let him claim her as his. A world where she was not his mate was not a world where he could live.

"When?"

"When are we going to talk you ask?" he queried. "Talk fourth on the list."

"If this is so important, shouldn't we talk first?"

"The shower would be a good place to begin. For now, unless you plan on showering in your clothes, you should undress."

He stepped back, folding his arms across his chest, grinning wanting nothing more right now. He needed to see her naked, touch her, explore every inch of her body prepare her for what he hoped would follow.

"What about you?" She turned her back, seeming suddenly timid and began to shed her clothing.

When she reached for the robe, she found nothing but air. She felt his big hands cup her breasts. "Are you so suddenly shy?" He turned her, "Let me look at you, feast my eyes on every sweet inch."

Her head rested against his chest, as he ran his hands along her back then to her butt, pressing her belly against his heavy arousal. "Guy..."

With a huge gulp of air, "We should go now." He helped her into the robe, tying it before he slipped on his.

He led her outside then around the corner of the house. "Where are you taking me?"

"It's an outdoor shower. Heavenly."

Inside, he turned on the water before shedding his robe. He gazed at her unable to say anything then he helped her disrobe and tugged her into the warm water. His mouth covered hers, slow, gentle, at first, then forcing her into a deep, wet, open-mouthed kiss that seemed to go on forever, his tongue plunging deeply, ravaging, subtly then moving with sensual, gentle abandon again.

Her hands had been set against his chest. Now they moved, stroking the deep, rich, crisp dark hair that grew upon it. He shifted against her, touching in turn, the stroke of his palm and fingers cradling her cheek, his thumb running from her throat to the valley between her breasts. His thumb and forefinger found her nipple, rolled and rubbed it, sending fiery burst of flame and heat through her breast to her whole body. She moaned against him instinctively arching toward him, her own fingers falling lower upon his chest to tangle into the dark hair there.

Picking up the soap, he watched her moisten her lips. With a groan of desire, the soap slipped from his hand and she was in his arms and he was inside her. She climaxed before he could barely touch her.

Limp against him, "How do you do this to me?"

He chuckled, needing the levity and, "Will you marry me?"

She stepped back, her hand on his chest. All emotion drained from her body. He watched her swallow before she bent over and picked up the soap. Ignoring him as well as his question, she began to wash the dirt and grime left from the trail before turning to wash him. It seemed she touched every inch of him, arousing him. Leaving him waiting for an answer to his proposal. He never meant to pop the question while they were in the shower, naked. Hell, it wasn't the most romantic way to ask but he had no regrets.

"Cas..."

"What?" She soaped her hair still ignoring his question, her back turned to him.

One of the twins must have left shampoo and conditioner in the shower before they arrived. Over her shoulder she handed him the bottle. It seemed she still didn't want to look at him.

"Will you marry me," he persisted, dumfounded by her seeming inability to look at him.

"Why?" She rinsed her hair.

Her breasts were so beautiful, not that large but perfectly shaped and their texture provocative. "Because you're my mate and I want you to become my wife."

"I see." She hesitated. "Not because you love me."

His mouth went dry. Weren't they one and the same? "You're my mate," he insisted coldly feeling the sting of a rejection he could and would not tolerate. "What does love have to do with anything?"

"Fairies like to marry for love, which is why I'm not marrying Cedric. Well, there are other reasons also. He's despicable and he sleeps around. I've heard rumors..."

Her few words rendered him speechless. "I knew this would not be easy, but I didn't expect a refusal."

"Is it because I carry your child. I will make a very good single parent. I have resources, you know. I don't need a man to put food on my table or to tell me what I can and cannot do." She grabbed the bath towel and began to dry herself.

"Hell..."

Where did that last part come from? He had no intention of telling her how she could live her life. He ran his hands through his hair, frustrated, angry and terrified as well that he would fail in this endeavor. Inhaling a long steady breath of air. Her yes answer meant so much to him. He felt as if she gut punched him.

"Cas." He wrapped his towel around his waist, reaching out to her, touching her on her shoulder. "I never thought about love, just sex. Don't know if we've known each other long enough to say the words. What I do know is that we are meant to be together, and I'm confident love will come in time. We need to commit to each other."

Her back stiffened as he slipped her arms into the robe, helping her. "I've loved you from the moment I saw you in my dreams." She turned around to stare at him. "This was not at all what I expected."

"Love at first site? A silly notion at best," he said, immediately regretting his words and understanding every tiny nuance in his voice, every word he spoke could have repercussions.

She started from the shower, her spine stiff, chin high. "Suppose I'll have to see you in your bedroom. Hope our clothes made it there. Feel way too vulnerable right now."

Fuck. He watched her back for a few seconds before racing after her with only the towel around him. When he reached her, he didn't touch her but fell into stride alongside her. "I've messed this up, haven't I?"

She lifted her shoulders in that utterly feminine shrug he was beginning to enjoy immensely, except for this moment. When she did that, he knew the winning hand was his if he played the game right.

"Can't say that you've done anything right." They strode through the bedroom.

He shut the door behind them, then leaning against it. "I see the food is here."

"I'm famished."

It seemed she tried to ignore him. He would allow that for a minute or two.

"Why do you want to marry me? I suppose that should be discussed."

Guy didn't really have an answer for that other than everything he'd already told her. He just did.

And that was that.

~ * ~

"Perhaps some wine would help. The alcohol might serve to relax me so I can think straight."

"Perhaps wine is not such a good idea." His gaze slipped to her stomach then back to meet her eyes."

Her lashes lowered, "You're right of course."

"I'll ask cook for some lemonade or something sparkling that's non alcoholic." He left, retuning in a few minutes with a bottle. "It's Chateau De Fleur a non alcoholic sparkling wine champagne. Perfect for your condition. Cook doesn't like the alcohol so she keeps this on hand."

He poured the Chateau for her and handed her a glass. The first sip warmed her to her toes. She thought for a moment it must be the suggestion of the alcohol. In any case she didn't care.

He poured the Pinot for himself.

She still wore her robe, knowing that before they finished the meal and the short nap that might ensue, he would have her out of any clothing she managed to put on. Wasting time on dressing would serve no purpose.

"You think better with the aid of alcohol?" she asked as she sipped the sparkling wine, watching the play of his muscles across his back as he walked.

He appeared a caged panther, roaming the room, back and forth then back again. Intermittently, he ran his hands through his hair. If he were in his shifter form, she imagined his tail twitching with frustration and annoyance, but the irritation was of his doing not hers.

"Always."

He downed the first then poured a second. Stopping for a moment, he stared at her, his eyes darkening and his brows drawing together.

Seeing the passion in his eyes she felt a ripple of energy surge down her spine. In another time she would enjoy the aftereffects. "Perhaps food would help me think straight. You've put a crazy spin on everything and you've only answered my questions with vagaries and innuendos, nothing I understand or agree with. What do we have for food?"

"Pre-dinner appetizers."

"Well, that helps."

She understood her sarcasm wouldn't relieve the tenseness of this situation, but she was upset about the turn of things, never thinking he would propose marriage this soon even though she'd hoped for exactly that. Knowing why he was acting so out of character was at the top of her list to discover. The man who always appeared so debonair and sure of himself was now acting the exact opposite.

"Cas." He was still pacing then he stopped and spoke determinedly his fists clenched tightly at his sides. When he turned to speak, his voice as well as his eyes were cold. "I need to marry you and mark you as mine to keep you safe, to keep Cedric away from you. The mark he can never rid you of, not even with magic."

She held up her hands as if that innocent gesture would stop this horrible tumble downhill. Every time he spoke, she understood less and he confused and rattled her already shaken nerves. Rubbing her arms as goose bumps rose, "Mark me? And not because you love me."

"Yes, damn this isn't going at all as I planned. You are my mate," he insisted forcefully.

"And how was that? The plan?"

She really wanted to jump in his arms and say yes to his proposal, but he would have to do a better job at explaining his thoughts about a marriage or love or not, it would never take place. This marking thing needed an explanation also.

"Cas," he began slowly at first, seeming to carefully measure each word, "the moment I saw you I knew we were meant for each other."

"Isn't that the same as love at first site? Oh, I forgot. I used the word love and you don't love me."

She didn't want to enjoy his discomfort, but this was so new to her. He had always been self-confident, on top of the world. Now he was shy, no withdrawn in a way, almost as if he was asking a girl on a first date. Instead, he was just trying to explain things to her, things only a shifter would know. Marking a mate had never turned up in any of her research.

"I don't know. Maybe?" He was roaming again, running his hands through his hair, picking up objects then setting them down again.

"Go on," she encouraged, trying not to smile. "What did you mean to say next? Just curious."

"I don't remember," he paused, his jaw clenched tight, his fist tighter.

"When you saw me, you knew we were meant for each other." She filled in the gap in his mind, hoping he'd figure out that his thoughts were the same as love at first site.

"That. Yes, it's true. You seemed just as eager as I was to get to know me, but there was no fairy dust." He tossed that out as if he wanted to test her.

He still didn't trust her. That bothered her. "None." She stiffened at his words, her fingers closing tightly on the stem of her glass. "You were my shapeshifter and I ran to you because I knew you would protect me. Nothing more."

"How? How would you know I would do that?"

She tossed her hair out of the way, trying to make sense of her thoughts. "A gut instinct and like I said before I fell in love with you that first night you came to me in my dreams. There was no question in my mind. Still have no doubts."

"Keep going." He seemed more in control of himself now that she was answering questions. "I like to hear how you feel about me."

"I believed Cedric might not want me if I wasn't a virgin. I didn't know anyone else well enough to climb into bed with them. I wasn't eager to pick someone up at a bar for a one-night stand. Didn't want to risk pregnancy with anyone but you."

That was exactly what she did. She'd gone to the Red Neck Saloon with the express purpose of going to bed with Guy McKenna, her shifter. Strange at the time she wasn't positive though if he was her shifter. The one-night stand didn't happen until the next day.

"Do you hear yourself?"

She stared into her glass of sparkling wine for so long it seemed she lost track of time. "Yes. I know I'm not making sense."

"You seduced me with that skimpy thong bikini so you would get pregnant. You didn't even give me a hint of what you were trying to do. You could have told me."

"You would have said no."

"Possibly, but if you explained why..."

"You still would have said no."

"Maybe." It seemed he meant to stick by his statement.

She expected to hear anger in his voice, but it resonated with determination as well as a purpose she didn't understand. "I did all that. Yes. Took advantage of you but I didn't think of it that way."

"What way were you thinking?"

Unable to look at him and see the expression of disgust she was sure would be there, "Just about myself and my needs. I was selfish. Not going to argue that point."

"You never told me. You never gave me a choice," he accused, his voice and his eyes cold once more. "That wasn't right."

"Did you want a choice? It seems even though you didn't know my reasons why, you did make a choice. You made love to me and seemed to enjoy it. What was it you said? A ride you wouldn't forget." She wasn't about to let him blame everything on her. "Besides, if I wasn't pregnant, would you be asking me to marry you?"

"Yes."

It was his turn for one-word answers. "Why are we arguing?"

"Because you haven't agreed to marry me and I'm trying to convince you it's the best course of action."

"You have a strange way of doing that."

"Like I told you before, this isn't going like I planned." He sat down beside her, touching her leg with his.

"You haven't explained this marking thing. Not going to agree to anything I'll regret." Marking sounded as if it would hurt.

He suddenly appeared relieved, the first smile since their discussion began gracing his handsome features. "If you agree, next time we make love, I'll let my claws out and you'll have ten tiny puncture marks on your shoulders."

"Will it hurt?"

"I don't know, but I'm sure the pain will subside, probably nothing more than when I took your virginity." He appeared smug now.

She had to think about this for a few seconds. "Easy for you to say. What happens next?"

"You will be mine through eternity." Through the terrycloth robe he squeezed her leg as if that would make everything perfect.

"Sounds a bit one sided to me. What about you? Do I get to mark you?"

He let out a roar of laughter. "The same for me. I will be yours forever and always. It's more binding than a wedding ceremony as well as more enduring. This is serious though." He paused in thought. "No, you don't mark me."

"So," she began considerately, "we both want to commit to each other but you don't love me. The question is whether I can commit to that. I want to marry a man who loves me." She supposed though her love for him would have to be enough for both of them.

"The bigger question is if you want to risk a life with Cedric? Isn't it enough that I crave you and honestly don't believe I want to live without you?" It seemed he was using every argument he could think of to convince her to say yes.

"Not wanting to live without me isn't love."

"Do you want me to lie?" he asked, his voice soft yet compelling.

It seemed he tried to seduce with his voice as well as his words. Sometime he managed to slip the cloth from her leg and his fingers now massaged her inner thigh.

She closed her eyes trying not to give into his seduction. A small lie would be nice.

Thunder echoed throughout the room. Neither one had enough clothing on to venture from the room to see what it was. Cas raced to the window, trying to see what was happening but she knew.

"Cedric's trying to breach the barricade."

Her hand rested on her throat. The sound of her heart seemed to be louder than the swarm of faeries battering the protective wall Maska built around them. Lord, she prayed the barrier would hold.

"Cedric." Guy was hopping from one leg to the other trying to get his pants on then a pair of sandals. "Get dressed and meet me outside."

He grabbed a t-shirt. He vanished.

As he raced from the room, "That's a yes..."

She knew he didn't hear her words. In a perfect universe, she'd have time to get to know him, every facet he'd share before they wed, before he marked her as his. She could ask questions of Sadie and Margo so she wouldn't be so frightened.

Obviously, this was not a perfect world.

Rummaging through her bag, she found a clean pair of shorts and t-shirt along with some underthings. She wasn't in a hurry to witness the events. If Cedric broke through, she had no way to defend herself. Guy's family would be the only barricade between her and the man she detested.

A horrible life with a man she detested.

The McKennas seemed to think they were invincible, as did Cedric. Uneager to meet her fate, she dressed slowly before walking outside. Her heart in her throat, she focused on the dark cloud now hovering above them. The loud roar and the pounding stopped.

The fairy swarm hovered in the sky while a few of them littered the ground outside the bubble. The McKenna's watched but Kimi stood with her fingers at her temples, her eyes closed.

From afar, Cas heard their great grandfather chanting, the rumble of wings above them, and an eerie whirring. As she approached, the silence between the McKennas was unnerving. The men all stood with their feet braced apart and their hands on their lean hips.

Kimi turned, her hands in the air. "Guy, take Cas to the house, now! His anger grows. She should not be seen."

The sharp breath Cas inhaled startled her as her body trembled with the thoughts emanating from Cedric. Her knees buckled and to Cas it seemed the ensuing time existed in slow motion. Before her hands hit the ground, Guy caught her, sweeping her into his arms, cradling her close to his heart. She heard the rapid pounding and understood his fear as well as his reluctance to leave. At that moment she felt his love, knew some of

102

his thoughts as he did everything in his power to protect her.

His long strides brought them to the house. He sat down on the sofa with her on his lap. As he stroked her arms, "What just happened?"

"Cedric spoke to me. Cursed might be more appropriate."

Nestled close to him, her body shook. She could barely inhale a breath of air. "I could hear his thoughts, yours as well."

"You could hear my thoughts?" he asked, seeming surprised. "That's what Kimi can do. She can understand what others are thinking."

She couldn't stop shaking her head then touching his face. "It wasn't words I heard but emotions I felt."

He remained quiet for a time, then. "You know it's going to be alright," he told her as he massaged her back. "Nothing is going to happen to you. You know that, right?"

She tried to stifle a sob, letting her head fall against his shoulder. "I don't know anything."

"Together the McKenna's magic is strong, stronger than one man or a few fairies who have some magical powers."

Wiping away tears from her eyes with the backs of her hands, she sat up. Shrugging out of his arms, she started for the door.

"I'm not..."

"You can't go out there, Cas." Suddenly he stood in front of her blocking her way. "Kimi understood Cedric's anger when he saw you. It will risk everything if you don't do as she says."

She comprehended the facts, knew Guy was right. Outside where Cedric could control her mind was the last place she should be, leaning into him for support. "I know."

"You said he spoke to you. What did he say?"

"It was more his emotions that swept through me but some words as well."

"What was he feeling toward you."

For a few moments there was an inexplicable distance between them. Something she never felt before. "Nasty horrible emotions. He called me a whore and a slut and that I was just fuc..." she moistened her lips needing distance from her thoughts. "In any case it wasn't nice. He told me when I was his wife, he would make me pay for my indiscretion and disloyalty."

"Does he know about our child?" Guy placed a possessive hand on her belly.

"I don't think so. He didn't say anything about that. Just knew I was intimate with you. Don't know how he knew unless Destiny told him."

Destiny appeared from the shadows. "I did. I admit it. Thought the simple truth would dissuade him and this would all be finished. You'd be free of him. That's what we all want."

"You were listening to us?" Cas asked feeling betrayed by her friend.

"The two of you were inside and talking before I could show myself. I'm sorry."

"I hoped he'd stop pursuing me when he discovered the truth. Obviously, I was wrong."

"Didn't tell him about the child because I didn't know." Destiny settled on the top of a vase, daintily crossing her legs.

"What's Cedric going to do to you when he finds out the part you've played in all of this?" Cas waved her hand through the air.

"I'm hoping to stay with you and Guy."

"Three's a crowd, Destiny. It's not that I don't like your company but..."

"I don't belong. I can't change to human form like you can." She heaved a long dramatic sigh. "Still, I know how to make myself scarce."

"I'm only half fairy," Cas reminded her. "In any case..."

"I can't go back there." Destiny picked at imaginary pieces of dust on her clothing before looking at Cas with tears in her eyes. "I did this for you. When he realizes I betrayed him, he'll punish me."

Cas looked to Guy searching his face for some sign, a clue that he might be acceptable to Destiny living near them.

"We could build a fairy house out by his pool. Would you like that? What would you do for company?"

"I have a beau, Cas. He would come stay with me if you all agree." She fluttered above the vase for a few seconds before she settled back down, her smile tearing at Cas' heart.

When Guy didn't answer. "Of course, both of you can stay."

"Caucus," Brody said as the clan walked into the room flanked by Niagel. "Everyone is here."

"Destiny can stay here at my ranch if she'd like along with her boyfriend. I'll even marry them in the ways of the ancients if they'd like that," Niagel spoke slowly each word defined by itself. He smiled, clearly pleased.

Destiny blushed, lowering her head. "We were handfasted in the ways of our ancients, but I wouldn't mind renewing my vows in another way."

"Back to the business at hand," Carr reminded everyone. "The two of you," his glance swept from Guy to Cas, "must commit and do it as soon as possible. There is not a second to lose. You must also consummate the marriage in all ways."

"I don't trust Cedric," Kimi said. "There was something in the way he avoided my most urgent questions or walked around them with his answers. The two of you must present him with a strong united front and marriage along with the marking is the best way to achieve that."

"As well you shouldn't trust him," Cas said. "I suppose he told you how much he loved me."

"No, no he didn't and that is what terrifies me," Kimi said. "He told me only that you are pledged to him, had been for twenty plus years. I don't think he even knows how old you are."

"Neither do I," Guy admitted. "Suppose there are a lot of things we don't know about each other."

"Well, for all of you, I'm twenty-three years old. How old are you?" She turned to Guy.

"Been waiting to meet my soul mate for twenty-five years." He laughed then. "What's your favorite color?"

"Children," Lynn said, "that's for another time.

"Sounds like bedroom talk to me," Carr said only to find Margo hitting him in the arm.

"Doesn't sound like any of your bedroom talk," she said blushing prettily.

Carr pulled her into his arms, kissing her soundly, changing the blush from a light pink to a bright red. She hit him again. "Stop that."

Brody whistled gaining everyone's attention. "This is serious. We have the fairy king's son sitting outside our walls and he wants his woman back."

"She's mine," Guy growled.

Kimi spoke then repeating her earlier statement. "The two of you need to marry as soon as possible. Great grandfather will perform the uniting ceremony." She paused, glancing at them. "If the two of you agree. Have you talked this out?" she looked to Cas for an answer seeming to know Guy's.

A few seconds passed before she responded. "I said yes but I do have reservations. There are some things he failed to explain. I need clarification before I commit."

"There is no time," Niagel spoke again, his voice firm. "If you said yes, so be it. The elements as well as the gods have spoken to you, even for you perhaps. My housekeeper will give you the appropriate garments."

Cas' heart leapt to her throat. This was all happening too fast for her peace of mind, but she as the others, saw no alternative. Marrying Guy was what she wanted. Perhaps when she found herself in Cactus Junction that had not been her agenda.

But now...?

"They are laid out on the bed in Guy's room."

"Guy and Cas should go now before Cedric changes his mind and bombards the wall again," Brody told them.

Guy stood then holding out his hand. "Are you coming?"

Hesitant at first, she thought on everything she'd been through and held out her hand. With a huge gulp of air, "Yes."

"Are you sure?"

"More than anything, I'm positive."

~ * ~

Cedric retreated to a makeshift tent near the ranch house. His wings fluttering, he paced, agitated, angry, stressed. His woman slept with another man. How dare she?

"Casidhe is a whore. She fucked him, let him take what was mine, what was promised. I'll see her dead." Spittle flew from his lips his fists hitting the walls.

"Why don't you just let her go?" The young woman he had brought to him to ease his stress asked. "She is nothing to you now."

"Because if I can't have her no one else will." His growl of loathing gave him immediate pleasure when the naked woman on his bed shuddered. "What is your name?"

"Kendra. Is it to your liking?" she asked a tiny smile on her face as if she was shy but also pleased to be summoned by him.

"It's not Celtic. It's Anglo." He waved his hand in the air, slowly approaching her. She was his prey, but she didn't understand it yet. "Suppose you'll have to do for now."

He came down upon her then, took her without care. When he was sated, he adjusted his clothing. Sitting down on the bed he poured them both a glass of wine ignoring her tears as well as the blood-stained sheets. He hated the mess even while he enjoyed having a woman for her first time. Perhaps he was happier Casidhe was no longer a virgin.

Ringing a bell, he waited for a servant to appear. "We need clean sheets and a bath for Kendra."

The servant nodded backing from the room seeming to need escape. "You did well," Cedric turned to the girl. "Perhaps you'll find some pleasure as the night continues."

"I thought..."

She gasped when he came down beside her again, touching her intimately. He laughed at her sharp cry. "You like this."

"Y-yes," she stammered, her dark sooty lashes fluttering on alabaster cheeks.

"What did you say?" he commanded.

"Yes. I like this."

"Good," he murmured as he licked her bottom lip, biting until he heard another cry before licking the blood away with the tip of his tongue. He didn't care if it was a cry of pleasure or pain, both excited him. Both made him hard, he needed her again.

"Cedric," she said his name.

"Lie back and spread your legs for me. I want to see all of you."

"No."

"But you will or you and your siblings will forever regret this night. You will do it every time I tell you."

Chapter Five

As the housekeeper told them, the clothing had been set upon the bed. They were told to dress only in what had been set out. For a moment, he paused realizing there were no undergarments.

Cas seemed to hold back for a moment even while he was eager for the ceremony. He slipped out of his clothing and into the lightweight linen pants. After tying the drawstring around his waist, he put on the beautiful white doeskins shirt that had been embroidered with Native American symbols. They were symbols that were known to his great grandfather and probably only a handful of surviving Apaches. Thankfully, the vest covered his private parts that seemed to be visible through the fabric of his pants.

"You still have reservations?" he queried glancing her way before looking at the dress that had been set out for her and praying she would not change her mind. What could possibly be holding her back?

She said yes.

Cas was fiddling with the hem of her t-shirt, seeming unsure of herself. "Some," she whispered, her hands shaking. "I understand there is no choice. Marrying someone because it was the only plausible way to stay alive and sane has never been a dream of mine."

Stepping close to her Guy drew her into his arms. "I'm sorry we can't do this the way you'd like, something more comfortable for both of us. I promise you, we can have a normal wedding when this all said and done, we'll have a normal marriage. I promise."

"Really?" She looked at him with moisture filled eyes. "It's increasingly hard to believe there is anything normal about either of us. We are both so different. How can anything between end up normal?"

He held her face in his hand and with his thumbs he brushed the tears from her eyes and lightly kissed her. "The girls will love to plan a wedding with you. They will have you thinking you are crazy by the time they finish all the details. I promise you there will be another wedding, just what your dreams have always been."

"You think they accept me now?" she asked still fidgeting with her clothing and looking at the wedding dress lying on the bed. "I had hoped but when they showed up in the guise of a barbecue, I didn't feel friendly vibes coming from them. They didn't trust me."

"The girls no longer have a choice. The McKennas have banned together to protect you. Wedding or no wedding you are one of us and you will never escape the fact you carry a McKenna child in your womb."

"Still..."

She seemed so unsure of herself and his heart went out to her. "Still...?" One eyebrow arched skyward.

"Would you leave for a few minutes so I can get ready?" She slanted him a tiny smile. "I need a few moments of privacy to gather my thoughts."

"You're not going to balk on me and run away?"

He suddenly felt insecure. She had been hesitant since he posed the question. Now she wanted to be left alone.

"Where would I go? Into Cedric's arms? There is no way. I just want to look presentable when we are married. Don't want any regrets."

"No regrets," he repeated as he backed out of the room.

The door closed behind him with a soft sound. For a few seconds he leaned against the solid wood, eyes closed, wishing he could hear her thoughts, wishing he knew if she was dressing.

He could not. So, he pushed away from the door, hoping for the best.

Walking into the living room, he was met by his chattering siblings and their spouses. The sight gave him reason to smile. They were all close and the fact they accepted Cas pleased him. For now, it seems as if the Cedric has stopped the attack.

"Well, where is she? Thought she would be right behind you." Brody asked as he rose to greet him. "Your soon to be wife needs to show herself."

"She's still getting ready." Guy held up his hands to ward off what he knew would be his brother's hasty comments. "I understand the wedding needs to be sooner not later, but she wants to look her best."

"Her best when time is of the essence?" Carr asked a smattering of disdain in his voice.

"You're a man. You can't possibly understand," Margo laughed. "Perhaps I will go help." She looked to Sadie if she would want to go with her.

"I most certainly do."

"And too practical when it comes to things like this." She sighed. "There was time not so long ago you were the playboy of the family. I remember when I first saw you atop that table in Las Vegas in little but your..."

"Hush, Margo," Carr laughed, seeming to take his wife's teasing in stride. "That story is not for my family or anyone else for that matter. It's most definitely private between the two of us."

"As we all have a few tales that are for our memories only," Deacon said, staring at Lyn, his eyes simmering with unleashed passion almost as if he thought there was time he would sweep her into his arms and their bedroom.

"There are certainly things I don't wish to share," Maska agreed.

"She'll be out in a few minutes, I'm sure." Guy tried to reassure his family as well as himself but he thought it was more for himself than his siblings. "If it makes any of you feel better, I'll go to our room and see what is holding her up," knowing he wanted to make sure she was still in the room and willing to wed him.

"I'll go to your room and see what I can do," Lyn volunteered, rising from her place on the sofa. "I know exactly how she feels. As random as this happened it's still her wedding day. She might want to confide in someone or ask questions. All of this must be overwhelming."

"What could be overwhelming?" Brody asked seeming confused.

Lyn turned to Guy. "Did you tell her about the marking ceremony? That in and of itself could make her want to run away. She will wonder what the procedure entails. I'm sure you explained but from a man's point of view, hardly suitable for a young woman who has never been around shifters.

"I did tell her, explained as best I could."

He suddenly had so many doubts and reservations he didn't understand. She was so tiny all he yearned for was to protect and shelter.

"I'm sure you did just fine," Kimi said slanting him a warm sisterly smile.

Guy stood and watched Lyn walk from the room, Margo behind her, glancing down at his watch. "I just want this to be over with? Feel as if I've waited an eternity to find my mate. Now that she's here and willing to marry..."

"Pre-wedding jitters, old man," Carr laughed patting his baby brother on the back. "I remember them well. Seemed like I couldn't shake them until the words were said and we were cutting the cake."

"She loves me, or so she says," Guy murmured, almost believing he was talking to himself despite the fact his family was in the same room. "Should I feel that way too? That's one of her objections. I can't say the words." He sat down head in his hands for a moment before he looked up. "Don't really understand the difference between a mate for life and love."

"Of course, you love her. Cas is your mate," Kimi said. "You love your mate. It's a given. Just come clean, vanish that stubborn male pride of yours and tell her you love her. She did the hard part. She told you first."

He was stymied now, looking up, "This has happened too fast. No time to date or get to know her. Hardly know anything about Cas except I want her, need and crave her just about every second of the day."

"Maybe you should reconsider this wedding and marking. It's quite the commitment for a man to make if there is no love involved," Brody said blandly. "If you don't love her..."

Guy closed his eyes inhaling long and deep, thinking about everything his brothers and sisters were telling him. Finally, "No, giving up is not possible. I can't live without her. That is what I do know."

Brody handed him a glass of whiskey, grinning as if he knew things. "Drink this. It will steady your nerves. Might make your thoughts clearer too." He slapped him on the back, laughing. "Glad to hear she loves you though, even if you can't return the sentiment."

Sitting again and resting his forearms on his legs, his glass in both hands, Guy said, "Thing is I want to say the words. Tell her I love her. Seems they get stuck in my throat and won't come out."

"In time the words will be easy to say," Maska told him, joining in on the conversation. "You might be surprised. After I abducted Kimi, she didn't want anything to do with me, didn't trust me."

His heart pounding in his chest, he glanced at his watch again then the hallway leading to his room. "She's already so beautiful she melts my heart when I look at her. What the hell is taking so long?"

"It's only been ten minutes," Kimi said sarcastically. "If she is going to look amazing for you and this special day, she'll do her hair and makeup. That will take at least fifteen. Don't be so impatient."

"This ceremony was supposed to be urgent," Guy shot back clearly at the end of his patience, "I'm going to see what's taking so long."

"No, you aren't." both Sadie and Kimi stepped in front of him. "You'll have to go through us and that wouldn't be pleasant as you learned when I was growing up."

"Give her the time she needs," Sadie said, her voice soft. "I promise you she won't disappoint. She might also need time to reconcile to the marriage. I know it wasn't easy for me either, not being a sifter."

Turning on a heel, he strode to the front door, looking out on the porch then, "Where are we going to do this? Outside?"

"Outside would infuriate Cedric if he's watching," Kimi said, her voice soft, "We don't want to anger him anymore than he already is. At the moment he's entertaining himself with another woman, but she doesn't deserve anymore of his wrath. If we were to toss this in his face, he might kill her."

"He's mistreating this lady?" Guy asked, his muscles tensing. "Can't you do something about it?"

"Unfortunately, no. Not unless you want Maska to break the shield so we can have that battle we're all trying to avoid by this rushed marriage. I hear his thoughts as well as the young lady's but nothing can be done. Cedric is a man set in his ways, one who is used to having what her wants. Cruelty to women for him is not uncommon."

"Cas will avoid Cedric with your marriage. She is after all, the woman he is seeking, has been promised. With this new knowledge we can't possibly let her go to Cedric whether she was your mate or not." Carr's brows drew together seeming to understand his distress and agitation.

"Another drink?" Brody asked, handing him one. "Still need to relax and clear those thoughts?"

He pushed his hands through his hair before rubbing the back of his neck. "Sure. If it will help pass the time."

Restless, he roamed into the family room then the dining room. A three-tier cake sat on the table. "What the devil," he murmured looking for the cook who appeared from the kitchen with a plate of cheeses and meats. Crystal champagne glasses adorned the table as did cooled bottles of champagne along with the sparkling wine for Cas as well cook's special appetizers.

"I didn't expect..."

He smiled fondly at the woman he'd known for all his years. She had always been there for his family during good as well as difficult times and she was here for him now. She must have started baking as soon as they arrived. He was amazed.

He opened his arms wide for a quick hug. She set the platter she carried on the table before walking into his arms.

"What did you expect?" she asked stepping back.

"Nothing I suppose. Didn't think we would celebrate." What he'd believed was that they would have the ceremony then he would take her to bed for the second ritual.

"Only the best for the littlest of the clan," cook said, laughing at her joke. "Nothing makes me happier than to cook for the McKennas. Seems they don't come around as often. Perhaps when your little one is born you will find a way to let me see him."

"Youngest but not the littlest," Guy corrected her with a laugh. Stealing an appetizer, he popped it in his mouth. "You're still the best damned cook in California, and I promise the babe will be in your arms as soon as Cas feels comfortable enough to bring him here."

"Sierra Madres," she amended, blushing from his compliment.

114

"Would never want to take on the entire state."

He grabbed another morsel of food expecting her to swat his hand as she used to do when he was younger. When she didn't, "You're getting slow in your old age. You always swatted my hand away."

"Bite your tongue, young man. This is your wedding and you can have whatever you want. Eat everything before the others get a chance as long as you leave the wedding cake until your bride is with you."

His emotions bursting with feelings for her, he gave her another quick hug. "Should I tell Cas I love her?"

She was wagging her finger at him, her smile changing to a scowl. "Only if you do love her, but you shouldn't be marrying that pretty little woman if you don't love her. What is this talk anyway?"

He couldn't help but shrug, feeling a bit of tension ease with the movement. "Thing is, don't know if I do?"

"Sit down and explain yourself. You know I'll listen, always have," she said watching him with a strange expression on her face.

He proceeded to tell cook the story while she seemed to listen attentively. "There it is. What do you think?"

She tenderly placed her hand on his. "You love her. Tell her before she pulls away from you." She stood, smoothing her dress with her hands. "You know my advice is sound. "Tell her when you claim her tonight it will make everything better. She'll forget the pain and love you even more than she already does. If you don't say the words she craves, the night will be more tempestuous as will the days after."

He stiffened understanding the omen. She was almost as in tune with the elements as his great grandfather. While he didn't want to lie to Cas, it seemed everyone believed he was in love with her and he wanted to make her happy.

Brody appeared in the kitchen, grabbing an appetizer in the process while cook swiped at his hand. "It's time."

"Bout time."

Guy inhaled a gulp of air, stealing himself for the ceremony. In a few minutes he'd be married and a few months later a father. Perhaps he should take cook's, as well as his sibling's, advice and tell Cas he loved her. Conceivably, all his insecurities and the speed with which all this

115

took place had him wavering, doubting himself.

When he followed behind Brody, he saw everyone except Niagel gathered in a circle in the middle of the living room. Chairs and tables had been pushed back to make room. Never witnessing a marriage such as this, he wasn't sure what to expect.

Carr met them, "I've been told that you need to stand in the middle with the rest of the clan surrounding you."

"Where is Cas?" He'd expected to see her when he left the kitchen. The room seemed empty without her.

"She will be here." That was all Brody would tell him.

"All right then. I will have to trust my big brother and head of clan McKenna." Guy stood in the middle of the large circle, directing his attention toward his room where he expected her to emerge.

She appeared then, holding his great grandfather's arm as the old man ushered her into the room. It seemed there were elements of a traditional wedding as well as the ancient.

Cas wore the white gown that had been laid out on the bed. Unlike his garments they were not made of doeskin but a lightweight material that seemed to cling to all her curves.

His breath caught when he saw her. He knew she wore no undergarments beneath the gown but at the moment she wore a doeskin cape, tied at the neck and falling around her, covering all of her. When she took the cloak off, parts of her would show that were meant only for his eyes. If he could see that fact, so could everyone else.

Brody, still close to him, whispered. "The ceremony is ancient as well as traditional that the bride and groom be naked for everyone to witness. Be pleased Niagel considered the more modern days feeling about nakedness."

That didn't make him feel much better. He wondered if she knew everyone would soon be able to see all of her. If she didn't know, he wasn't going to be the one to tell her. Instead he meant to feast his eyes on her, realizing by this evening she would be truly his.

They stopped in the middle of the circle and Niagel handed her to him. "Please face each other. You must first divest yourself of the vest."

He looked to Cas glad that their nakedness would not completely be shared with the others even for tradition.

Lyn was behind her. "Undo the bow." When that was done Lyn slipped the cape from Cas' shoulders.

"Take her left hand in your right," Niagel told him.

After that, Brody wrapped a leather thong around their wrists, binding them together. He felt a wave of happiness and completeness wash through him at the contact. When he looked into her eyes, he saw the same emotions. It seemed his heartbeat melded with hers as did each breath he inhaled became one with Cas.

Niagel, his aged face smiling at them, took their hands in his and began to chant, at first soft but growing louder as the time seemed to speed by. The tongue was ancient and he felt the elements as he called upon them to bless the binding together of their lives.

Wind, water, fire and earth, he felt their calling, their warnings as well as the intensity of the threats that seemed to come along with the ceremony. His legs began to cramp. He felt her distress as if he was one with her. This needed to end or she would be a crumpled ball on the floor.

Still the room turned on its axis, slowly then faster just as Niagel's words grew in speed and force. Dizziness assailed him as Cas seemed to lean into him, her eyes closed, features stretched thin. Tangible strain was etched in the fine lines of her delectate face.

As if Niagel understood or the ceremony was indeed finished, his chanting ceased. Slowly he bent over and kissed their bound hands. Then, "You are wed. All of the gods have witnessed the joining of Casidhe and Guy. Through all eternity you are bound to each other. As time goes by and the bonds of earth let you go you will find each other in another time just as you have now. Tonight, if the gods are pleased with this union, you will witness some of your past lives."

At Niagel's words he heard Cas suck in a breath of air and he understood then she would see them as they existed before when they made love, when he claimed her as his through the marking ritual.

He directed his attention toward his great grandfather, "We are husband and wife?" Guy asked unsure what to do. "May I kiss her?" He was hesitant to ask the question.

Niagel nodded, a smile on his face. "Whatever you do until and while you mark your woman must be done while your hands are bound together. Keep that in mind and don't allow the spirits to look unfavorably on your joining."

"Will you put your lips on mine? Kiss me chastely now and save the best for private?" he whispered to Cas, hoping no one else heard, but the laughter and applause surrounding him told him different.

When she tilted her head slightly before nodding her permission, he brushed his mouth across hers. Once then twice, wanting to deepen the contact but not with all the onlookers.

Cas was his now.

He pulled away. "Are you hungry," he asked. "I believe we need to cut the cake first, drink a little champagne, eat something so we can survive the nightly activities I've planned for the two of us."

"We need to make love and you need to mark me. Lyn explained everything to me. I'm not afraid anymore." Yet the way she caught her full and very tempting bottom lip between her teeth and the strained smile told him differently.

Tonight, he would take great care and consideration with his bride, his mate.

"We need to celebrate first." He led her to the dining room before pouring her a glass of champagne, lifting his glass and waiting for Cas and the others to follow suit. "To my beautiful bride."

Then Brody stepped forward, "To the newest McKenna. May she make my baby brother the happiest man alive."

~ * ~

"Knock, knock," Lyn peaked into the bedroom. She had champagne glasses in one hand a bottle under an arm and a platter of appetizers resting on her second hand. Margo stood behind her. "Can we come in? We bring gifts and food to eat as well as something that might relax those nerves I'm sure you're experiencing. A little of your sparkling champagne since we heard you're pregnant. Something nice before a harrowing experience is always a good idea."

"You two are goddesses," Cas smiled feeling suddenly relieved she didn't have to do this by herself. "Thanks for coming to my rescue. I had serious thoughts about running away."

She had been sitting on the bed staring at the wedding dress that wasn't much of a dress, knowing everyone would be able to see all of her and she didn't know how she would be able to present herself for the wedding. This was a dress that left nothing to one's imagination.

"I can't wear that thing." She lifted the beautiful yet sheer gown high so the women could take a good look at it. "See?"

"Umm... I see what you mean," Lyn's pause seemed extra-long. "You don't have a choice though and I truly believe there must be a reason great grandfather insisted on this dress."

"I'm sure Lyn is right," Margo said, critically eyeing the dress.

"What possible explanation could there be?"

"When you go out there, I can walk in front of you. I doubt if it was Niagel who suggested this dress, he had the intention that everyone would see all of you when he had Cook set this on the bed." She picked up the gown, holding it into the sunlight, which glistened through it as if it was nothing.

Cas felt the ensuing shudder shimmy down her spine. Tears tumbled from her eyes. Wiping them away with the back of her hand, she was shaking her head over and over, not understanding why all this had to be so difficult. She would have been just as happy to elope. She would rather wear her shorts and tank top.

"I can't wear that. This has gone too far. I'll find a way to stay away from Cedric but wearing that," she pointed a finger at the dress Lyn was holding up. "I can't do it. I won't."

"Not even for a lifetime of happiness with your mate. You love him, I'm sure of it. Have you told Guy?" Margo asked.

"I did tell him. I've been completely honest and open with that man and you know what he told me? He said he didn't love me. Why the hell did he ask me to marry him? He doesn't have to be a martyr."

Lyn drew Cas' hands into hers. "He loves you. Don't ever doubt it. He's a McKenna male and those words don't come easy to any of them. Every time he looks at you his eyes darken with desire."

"That doesn't make it right." Cas looked away even while she appreciated Lyn's efforts on her behalf. "Desire is not love."

"No, no it doesn't but it's the way it is for now. He'll come around then he'll tell you the words more times than any woman needs to hear. Deacon isn't even a McKenna and that is the way he is too."

"That might be meant to reassure but..." Cas swallowed trying to erase the fear that she was just about to make the worst mistake of her life. Marriage was for a lifetime and it seemed these people believed it was for eternity."

"It took Carr a long time to say the words to me," Margo said with a whimsical smile.

"I'll bet he's said other things though, affectionate and endearing things, words that mean he loves you." Lyn twirled around the room with the dress held to her shoulders. "This is by any and all standards the most unique wedding dress I've ever seen. Deacon would love it if I showed up in our bedroom with nothing on but this confection."

"Like what other things?" Cas asked, watching Lyn as she danced around the room.

Lyn stopped, seeming to think "Like, oh, he can't live without you, comes to mind. Has he told you that?"

Cas slowly nodded, hearing the same argument Guy made to her earlier. She could be wrong but Destiny pointed out that he loved her, now both Lyn and Margo did the same. It was his actions that cemented his love for her. Her friend insisted actions speak louder than words.

She'd certainly appreciate hearing the words.

"Yes, he has, but I need to hear, I love you, come from between his lips."

She didn't want to be stubborn about this issue but she was, even while she understood she would marry Guy without him telling her he loved her. Sudden sadness enveloped her as she tried to push the debilitating emotion from her mind and focus on what was good about today.

After setting the dress on the bed, Lyn poured champagne for both of them. "Before you put on that dress, you are, we are going to have at least two of these glasses and perhaps one of Cook's wonderful little appetizers. I don't care how much time it takes. The men can wait."

"I think I'd like that. Always can use a little false courage." Cas sipped the sparkling beverage, enjoying the bubbles hitting her nose. "False courage," she repeated wondering if that was really what she was trying for. She would have to imagine the alcohol as well as the courage.

Lyn wrapped an arm around her, giving her a quick hug. "I know we were hard on you that first day. The brothers were sure you sprinkled some of that fairy dust in Guy's eyes and convinced him to do things out of character. No one trusted you or your intentions. We are a very and at times over protective clan."

Cas bristled at Lyn's words. She said, "I thought about doing the dust for a second but knew if I did, I would regret it."

"I'm glad of that."

"Knock, knock," Cook poked her head inside. "Everyone busy getting ready for the ceremony?"

"Come in," Lyn answered for her.

Cook stepped inside, brandishing a solid white cape as she'd become a matador. "Got something for you to wear over that dress, at least for a little while. Think it will make you feel better about... Well you know." She slanted a pointed look at the so-called wedding dress.

"Thank you, thank you so much. I can't tell you how much this means to me," Cas felt as if she gushed but every word was true. By bringing her the cape, Cook lifted a huge burden off her shoulders.

"Seems we better get on with the preparations for the ceremony. I brought a few things at the bequest of Niagel. One is the cape. It will be something new for you."

Lyn scrunched her eyes. "In all the rush, I forgot about our traditions, but what will she do for blue and borrowed?"

"I've the blue also." Cook held up a garter with a blue bow nestled in the lace. "Not too sure if that's allowed under the circumstances but I don't care. The old man will have to put aside a few of the ancient rules for a couple of modern ones even though he'd said she was to wear nothing but the dress."

"The old man?" Lyn laughed, seeming pleased at Cook's words. "You talk to great grandfather that way? He's always so serious. I would expect him to conjure up a bolt of lightning to strike you down."

"The man does have a sense of humor. If you thought about it, you'd remember all the times he's made you laugh. In my defense, he is old. We are both nearly ancient." Cook admonished Lyn. "I love the old man dearly and when we're here by ourselves we don't hold to the niceties. We always say it the way it is."

"Well, it's all new to me but I've figured out what you can borrow, Cas." She unfastened a delicate gold chain that held one piece of turquoise. Deacon gave it to me just because he wanted to. So, it can be your borrowed."

She handed it to Cas who turned the piece of jewelry over in her hand. "It's beautiful, thank you." She started to tear up again but this time was able to push the moisture to the back of her eyes. "I'll never be able to repay all of you for everything you've done for me."

"Let me help you with that," Cook volunteered, taking it from Cas before fastening it for her. "One piece of jewelry seems sensible for something like this. Wouldn't want the old shaman to shoot angry looks at you when he sees what we added to her attire." Cook laughed.

"Now for the dressing of the bride and first undressing of the bride," Margo laughed, seeming to be thinking of the wedding night.

"Would you like some privacy? You can knock on the door when you have the dress on and we'll come back and help you with your hair."

Cas lifted her shoulders feeling a bit of dread at the daunting minutes ahead of her. Once again, her body shuddered. "What difference does it make? You will see all of me when you come back in. It's not the two of you seeing me that makes me want to run away. It's the men."

"Yeah, I'm sure Guy isn't going to like it at all, but there is nothing to be done about it. Now let's hurry up and get this over with. The sooner we get the two of you wed the sooner we can move on to things that are more fun."

"You both are right. If I don't show myself soon, Guy will be knocking down the door just to make sure I'm alright."

Determined to be brave Cas stood. In seconds her clothes littered the floor and Lyn stood beside her. "Lift your arms."

Cas did enjoy the sensations as the garment slid down her body. The shoulders were fashioned together with a bow that could be easily untied. She wondered about that but was sure there was some reasoning behind it. Was also pretty sure she would find out soon enough. Perhaps sometime in the ceremony she would have to be stark naked.

"There," Lyn stood back seeming to admire Cas. "Would you like your hair swept up or do want to leave it down?"

"You are a beautiful bride," Margo added.

"If I leave it down, it will cover my breasts." She stroked her hair trying to place it strategically to conceal.

"Perfect, then all we need to do is your makeup."

"I don't wear much."

"Don't make her feel like a clown," Cook advised. "If she's not used to it, too much makeup on that pretty face will not allow her to like herself and her appearance."

"I will do it myself and you can curl my hair." Cas sat down in front of a mirror trying her best to make all of this work.

Cas applied a bit of makeup a little blush and concentrating on her eyes she made them look bigger with eyeliner and a pale shadow as she applied a nude colored lip gloss.

"There." She sat back, staring at herself in the mirror before turning to look at the two women. "Am I presentable?"

"Beautiful," Lyn whispered, smiling.

"Breathtaking," Margo murmured.

"You will steal his breath before he has chance to inhale." Cook added with a huge grin.

"Come here," Lyn said, "and I will help you with the cape. "No one will see anything. These clothes must be for after the ceremony."

"If that's the case someone should have asked me my opinion," Cas murmured wishing she'd had some say in any part of this.

"Because of the threat of Cedric, the ancient ways needed to be adhered to," Cook repeated what they already knew. "The dress is special for ritual. As I said earlier, in the ancient days the couple wore nothing at all. This is a huge concession on Niagel's part. I know he struggled over this decision for many days."

"Days?" Cas suddenly felt overwhelmed by what she said.

"Yes, days. He knew of your challenges. Saw you in his dreams before you even reached Cactus Junction and Guy. There has never been a question in his mind that you are Guy's mate."

"I wish I understood more of this, but fairies do have their ceremonies and ancient traditions too." Cas walked to Lyn who was holding the cloak, unwilling at the moment to comment on Cook's revelation.

Lyn slipped the garment over her shoulders before tying it closed with a bow and adjusting it so it covered her. "Everything is tied with a bow. Is there some significance in that?" She glanced Cook's way as if hoping the older woman would have an answer.

Cook chuckled softly. "To make the disrobing easier, maybe. Other than that, I don't believe the bows mean anything."

"What do you know that we don't?" Lyn was quick to ask, seeming to misinterpret Cook's comment.

"You will see in a few minutes and I suppose you can make guesses about after the ceremony. Now, I'll fetch Niagel and we'll proceed." Cook left shutting the door quietly behind her.

Then, "Tell me what you can about the marking?"

"For everyone the sensations are unique. I was not marked by another panther but rather a tiger. Deacon is a shifter but his animal form is that of a white tiger. I will be honest with you. It did hurt but only for a short time. Kimi was never marked, because her soul mate is a witch and Sadie, well, I think the process was very painful for her. She never speaks of it except with a grimace and to look away. Brody won't talk about it either. It seems the two of them want to leave it in the past."

"So, because I'm a fairy it will most likely hurt more. Well, that's reassuring." She let out a long breath of air, telling herself it will all be over in a few hours and she would be able to enjoy the rest of her life with Guy. *Don't worry yourself sick over this,* she admonished herself.

This was a small price to pay.

Cook opened the door. "Niagel is here to serve as both the shaman and the man to give you to Guy."

Niagel offered his arm and Cas accepted it. "We will go now and you will become one with Guy. All the gods in the universe will accept your marriage as the one true one. You will have naught to fear. Cedric can rant and rave but he will be unable to change what is done here."

Her heart pounding, she walked from the room with Niagel. No more words were spoken until they stepped into the living space. The sight of Guy stole her breath. His dark hair and deep tan against the white of his garments painted a picture she would never forget. The steel blue of his eyes simmered with desire. He was her heart and she would do anything for him and to keep him by her side.

He smiled at her. He seemed to offer encouragement. When she stepped into the center of the circle formed by the McKenna clan, Niagel asked them to remove the garments that concealed them from the others. She inhaled sharply as she lost the protective covering.

Her gaze roamed to Guy as she tried to settle her focus on his chest, yet she could not help but see his private parts as she knew he saw all of her. He was so beautiful though. She also realized Niagel had turned them so they were the only ones who could see anything of them but their backsides.

Heat rushed through her, as a fine trembling seemed to take over her legs as they threatened to buckle. He was looking at her, his eyes smoldering with desire and raw passion. She sucked in air, her nipples tightening at the thought of his mouth closing over them.

Then their wrists were tied together, his thumb tracing gentle circles on her wrists to reassure or to seduce she couldn't be sure.

"You will be fine," he mouthed. "No one but me sees you."

She nodded a few times still so embarrassed she knew heated color painted her face as well as her body. He stepped closer to her as Niagel began to chant. The song seeming much like the one Guy chanted to her when he tried to calm her nerves that first night they met.

The effect of Niagel's words were nothing like the song Guy sang to her. As the time passed, she closed her eyes as it seemed the elements of the earth took over her soul. The world rumbled around her, seemed to toss her body back and forth until she wasn't sure she could remain standing then everything stilled and for a moment calmness entered into her soul.

Soft winds caressed her yet slowly they grew stronger until it seemed she would be swept off her feet. Just as she knew she could withstand nothing more the earth began to spin. Dizziness assailed her. With her eyes now open, she watched as the walls of the ranch house swirled around her. When she thought to crumble to the floor, Guy held her up, his hand encircling her waist. In her heart she felt his words of encouragement and stood straighter because of them.

"Please, whatever gods are out there, let me survive this," she thought she whispered.

The roar of the water surrounding them would have made the words vanish as if they'd never been spoken. Perhaps they had not been spilled from her lips. The liquid fell upon them, seeming to wash away the sins of their lives.

Perhaps their past lives too.

Her hair was plastered to her face and dripping between her breasts. Her dress molded to her body, to every curve her nipples hard, pressing against the fabric that did nothing to conceal only reveal. She felt his arousal against her belly while she knew they stood so close he would feel all of her also. Moistening her lips, the moisture from the water falling around them left droplets there. She wanted him to kiss her. Instead his large hands cupped her bottom drawing her so close nothing separated them.

Flames leapt from the floor, surrounding them in heat. The liquid slowly evaporated leaving her flushed, awakened, excited. Perhaps ready to mate. It seemed the fire seared her skin. She let her head settle against Guy's chest even while she yearned for the return of the cooling moisture.

Exhaustion so intense her knees should have given way assailed her. Guy held her in his arms and she understood this relationship between them was good and lasting. Slowly the chanting began to fade until Niagel stopped. Silence enshrouded them.

Guy's lips found hers then, opening around hers, parting, stroking, enticing. He touched her tongue with his, drawing it into his mouth. She opened for him, as he brought her inside him, just as she would bring him inside her. Their bound wrists settled on his chest. He kissed her again and again as if he too was driven by the heat of the fire and the need to complete their union.

When he finally stopped, his gaze was raw and hot with the fire that had recently wrapped around their bodies. She understood so much more now yet nothing.

"You are husband and wife," Niagel murmured. "You will consummate this union later today and Cas will be marked by Guy as his one and only person to be with him through time."

Applause rang out around them. Conversations seemed to encircle her yet she understood nothing. Could not think of anything but Guy and what they still needed to do. She heard Lyn speaking then Kimi. Brody's voice joined them as did Carr's.

She floated on a cloud of nothingness as if she was removed from her body and could see everything but understood nothing. Before she heard the words, Guy's lips touched her ear, soft, teasing, tantalizing leading her to expect more.

"You are wed. All of the gods have witnessed the joining of Casidhe and Guy. Through all eternity you are bound to each other. As time goes by and the bonds of earth let you go you will find each other in another time just as you have now. Tonight, if the gods are pleased with this union, you will witness some of your past lives."

Guy directed his attention toward his great grandfather, "We are husband and wife?" he asked unsure what to do. "May I kiss her?" He seemed hesitant to ask the question.

Niagel nodded, a smile on his face. "Whatever you do until and while you mark your woman must be done while your hands are bound together. Keep that in mind and don't allow the spirits to look unfavorably on your joining."

"Will you put your lips on mine? Kiss me chastely now and save the best for private?" he whispered to Cas.

She tried to nod her head in understanding and acceptance but it didn't seem to move. He looked concerned and she wanted to touch his face to reassure him that she was fine, but her hand wouldn't move. He held her close as she heard others talking to him then Niagel's voice and Cook's.

When she tilted her head slightly before nodding her permission, he brushed his mouth across hers. Once then twice, wanting to deepen the contact but not with all the onlookers.

She was his now.

He pulled away. "Are you hungry," he asked. "I believe we need to cut the cake first, drink a little champagne, eat something so we can survive the nightly activities I've planned for the two of us."

Slowly she began to slide into her body. For the first time since they began the ceremony, she was beginning to feel complete. She needed to ask someone what happened to her. It didn't seem as if Guy was affected the same way. He could talk and laugh, move as well.

Her fingers and toes began to tingle with sensations. She wiggled them against his chest and he laughed.

"Good girl," he whispered close to her. "You are coming back to me. I was worried until Niagel told me this was normal."

"What is normal in all this?" She tried to speak but still no sounds came from her.

Now, it seemed she could stand. He slipped the cloak around her shoulders then turned her so Lyn could tie it closed. He also put one arm in his vest, draping the other side over his shoulder. When she looked down the vest covered him in part. Yet he didn't seem concerned. Perhaps shifters learned modesty could rarely be a part of their lives, since they had to remove their clothing to change shape.

"Can you walk to the dining room? We should cut the cake, have a bite to eat and drink then find our way to the bedroom. I'm sure Cook will have plenty of food and drink prepared for us there. We will not sleep very much tonight perhaps only for a few hours."

She understood his primal need to mate. She felt it also. He was aroused as was she and could think of nothing save the mating. "I believe so."

This time he heard her reply because his hands around her waist tightened for a moment before he laughed.

"My sweet imp, I can hardly wait to get you alone. I want to spend the entire night making love to you, giving you pleasure."

"I can see now," she told him her voice still whisper thin.

He roared with laughter appearing to catch the attention of the others. He cleared his throat seeming to want to avoid telling him exactly why the laughter. "She is coming around. Cas will be herself soon."

Slowly and with his help, they walked into the dining room. The cake was beautiful and she wondered if Cook made it. Of course, she made the sweet confection as she also prepared the appetizers.

"Can you hold the glass?" he queried but offered her a sip after what seemed as if a toast had been made to them.

"I can try."

He waited to see if her fingers would close around the stem and hold it. When they did, he tapped her crystal glass with his. "To my beautiful wife." Bending once more so she would be the only one who could hear, "Do you want to sleep with me tonight?"

She smiled then, "Yes," she whispered back, "but could we put off the other part?"

"No, but I will try to be gentle."

Honestly, from what Lyn told her, she didn't think he could control that part of the ritual. The marking just happened the way it was meant to happen and when it was supposed to happen.

Everything slowly became clearer, her body normal, yet when Guy touched her or this thumb brushed the underside of their bound wrists, the flames seemed to grow brighter and hotter.

As he spoke, he bent close to her. "We should cut the cake. Do you think we can do it together?"

He touched her ear with his tongue and she thought she might truly burn as the flames had seared her body. His touch seemed to do the same thing.

"If you help," she murmured.

There was laughter in the room. "Do you like the icing to stay on the cake or should I put a bit on your lips? Perhaps smear it all over your face?" He was teasing her now.

"The cake please," she told him as they reached for the cake knife.

Someone took her champagne, setting the glass on the table. He wrapped his hand around hers, directing the knife, cutting it and settling the piece on a plate, which he left on the table.

"Me first." With his free hand he placed the cake near her lips. When she opened her mouth to take a bite, he was polite. After he put the cake back on the plate it seemed he smeared his thumb with the icing, rubbing it on her lips, watching, touching gently.

She was startled, suddenly more alert, hotter than before, "Guy."

The icing covered her mouth as did his lips, kissing her again, deepening the intimacies. He seared her flesh with molten heat everywhere he touched her. Set her on fire, flames seeming to lick everywhere. She closed her eyes, letting her head fall back to give him more access.

"Not yet, imp." He drew away from her. "It's your turn, then we'll retire for the night."

"My turn?"

"To feed me our wedding cake. Everyone is watching. When you do this, we can leave and let everyone celebrate our joining."

She nodded, thinking she would put icing on him but if she did, they might not make it to the bedroom.

He took the issue away from her, smearing the icing himself as he ate his bite. "Now, you must appease our guests and delicately lick the icing off my mouth."

Her body shook and the tiny mew of desire reverberated through her body as she burned hotter and brighter than ever before.

~ * ~

"No!"

Cedric roared so loud the single word shook the walls of his living quarters. The woman in his bed screamed, covering herself with a sheet.

"It has happened." His wings fluttered faster than a hummingbird's as he rose off the floor. He thought his heart would pound out of his chest. Rage filled him.

Energy pulsed through him, alarming him, inflaming his senses. Flying outside he soared high into the atmosphere then turned diving toward the protective barrier that had been made with magic for the sole purpose of keeping him out, keeping him away from his promised fiancée.

"No," he cried out, as he hovered over the bubble, looking down on the ranch house, wishing he could pry his way through.

All along he'd known this would happen, had tried to prepare himself for the inevitable but nothing he'd tried worked to that end. The magic of the McKennas was too strong.

Something different had taken place there today. He realized his people recognized this marriage. How the ancient man pulled it off, he could not comprehend but somehow, he did. All the gods known to mankind recognized this union. Nothing he could do would ever pull it asunder.

No power on earth could change this and the shifter had yet to mark her. He would have her at least once, Cedric decided. Clan McKenna could not keep an eye on her every second of every day for the rest of her life. There would come a time when he would find her alone and vulnerable.

He felt better then, knowing Cas would not be his wife but he would have her beneath him then he would give the damaged goods back to McKenna and he would laugh in his face.

"Yes," he spoke to himself still hovering over the bubble watching the earth. "Yes, this is what I will do."

Calmer now, he flew home, striding into his bedchamber to see his paramour dressed as if she intended to leave.

"Cedric?" Her eyes were wide, panicky. Frightened she held her hands to her chest as if she could hold her fear at bay.

"What are you doing?" He strode to her. "You're supposed to be in my bed. I don't recall giving you permission to leave." His fingers wound into the bodice of her dress. He wanted to rip it apart, needed to see her breasts spill free. His anger could only be assuaged through physical exercise, through sex with this woman who would resist him.

"You didn't," she licked her lips, her body shaking. "I didn't think you were coming back. You left in such a fury."

Deciding he would be nice to her, catch her off guard for a few moments, he poured a glass of wine for her and one for him as well. "Drink." He smiled at her hoping the simple gesture would put her at ease.

"If it would please you," she whispered accepting the glass but she didn't drink.

Foolish bitch, I wouldn't offer it if it didn't please me. "I want to make you happy today."

He wouldn't take his anger out on this woman, what was her name? No, he would wait until he had Cas beneath him for the anger to be part of the sex act. Cas would feel his vengeance before he finished with her. No one defied his wishes.

Sipping his wine, he sat on the edge of the bed, studying the girl. Her hands shook with fear of him. He'd always liked that. "Come here."

She held back. Her reticence pleased him. "May I leave? I'm quite fatigued."

"Of course not," he grinned, planning on making this night of love making one she would not forget. "I'd like you to disrobe," he hesitated, "no, on second thought. I'd rather take your clothes off for you. It would be so much more fun, don't you think?" He set his glass down before striding toward her.

Her eyes wide, she was shaking her head and fumbling with the fastening on her dress. On her back, her wings fluttered wildly.

"I'd like to go," she repeated breathlessly. Yet buttons popped free and he could see the gentle curve of her breasts beneath her fingers.

If she denied him one more time, all his patience would go out the window. This game was new to him. He didn't recall even in his youth being nice to a woman. He took what he wanted and that was that.

"You must share some of these fine candies with me." He held up a box of chocolates. "Just one, you don't want to eat too many and get fat but one might serve to persuade you to let me have my way. The candies go well with the wine. I personally picked out the right ones."

Hesitant steps brought her closer, "What are you doing?" She reached out, picking out a chocolate but didn't put it in her mouth. "Why are you being nice to me?"

"Go ahead, eat it," he encouraged, patting the place beside him on the bed unsure of how to make this joining good for this woman. He would find a way. "Then sit by me."

Her tiny pink tongue slicked the chocolate then she placed it in her mouth chewing slowly, savoring the sweetness.

He would savor her sweetness soon, perhaps lick all of her. He drew on everything he'd heard others saying what women liked. Touching her lips with a fingertip, he wiped chocolate away then placed his finger in her mouth, "You must get all of the goodness. Lick it."

Every part of him hardened and he was instantly ready for her. This might well be the most difficult night of his life but he was determined. He had always taken joy in a woman's pain. Perhaps there would be as much joy in her pleasure.

Chapter Six

He wanted to pick Cas up and carry her to the bedchamber but with their hands bound together, he wouldn't risk dropping her. She had been affected deeply by the ancient ceremony. For her, it seemed the joining had been more penetrating, all-encompassing. He wanted to hear all about it when she was more lucid.

Hand in hand they slowly walked through the hallway. At his door he stopped, bending to her level to kiss her. When his mouth touched upon hers, she whimpered then sighed softly as she leaned into him, her free hand on his chest. This was what he needed now, closeness with her, learning about her, not sex or the marking ritual.

"Cas," he breathed her name before opening the door, wishing for normalcy but that wasn't going to happen until they consummated the marriage, the joining of soul mates.

"Don't want bad luck to come our way," he murmured.

Understanding tradition, he managed to sweep her into his arms and carry her across the threshold. Standing inside the room, he pushed the door shut with his foot.

He didn't want to let go of her, but he let her slide down the length of his body, relishing all her soft curves and looking at her differently now that she had become his wife.

"Guy, can we wait a little, you know. I..." she moistened her lips, looking at him wide eyed. "I, I don't feel normal at all."

The mating was supposed to take place as soon as possible. Putting it off would only create more fear for her. He didn't want that. "Until you eat and have a glass of your sparkling wine. In the meantime, you can tell me what happened to you during the ceremony."

It seemed she tried to smile while she nodded, her head confirming his suggestion. "It was strange, nothing I've ever experienced before but I think you already guessed that."

"True enough."

On the bed there was a platter of food and on the nightstand two glasses of Chateau De Fleur had been poured. Two bottles sat nearby. "Seems Cook has seen to everything."

"Are you hungry?"

He suddenly felt awkward and unsure of himself. Waiting to have sex was not normal but he meant to abide by her wishes. He could wait.

"My stomach is churning," she said, sitting on the bed beside the tray of food. "Just looking at it..."

"What happened to you?" Guy asked as he untied the cape's bow, allowing the material to fall around her.

She moistened her lips while she watched him shrug out of his vest. "I…" she was shaking her head, her eyes closed as if she tried to remember, or perhaps forget. "It was..."

"Take your time."

He tried to encourage but knew he fell short. Just looking at her in the sheer gown was nearly his undoing. She was perfect, exquisite.

He watched her inhale a deep breath of air before letting it out slowly, her breasts rising then falling provocatively. "Do you want me to tell you everything?"

"Whatever happened to you, I need to know," He lightly brushed her cheek with the back of his hand, sensing the hesitancy on her part. "It seems you are suffering and perhaps I can take away some of the pain. I'd like to share the burden. That's what partners are for."

"It was just so strange." She scooted to the front of the bed, leaning against the backboard.

"How so?"

Looking over the rim of her wine glass, her eyes seemed to cloud over then she stared at him. "Your father called up the elements of the earth. One at a time it seemed they embraced me, took over my body. I felt every one of them."

"I felt some of that," he told her. "Obviously not the same way."

"Not, I'm sure to the degree I did. None of it happened at once but each element seemed to take its time," she paused, watching him for a reaction. "You think I'm crazy, don't you?"

"Hardly." He sat next to her, taking her free hand in his then bringing it to his lips, kissing the back. "There is more though. I feel part of it as if I was there."

"You're just being nice."

She laughed softly nestling into him, seeming to find comfort.

"No, when Niagel first began to chant, I felt as if the earth was moving and the walls of the house seemed to swirl around me, but that was all. I didn't experience the other elements and I'm wondering why. You're telling me you were able to experience the wind, water and fire also?"

She nodded, tucking her lower lip beneath her teeth. "I felt everything. After the earth a breeze caressed then intensified to the point where I thought I would surely be blown from the room, then the water roared to life and fire burned me, seared my flesh." She was breathing heavily, a fine sheen of moisture coating her body as she talked about what occurred. "Yet it didn't, not really."

"No wonder you've not quite been yourself. The events you describe are surreal, supernatural in ways." He wrapped his free arm around her pulling her tight against his chest. The need to protect encompassed him once more. Never in any of his imaginings could he have construed this scenario. His great grandfather must have realized what would happen to her.

"The flames, I think, were to get me ready for the mating or the marking, I'm not sure which. I think I was ready for you then, hot and wanting. You could have taken me in the room with everyone watching. I would have made no objection."

"Most likely. The ancient chants would have thought of everything. Wouldn't want a reluctant bride," he chuckled, stroking her arm, watching the goose bumps rise and feeling the shiver of desire they caused. "You aren't reluctant."

"No, I'm not. You can laugh but..." she waved her hand in front of her face. "I'm sure I'm still flushed and every time you touch me the flames and the fire seem to roar to life. I need you desperately, but at the same time I'm not truly ready for this event to take place."

"We should do something about that, don't you think? I believe you are just afraid."

Before he marked her as his though, he wanted to learn a few things about her. In the short time he'd known her it seemed they'd either been running from Cedric or making love.

"Yes, but..." Nervously she sucked on her lower lip.

"But what?" He was mesmerized by the play of emotions rushing across her delicate features. He needed to see inside her head, longing for Kimi's ability to read the thoughts of others.

"I don't know." Her shoulders rose a fraction before settling back into place, "I guess I'm still afraid of what is to come. The unknown, you know. The pain I've been told it will cause then what comes after. Who will I be? Will my identity be lost?"

"You have many questions. I can't answer even one. I'm sorry for that."

"No more than me."

"What's your favorite color?" He almost laughed at the expression on her face and hoped his diversion from the fearful topic worked.

"Why?"

"Just curious, I suppose. Mine is the alabaster color of your skin, ivory silk." He touched her then, ran his fingertip down her neck and across her collarbone, keeping his gaze riveted on her. He thought to coax and seduce.

Her blush seemed to rise from the tips of her toes and through the gauze of her dress. He saw the beautiful pink luster rise to paint her face. "Didn't mean to embarrass you."

"You didn't. If your words are foreplay, they are working magically." She leaned forward, caressing one of his tiny nipples with her tongue and teeth.

He inhaled sharply, craving air, his body tightening with need. Her actions were primal and provocative. "The words weren't meant to be, but if it works. What you just did is more potent than any words." He pulled one of the ties on her dress, undoing it then sitting back to watch the fabric slide downward to reveal one of her breasts. The rosy pink nipples seemed to beg for his attention and he meant to oblige.

This time she sucked in air as his mouth and lips stroked and teased her nipple laved it and nibbled there. He placed her free hand on the waistband of his pants. "Untie them," he told her then wriggled out of them. "This is it then? You are ready?"

"It is." He undid the other shoulder strap, watching the material slide to her waist. "Lift your hips." She did and the sheer wedding dress found its way to the floor.

He sat back then, admiring her body, enjoying the gentle rise and fall of her breasts and the way the nipples hardened in anticipation. She was his now and the fact was amazing, astounding really that this beautiful woman needed him enough to do all the things his family required.

"What do you want me to do?"

"Just be yourself and enjoy this for as long as possible. At least..." he stopped short.

"At least?" she asked seeming to wonder at the direction of his thoughts. "At least what?"

"You are not a virgin." He watched the reaction as she realized what he must be implying. She would not have twice the pain tonight.

"No, there is that. We've been there before and it surprised me. I'd never really thought about it before. I'm your only lover."

She smiled at him, touching his face. "Kiss me now before I change my mind."

His lips met hers as she opened for him, seemingly hungry for the contact. Her flesh was hot to the touch. He was reminded of the flames she told him about and how they seared her flesh.

Moving lower, he kissed his way to her breasts, rubbing his day-old stubble on her rounded curves, delighting in the sounds of pleasure he created within her. Her fingers entwined in his hair, seeming to draw him ever closer to her even as she seemed to respond sweetly to him.

As his hands crept nearer to her mound, he lingered at her belly, kissing her, thinking of the wee babe growing inside. As of yet there was no evidence she was pregnant, but he figured it would not be much longer before he could see the swell and watch the baby bump grow.

"Guy?"

"What?" He looked up to see her watching him.

"Do you have any idea what it's like to watch you take me into your mouth? My body flames even more. Molten lava could not be hotter or more potent than your touch upon me."

"Spread your beautiful long legs for me," he told her as he settled between them focused on her mound and wet swollen folds that invited his attentions. His body hardened with insistent need, but he wanted to make this beautiful for her, needed to give her as much pleasure as possible to offset the pain that was sure to follow.

He explored her, touched every part of her before giving his attention to the silken nub. Her hips jerked as she responded to the sweet sensations he created, and he could barely contain himself. Over and over again, his lips traveled across her body paying homage to every sensitive and erotic place he could find. His hands cupping her breasts, toying with her nipples he kissed her again and again, until his heart pounded and his breaths were short.

"Are you ready for me, little imp?" He had first and second thoughts about giving her fair warning, but he knew she needed to be told. "I will try like hell not to hurt you."

"Never more ready," she said her voice husky with the raw passion he created in her.

He hoped the sweet pleasure he gave would be enough to assuage the pain he would inflict and was dreading. When he pushed inside, her walls clenched around him sucking him deeper inside until he touched her womb. With each thrust he felt her body tensing ready to climax and it was at that moment he would mark her as his.

Suddenly, she cried out as he felt the spasms rush through her and over him. His claws emerged and he touched her behind the top of her shoulders, nails scoring tiny puncture wounds in her soft skin directly over the ones he must have put there in another lifetime. The marks would remain there through eternity, he realized. If there ever was, now there was no doubt in his mind that Casidhe was his soul mate.

She screamed, cried out his name, "Guy!" writhing in pain now, no longer pleasure filling her body. He almost withdrew but understood she could never endure this a second time. The act must be completed now. Minutes seemed to turn to hours as his nails remained embedded in her flesh for what seemed an eternity.

Her body stilled then, tears slipping down her cheeks. Yet she remained very still, her eyes closed tightly while she seemed close to death. He was suddenly afraid for her. A fine sheen of sweat covered her body. He touched her pulse just to reassure himself she was alive and breathing. The beat was weak but it was functional, blood still pumping through her.

"Good God, what have I done to you?" he asked himself as he slowly withdrew from her before untying the leather thong around their wrists.

He sat back on his haunches, watching, afraid and so impatient for her to wake. This was too much like their wedding ceremony for his peace of mind. Today she endured more than any human should.

He would make it up to her.

She wasn't human and neither was he. She was stronger, had more strength than he was apt to give her credit for. Her long beautiful hair was spread around her. He wanted to commit this sight to memory for she was his now in every way possible. He just needed her to wake up so they could talk. Needed to hold her passively as well as to reassure and give comfort.

He needed to know what she experienced and how much pain he caused her. The rest of his life would be spent making it up to her. He vowed there would never again be pain in her life.

Moving off the bed he gulped the glass of wine before pouring himself another then drinking deeply once more. Covering her with a quilt, he paced then, roamed the room feeling caged, trapped overwhelmed by the events of the day and this night. Helplessness had never been a part of his life. For long minutes he watched the moon then the protective barrier as it slowly faded.

The clan would no longer need the extra protection. They had known when he marked Cas. They had heard her scream and would condemn him for hurting her. Because it was an ear-piercing sound almost as if she'd drawn her last breath.

It was a sound he didn't think would ever leave him.

Once more, he sat down beside her, bent close to her face to feel the reassuring breaths of air. He ran his hands through his hair, pacing again, wishing she would wake up and smile at him.

At the window again, he saw the moon was full and watched wispy clouds as they floated across it. He wondered if she could fly as high as the moon.

Probably not.

He realized again he wanted to see her fly, view her in her tiny fairy form. His breath caught as he imagined her delicacy. She might do that for him now that she was safe. The soft feminine moan caught his attention, making him stiffen and turn his attention to her.

"Cas?" Quickly, he sat beside her, stroking her hair, feeling the silken heat radiating from the locks. The quilt he covered her with slipped as she moved.

Slowly she opened her eyes, blinking a few times then groaned. The sound was pain-filled and Guy grimaced knowing he'd done that to her.

"Guy?" She lifted her hand to touch him but didn't have the strength. "I can barely breathe. Was it supposed to be that way?"

With no idea about anything, he had no way to answer her. "I'm here for you, Cas. Just sleep if you want, rest, curse at me. Hit me if you like. You don't have to do anything. The rest of the night and tomorrow, forever if possible is for you, only you." He hovered over her, wanting to give her whatever she asked for.

She smiled then, "That was the worst thing that ever happened to me. I'm glad I won't ever have to do it again, at least not in this life," she told him seeming to remember something.

"I hope it wasn't the sex you're talking about." He tried to tease but had second thoughts after the words left him.

"You know what I'm tal... Oh...." She wrapped her arms around her body, tears sliding down her cheeks again. "No... I don't want these. Make them stop," she cried out.

"What? It isn't the marks." Yet the blood had dried and there should be no more reason for excruciating pain. The deed had been done, now there should only be recovery.

She was shaking her head trying to sit. He helped her sliding in beside her. "My mother."

"I don't understand."

"Neither do I but I feel her pain and the agony. Somewhere in this world she is hurt and needs help. She's alive. They lied to me." Then, "Cedric will seek revenge."

The astonishment in her voice unnerved him. He'd never really asked her about her mother, assumed she lived and perhaps guiltily slunk away after she promised Cas to Cedric.

"Slow down," Guy said. "You are feeling others. Can you read their minds as Kimi does?"

"No, I just feel what they feel. My mother is part of this, but I don't know where she is."

"How?"

"That's a question I wish I knew the answer to." She was grimacing again and holding herself with her arms wrapped tightly around her body. The strain would overcome her soon if he didn't figure out how to help her stifle the feelings washing through her.

"You have to close off the thoughts or you will go mad," he told her, understanding because of what Kimi went through and remembering those first few times when Maska feared for his wife's life.

"Really? How do I do that?" It seemed she was struggling against the constant bombarding of emotions.

He couldn't imagine the hell she must be experiencing.

"Think of something else, anything else. You need to learn how to call on the sensations when you want and know how to turn them off. I'm sure Kimi will help you with that."

"But not now. I will close my mind to all except you and our wedding night. Perhaps those memories are not so good either. We need to do something that will be pleasant. So far, I cannot speak highly of this night. "

"Good," he smiled hoping she would be able to do that. "Pleasure and good memories will be a part of this evening. I'm promising you."

"Not too sure you can promise something like that."

"Show me the marks and I'll tell you a bit about what happened during our mating."

She hesitated again, looking as if that was the last thing she wanted to do. "If you insist."

"I do, but you'll have to get up." He led her to a mirror then turned her so she could see the punctures now covered with dried blood.

"Those tiny marks were excruciatingly painful." She turned sideways then looked at her other shoulder. "Why? It shouldn't be nothing more than getting stung by a bee or pricked by a needle. Your piercing the shield of my virginity did not give me so much pain."

"I've no idea," he murmured, studying them closely and realizing she was right.

She turned herself to look at them again, "I'm going to try to forget everything, every horrible second. I don't want to remember anything, none of it."

"I'll wash the blood off." He left for the bathroom coming back with a damp washcloth and a bowl of water. Cleaning each wound he took his time making sure he examined the marks. "Does this hurt?" he paused, waiting for an answer.

"Just a little when you touch, nothing to worry about."

He did worry. She was far too precious to him, hurting her was not what he wanted their relationship to be about. Remembering the joining, the act was not horrible to him, it was exquisite, amazing, the most intense he'd ever had. If he could have remained inside her forever, he would have considered. It.

When he finished, he kissed her shoulders, each minute mark, hoping the gesture would help heal the memories. He wanted to make love to her again, but he felt her resistance.

"Are you afraid of the emotions that might surge through your mind if we make love?"

"I can't help it."

"We should eat and talk for a while. Seems I told you my favorite color, but you didn't reciprocate."

She tossed him a scowl, her brows creasing. "A favorite color is hardly important but I don't really have one. When I was little pink was always a preference. So, what else do you want to know about me?"

"Hmm..." He filled a plate for her before handing her the glass. "Should we sit on the bed and see if we can do this without spilling?"

"Won't make any promises." She looked up from the plate of food sitting in her lap. "If we make too big of a mess we can always sleep under the stars."

"You liked that did you?" His heart warmed even more for than he could have ever thought possible.

"Heavenly would be the only way I can describe watching the stars in the sky while you hold me in your arms. Perhaps I would be more conducive to sex with you if we were outside in a completely different environment."

"Hope this bed will not always hold bad memories for you." He was reluctant to take her outside even though the barrier was removed at least an hour ago.

"We should make new ones," she said. "I want good memories everywhere I go with you."

"As do I with you."

"My mother was supposed to be dead," she spoke softly.

He'd wondered when he could bring up the topic, she introduced a little while ago.

"Yes, there is that and you need to tell me what happened during the claiming. I know it was more than the pain that changed something about you as well as the marks on your beautiful body. You are different somehow."

~ * ~

"Good or bad different?" she asked terrified so much changed that he wouldn't want her any longer.

While she understood he didn't love her, she hoped these events didn't change him in any way.

"Neither." He lifted those broad shoulders she'd come to love, causing a masculine play of muscles across his chest. "Just different,

144

that's all. Nothing to think twice about."

"Just different," she repeated, feeling exhausted suddenly.

Her head on his chest, she closed her eyes trying to recall everything that happened to her tonight. She touched him then, understanding his potent strength more than before. Ran her finger along the broad expanse of his chest. Saw the rippling of his muscles as she felt a jolt of heated pleasure, warmth suffusing her.

"I can't really explain... different is different." He stroked her hair, her arm, tenderly setting his chin on the top of her head. "After what you went through, I would expect nothing less."

His gentle emotions filled her and touched her soul. Once she thought these sentiments she was feeling emanating from him was love, but he told her enough times to be convincing he didn't love her. So, what were the emotions she was reading, feeling so intensely?

She began recounting the tale slowly at first, her thoughts in a jumbled mess. Needing to remember everything for herself, "The moment your nails scored me, everything changed."

"How so?" He let her hair slide through his fingers once twice before tucking the strands behind her ear.

She enjoyed this gentleness. While he didn't seduce, she felt the closeness as well as the tenderness. "You gave me pleasure, you know, but the joy of the sex was overshadowed by the pain and visions as well. Everything seemed to consume me."

"You wound me," he laughed softly yet stopped suddenly as if wondering if he should laugh.

His conflicting emotions touched her soul, hardly fair of her to understand his feelings toward her. "No. I didn't." Her voice was curt and she needed a moment to distance herself from him.

"Then what?" He touched her, moved her so he could look in her eyes. Warmth and compassion filled his eyes.

"I saw us." She understood his need to learn more, but he would have to be patient in this.

"You saw us," he hesitated, an interesting look on his face she wasn't sure how to interpret. "All you had to do was open your eyes, but I know you didn't. So, what exactly did you see?"

"No, you're right. My eyes were shut tight. What has your brows furrowing together so tightly?"

She waited for him to say something, but he continued watching and waiting for her to say more. It seemed the conversation would be hers alone.

Cas moved off the bed, walking around the room, naked, pausing at the window for a moment before wondering if anyone could see her. Quickly, she moved away. She picked up a few things, turning them over in her hand. A large piece of turquoise caught her attention. In her hand it was smooth and startling cold.

When she turned to look at him, he was smiling and staring at her. "You are beautiful, you know, strikingly so."

"Thank you. This has been surreal, Guy. I'm afraid you might not believe anything I tell you." She understood that feeling too, the smoldering look in his eyes. His tender protective emotions changed to lust in a heartbeat. Well, he would have to be patient because she meant to take her time not to provoke or tease but just because she was having trouble finding the words.

A glass of sparkling wine would taste good as well as a piece of cheese to pair with it. "Would you like some?"

"If you're having one, I will also."

Her strength was something she would need before the night turned to morning. She refilled her glass as well as his then, sitting on the edge of the bed, understanding that even though he wanted her he wasn't going to touch, at least not in ways that would seduce.

"You want me."

She watched him over the rim, touching it with her tongue before she realized she wasn't helping him, rather hindered. The surge of lust he experienced just then she felt also. She inhaled a shaky breath.

"You don't need to be able to read my emotions to know that. All you have to do is look at me." His grin was infectious as he flirted with her, staring for a moment at his arousal.

"True." She found another piece of cheese, smiling and trying to use the levity of the moment to ease her tension. "I feel as if I've eaten nothing in more days than I'd like to count."

"You're hungry now."

"I am."

"Why do I get the feeling you're putting things off?" he asked with a bit of anger in his voice or perhaps it was a lack of patience.

Her hesitancy she understood tested him.

"Because I am. You know me too well." She needed to be honest with him now as well as with everything in their future. "And I really don't know why. Until I say the words, I'm free."

"That's easy, you're afraid. If you are going to take some time to eat then I am too. I can wait as long as you need. Gather your thoughts. I'm trying my hardest not to lose patience."

"You're doing a fine job," she murmured.

"Not really," he admitted.

She put her hand on his arm, stopping him for a moment. "Eat and I'll talk. It's just that I'm not sure you'll believe me. When I'm finished, you're going to want to make love again and that terrifies me. I only want to feel normal."

"Understand this," he began, his voice gruff. "I'm pretty sure Sadie never experienced more pain when Brody made love to her afterwards. Of course, I wasn't there but I doubt if they would have three children if pain was part of the scenario every time."

Cas mulled his words over in her head for a few seconds then, "My mind believes you but..."

"You're still afraid."

She nodded thinking she shouldn't be but she was, and there really wasn't anything he could say that would change her fears. "Like falling off a horse one has to get back on or they'll always fear the same thing." She tried desperately to convince herself.

"That's right, little imp, but we still need to talk which you've also been putting off with idle conversation. I'm ready anytime you are." He leaned against the headboard crossing his legs and settling his hands behind his head.

Smiling tenderly, she pushed his hair off his forehead before she began, "The first time you marked me, you had red hair and a bonny red beard. We were lying in the heather on a Scottish hillside. The day was sunny, the sky a beautiful shade of blue. Your kilt was still around your waist, but you must have been impatient because I was naked. Don't know what year it was but what I saw seemed to go in chronological order."

"Red hair, hmm... I was a ginger then? What did your dress look like? We might be able to figure out the time?" he asked smiling at her and seeming relieved she was finally telling her story.

"Not much design to it, but the fabric was blue, the dress simple. It was more like a sac than anything else."

"Must have been easy for me to take it off." He wriggled his eyebrows at her. "Right now, you've made your disrobing even simpler. Probably wanted you just as much then as I do now."

"Probably not as easy as the one I wore today," she felt a bit more lighthearted now that she was beginning to talk, letting go all her inhibitions as well as fears.

"Probably not, or what you are not wearing at the moment. All I have to do is reach out and caress you."

"There were more markings in between, too many to count. The vision came to me in blinding fashion. Occasionally, they would slow and I would get a better picture."

"So..." he prompted, "I want to hear more about my awe-inspiring prowess."

"The second time the visions slowed we were in a small hut. A black kettle sat above a fire in the fireplace. You wore just a nightshirt and I remember that I asked you to take it off. An old mattress was on the floor. I know I was a virgin. You had never touched me before. It seemed we were forced to wed, or rather I was." She blinked a few times trying to remember the vision as well as the thoughts that had bombarded her.

"You must have wanted me."

"From what I remember, yes, but only when I saw you naked," she laughed recalling the thought. "I did not think it was fair that you wore clothing and I did not. I was curious about the way a man would look."

"Curious, Cas...?" he smiled, laughing and touching her gently as if he tried to relax her get her ready for sex with him.

"After that, all I recall of that was seeing your claws emerge and screaming."

Cas enjoyed his eagerness as well as the teasing way he helped her relax. "So, the next time we were in a bedroom."

"Novel idea," he laughed. "Bedrooms are so much more comfortable than a rocky landscape or an old mattress on a floor."

She swatted him, punched him in the shoulder as she laughed. "Don't interrupt. I think it was a castle. This joining your hair was coal black and your eyes an intense shade of brown. We had been lovers before. I'm sure of it."

"Did you feel the pain either time?" His eyes narrowed in concern for her. "I don't like the fact it has been so many times."

"Not like this time," she told him. "Yes, it seemed the pain increased every time we mated, culminating in this last one. When we come back next time will it be worse?"

"I don't know. I hope not but I'm convinced we will be together again after our deaths in this life."

"Let's not speak of death."

"No, only life and our future. This was different because it's when you received the new, special powers so you can do more than sprinkle fairy dust in someone's eyes to have your way with them, me," he added smirking, still stroking her body, sending warm shudders throughout. She felt the desperate need to feel him fill her with his heat.

"Possibly," she thought over his words for a few moments. "So why did I get these extra powers? I never wanted them or asked for them. Don't even know what to do with them. Why should I know what others are feeling? Seems an added burden where there shouldn't be one."

"Don't know," His lips found her ear, touched, teased and explored before moving to the rapidly beating pulse at her neck.

She shivered, realizing despite her fear he could still arouse her, would indeed always have that ability but for now, "Stop," she told him the single word, weak and without purpose. "Just let me get this all out then I promise you I will make love to you. I will make sure I do the seducing."

"Aw, little imp, you ask me to stop this and this? An impossible feat." He trailed kisses down the length of her neck then across her collarbone then lower to caress each breast with a tender kiss, a gentle nip. He turned her away from him, kissing each engraved mark he left on her body. Seeming to feel her response to him. "You feel this and you like it."

"I've always enjoyed what you do to me. It doesn't mean..." She was at a loss for words.

"Of course it means you want me. Did you see any other times of our mating? It's kind of like voyeurism except it is us." Again he found a nipple, gently sucking it into his mouth, caressing, nipping, craving her.

She gasped for air, letting her head fall back unable at the moment to answer his question. "I think the next time was during the roaring twenties. We were in the back of a car, the rumble seat I believe or not. It was all rather vague and disconcerting. I think we were hiding from someone or something, and I felt the danger surge around us. Not romantic at all or comfortable but you had blond hair and green eyes. They were such a vivid color I nearly swooned. It must have been your eyes that swayed me to let you have sex with me."

"Ah, you don't like the color of my eyes now? They don't make you swoon with a fever of lust? You don't want to throw yourself on me. I'm disappointed in that." He turned his attention to more erotic parts of her body. "I'll have to see what I can do to make you swoon and throw yourself at me."

"Short of cutting off my air, there is no possible way," her voice prim she tilted her head to one side, daring him.

"You couldn't tell me how good I am if I did something like that." He kissed her lips, sucking them into his mouth, exploring with his tongue.

She was panting now, unable to control any of the events of this moment. "Love the color of your eyes. They seem to pull me deep inside, touching my soul but since I don't wear a corset, it's very hard to swoon. I would have to stop breathing for a while and we just established the fact that it wasn't possible."

"Is that the last time you watched us in the most intimate act between a man and a woman that God created?" he asked, his hand exploring cherished parts while she allowed him access, her body responding with a gentle flow of warmth, not the searing, branding heat

150

she experienced before.

"The last real vivid one but I swear, Guy, you must have marked me a thousand times through our history, through the history of the world. The images flashed by with such speed and each time... the pain seemed to increase."

"I'm sorry, so sorry. You can't imagine how I feel. No wonder you're reluctant, but I promise you I will stop if there is any hint that I'm hurting you. Good Lord, what am I to do to convince you?"

Guy fell silent. He was still staring at her, at all of her. She knew his feeling but she needed to know what he was thinking.

"No, you can't imagine the agony. I know what you feel. You can't hide it from me and with you I don't seem to be able to turn it off. But I need to learn what you are thinking." The tone in her voice was not what she wanted to convey to him but it was how she felt.

"I'm sorry," he told her again sighing deeply before replying, "I didn't mean to imply I have any idea what you've been through. I can only go on what you've told me. As for my thoughts, I was thinking that your breasts are very high and full, as white as your belly. Thought the same thing the first day I saw you naked. I wondered just how someone like me got so lucky."

Hearing his words, tender thoughts for her husband of only a few hours assailed her. He was caring and gentle. The pain was not something he intended. She paused for a few seconds trying to figure things out.

Then, "It seems one marking should be enough if I'm your soul mate. Do men just want to do that to their woman? There should be a rule or a law, perhaps an ancient written document that says once a woman becomes a man's mate it's a done deal no matter how many times they find each other in the future."

"That's something we can fully agree on," he told her as he explored the length of her body with his mouth.

The heat he created was a slow burn, erotic as if the warm heat from the Sierra Madres flowed across her and through her as well. The tiny sound she made in the back of her throat brought his gaze to hers and a smile on his face. He bent to kiss her again.

"No pain this time, little imp? No fear?" he asked before returning to his unhurried discovery of every part of her. "Only pleasure that will melt every bone in your body, just like all the other times."

It seemed to Cas this joining would be different from all the rest. She didn't know why but assumed it was because of her new power.

With each tender caress, it seemed the warmth and the pleasure grew as well until her hips were arching trying to find him, seeking his body. He held back though, and it seemed he didn't want to rush this joining. It would not be hot, fast and furious as so many times before but warm, languid and gentle. Yet she knew in the end, the heat inside would rise to a fever pitch.

He rose above her then and she slid her arms around him, kneading the muscles of his back with her fingertips and scraping her nails down his spine, wishing she had the ability to mark him in some primal way.

Her breasts pressed against his chest. She was shocked to discover her nipples were sensitive. Not hurting, just... alive, vibrant with the sensations they created by lying together. More so than ever before.

When she moved subtly against his chest, more warmth rippled through her from her breasts to her toes. Compared to before it felt so amazing that she arched her back slightly and rubbed against him again, more slowly, needing more and more contact. Yet it seemed he held back from pleasuring her as if he waited for her consent. It seemed to Cas she was begging for his attentions.

"You want me?" he teased.

"Yes, desperately and I don't understand, but the fear has vanished and yet you do nothing to assuage me. Before you would have seduced in your manly way, brought me to an uncontrollable climax." Her voice frayed into silence while she waited for Guy to respond in some erotic and seductive way. He was not his usual self, she determined.

"I'm glad," he told her. "It's just as I've promised you."

She licked suddenly dry lips, once again wishing this was done, finished, completed. "Now I'm impatient, I guess."

She closed her eyes, feeling a dreaminess take over her mind as Guy's fingers found more and more sensitive spots. It seemed to Cas he listened to her pleas and was now going to do something to ease the building arousal within her.

She rested against him enjoying the song he began to sing, a chanting much like the first time they met so different from the wedding ceremony, so poignant. His hands roamed as his fingers stroked a fantastic mercuric dance upon the bare flesh of her thigh and formed over the soft tender curve of her derriere. She murmured, and she would have cast her arms around him again but he held her hands still.

His touch was no longer gentle but demanding, challenging as his hands latched firmly on her hips. She gasped, surprised by his sex thrusting deeply into her.

"Hush," his whisper came to her and held her tight against him, unmoving. "No pain?"

"Only pleasure," she whispered as his body moved over hers. The universe erupted into life and vibrancy and sweet warmth, heated warmth but not searing flames of unrequited desire.

This was peaceful yet even as time passed the sensations increased. He carefully moved against her with the gentle force of the wind and waves not the tempest that encapsulated her before. It swept her gently onto a plain, floating pleasantly with Guy beside her, above her, their bodies joined.

The moment came upon her by surprise, but it enwrapped her completely in its splendor. It coursed within and around her, and it left her crying out softly, reaching for the moonlight, reaching ever higher for a grasp of rapture that only her mate could give to her. It burst upon her, as sweet as silken drops of harmony and agreement, filling her limbs, her body, her very center with warm liquid ecstasy.

She watched him wide eyed now as his eyes focused upon hers. His groans filled the moonlit room as she felt him shuddering and holding her fast one last moment as his body surged hard into hers, seeming to touch the length and breadth of her in one sweep of ancient mercuric magic. She felt as if he must have dusted her own fairy dust into her eyes to convince her of the wondrous moment between them.

That was not possible though.

Then he fell still above her, resting on one forearm, his other hand placed lightly upon her naked thigh. Now she heard the sound of his rough breathing, slowing gradually until each breath was long and deep, peaceful. She felt his limbs entangled with hers as well as the fine sheen of sweat covering his huge frame. He was powerful, still an enigma to her.

He slowly withdrew from her, turning over to lie on his back, seeming to study the moon outside the open window. She had known only pleasure. He had indeed been right in his assessment of their situation of the lovemaking between them. In any case, she would never have denied him, couldn't for that matter.

Rolling over she put her hand on his chest. "You were right, you know," she whispered, placing tiny biting kisses along his chest moving from one nipple to the other enjoying the low sexy grumble emanating from him.

"I'm glad of that." He pushed tangled hair behind her ears gazing at her as if he'd never seen her before.

Her kisses moved lower and it seemed he reached out to stop her. "You don't want..."

"Of course I do. You can have your wicked way with me again then we'll talk some more. After all this is our wedding night. We can do whatever we want."

~ * ~

Etain huddled on a bed, her knees drawn to her chest, her body shaking. One leg was shackled to the wall of the tiny room. The chain was just long enough for her to reach the bed. In the cubicle there were no windows.

Years ago, Etain lost track of the days and weeks. With no idea of the time she spent locked away from her daughter, she slowly became more lethargic with the passage of time.

Shocked by the sudden presence in her head of a woman she thought to be her daughter, she was struck with the possibility of escape. The woman had somehow seen inside her soul and knew how she felt. That had not turned out the way she hoped.

Not at all the way she anticipated.

She rested her cheek on her knees, gazing at the door with the hopes Cedric would appear, or his father to remove the shackles. After all, she promised not to try to leave again.

Her promise was her bond.

"Casidhe, are you out there somewhere?" She whispered hearing her words float in the darkness of the night.

Closing her eyes, she tried to reach out to her again, to no avail. She let out a long thin breath of air.

For a moment in time she'd seen the daughter who'd been taken away from her then told she was dead. Now she knew they meant dead to her until she wed Cedric. The man had known she would never allow such a joining and so they captured her, kept her chained and locked in a room.

For a time, she had been given more freedoms. They allowed her to walk outside, breathe fresh air and enjoy the changing of the seasons. As time passed and Casidhe would have come of age her restrictions grew.

A room much better and larger than this one had been hers once. This space resembled a dungeon rather than a habitable room.

Perhaps she should not have wished for the door to open. She had only thought about her need for someone to speak with. When the door creaked this time, it was Cedric who appeared, a scowl on his face.

"You must be pleased with yourself."

His growl of wrath sent her stomach to churn.

"I don't know what you're talking about." Yet she had the distinct sensation her daughter felt her terror as well as her lifeblood. Often, Cedric taunted her with the knowledge her daughter was wed to him, and at his mercy.

No longer because the taunt would be a lie.

"I believe you do."

He pulled up a chair, straddling it so his arms rested on its back, scowling ferociously at her.

She didn't say anything for more seconds than Cedric seemed willing to wait for a comment to his insinuation. The satisfaction he was looking for would not come from her.

"Casidhe knows you're alive." He challenged her with every

spoken word as well as the unspoken ones he insinuated. "She has more powers now. Do you know anything about that?"

"I haven't seen my daughter in more years than I've been able to count as you've isolated me here. Until recently, I believed she was dead, had been told that by you."

"You have powers. Use them, I'm sure you have the ability to contact her."

He spat on the floor, striding to Etain, lifting her by her shoulders before shaking her until she was sure her teeth rattled.

Her head shook wildly from side to side. She closed her eyes trying to ward off the pain he created.

When he stopped and let her fall to the bed, "I've reached out to her but," she paused for several seconds mulling over the words she sought. "If she is alive, she has not answered me."

That much was true, yet she felt her probing and knew Cas felt her pain and suffering. Somehow Cas received the same powers as she had.

He waved a hand in the air, enough of this. "I know you're lying to me and you tried to escape. You would have only done that if you heard from Cas. By now you must know she is wed to a shifter," he said the word angrily a bitter tone to his voice.

"A shifter you say." Inwardly she smiled, knowing the man would protect her with his life. "Realize I have not heard or felt anything of this nature."

While she knew Cas wed, she did not know the man was a shifter. That fact explained a wealth of questions she had. When the man marked her that was when the powers kicked in and that was when their minds made contact.

"Liar," he accused.

"No, I didn't know."

She was shaking her head in denial, all the while feeling the joy that her daughter found someone who could defend and shield her from this man.

Even if she spent the rest of her life in this cubicle, she could spend it content that her daughter was not subservient to Cedric. Unable to help herself she grinned at Cedric, pleasure at the news radiating from every pore in her body.

"Wipe that smirk off your face. I could take the same liberties with you as I do the other fairies who displease me."

"As you planned with my daughter? I don't care. Do what you want. If she is safe and happy, that is all that matters to me."

He approached her again before backing away. "You've wasted away to nothing. There would be no enjoyment for me."

"That is what you are about. Your enjoyment and damn anyone else." Hoping Cedric didn't notice but she'd heaved a sigh of relief when he didn't want her.

Despite her thoughts, she vowed she would not enrage him.

"You will help me capture Casidhe. She will come to you if you call her, needing to rescue you."

"If he is any kind of a man, her shifter will never allow her to put herself in danger. If he comes for her, he will not come alone."

"I can make your life a living hell."

"You've already done that."

Chapter Seven

On the bed, replete, satisfied and anticipating a long life with his mate, Guy watched Cas sleep, gently touching her cheek with a fingertip. That day when he met her at the Red Neck Bar and Grill, he knew she was his mate, but never understood what that entailed or how he would feel.

He would wake her soon, make love to her again and again until neither could move a muscle then they would sleep and start over. It was their honeymoon after all and they would stay here as long as both of them wanted.

Before they left the room, however, he meant to shift for his new wife. He wanted to see her reaction to his cat form. Guy grinned, understanding he wanted more than just that, he needed to tease her a bit.

Her only contact with his cat was in her dreams, hardly realistic and when he shifted to run away from her. He didn't have the chance to watch her face. What she remembered was his naked body not his cat. They were the same but very different too. The fact she'd seen him shift was nice as well as encouraging in the forward movement of their relationship, a marriage that would, god willing, span decades and beyond.

Smiling, enjoying watching her sleep, he trailed a fingertip along her chin. She sighed, swatted at his hand before turning over. Her covers slipped to reveal the curve of one of her breasts. Once more he repeated the light caress. Slowly her eyes opened.

She smiled at him and he wondered just what she was thinking.

"Did you sleep well?" he asked, knowing during the night they slept very few hours. She should be exhausted yet she appeared wide-awake, refreshed and seemingly ready for anything the day might bring.

"What time is it?" She sat up pushing hair from her eyes, her breasts moving provocatively, tempting him to forget his plans.

He tried to hide the masculine groan, understanding the instant arousal and craving for his wife. He would never in a million lifetimes together get enough of her. "Ten o'clock."

"That early," she laughed, running her hand lightly along his shoulder. "Anything planned for today besides lying in bed and recovering from last night?"

One eyebrow rose, suggestively. "Making love, sleeping, eating. I'm sure my family doesn't expect us to appear until dinner if then. When we finish one round, we can begin all over."

She looked to the small table, her stomach grumbling with anticipation, "Is that breakfast? Looks good but there's something missing."

"Mimosas and croissants, mimosa for me orange juice for you but we can order anything you like. I told Cook something light but delicious. Hope I chose well." He poured two glasses before joining her on the bed.

"If I'm going to do anything at all today, I need coffee, strong coffee," she murmured. She accepted the drink he offered. "You always drink in the morning?"

"Only the morning after I married my soul mate. I'll get you some coffee later."

At the moment he had something else on his mind.

Slowly sipping the orange juice, she hesitated a moment before looking at him, the gaze and shimmer in her eyes provoking every male instinct he possessed. "I'd like to see you in your cat form. If you don't mind..."

"I wanted to show you. But..."

He was overjoyed she asked him. She was invested in their relationship. It was a good thing. She was his soul mate yet was he hers?

"But..." she prompted.

"I don't want to unnerve you or terrify you. My cat can be imposing. I'm not a kitty cat. I'm big and very real." He thought of all the ways he wanted to show off for her, tease her as well.

"Are you fierce?" Her voice sounded a tiny bit hesitant, but she slanted him a siren's smile and laughed softly. "Or are you Guy, my Guy."

"I'm just a pussycat," he smiled, wondering if she would rub his ears, discovering strangely he wanted her to do just that. Strange the way that thought made him feel, not sexual at all, just content.

"So you say." She pulled apart a croissant, daintily eating the pieces and sipping her juice. "I'm sure the enemies you've fought wouldn't give me the same answer. Let me see, you and your family have battled a sea demon and Jokul, what was he?"

"An ice demon," he told her, "and a Chullachaqui."

"What is that?"

"Let me see. A simple description should be in order. A Chullachaqui is capable of disguising himself as anyone and can take the form of any animal. I never understood the reasons they sought out humans. All I know is that they do and one wanted Sadie really bad."

"You're right as usual, but they were enemies not my mate. I would never hurt you. I hope you understand that. Not even in my cat form."

This conversation was going exactly as he'd hoped. She was still curious about him and that pleased him. She would do well when she saw him.

"So when?" She popped another piece of bread in her mouth.

"No patience? I believed you had more than that. However, I think it would be nice to finish breakfast first. You have to promise not to panic when you see me."

Perversely he wanted to see how long he could fend off her request even though he was just as eager to show himself to her.

"Very well then. I promise." She sipped slowly, watching him, running her tongue along her lips, enticing him, "I'll take my time. Perhaps you could get Cook to bring us some bacon along with the coffee."

"Bacon?" he asked.

"Breakfast isn't breakfast without bacon." Her smile was coy. "Coffee as well."

He understood exactly what she was doing and applauded her. In actuality though she was proceeding just as he asked her. However, he never bargained on her wanting more food, food that needed to be cooked. He wasn't going to let on that he was suddenly annoyed, not by Cas but because of himself along with his need to tease and show off as well. He thought he'd considered everything when he planned this, but bacon and coffee?

He couldn't help but lift an eyebrow. "You just sit still. Don't go anywhere. I'll find Cook."

On his way to the door he pulled on a pair of jeans, fastening them as he walked out of the room. He would give her whatever she asked him for. When he heard her voice, he stopped for a moment, turning.

"That's okay." She reached out a hand to him. "You don't have to give me everything."

"I'd give you the world if you asked. Bacon and coffee are simple things."

When he stopped to look back at her, she was framed in the sunlight filtering through the room. Good god, she was an angel not a fairy.

"Really, Guy, you don't have to do that."

"No, if you want bacon then I'll get you some. Be back in as long as it takes to cook it. How much would you like?"

"Whatever," she said, with a feeble shrug, looking at him as if she was tempted to call him back again and he hoped into his arms.

"Enough for the rest of the day then."

He shut the door behind him, whistling a lewd tune.

As he walked down the hall toward the kitchen, he was greeted by his family, good-natured comments bawdy and otherwise assailed him. He would have acted the same. In fact, he had when his siblings wed.

Kimi latched onto his arm, "You have a good wedding night, lil bro?" She slanted him a wicked grin matching him step for step. "Couldn't possible have been as wonderful as mine."

"None of your business, big sis," He kissed her on the cheek. "You know we McKenna's don't kiss and tell."

"Didn't expect to see you this morning. Why did you come out of your lair?"

She let go of his arm when they entered the kitchen. Leaning against a counter, she stole a leftover croissant from a tray.

"Hungry, ravenous, in need of sustenance to continue with the day," he added before he pulled Kimi into his arms for quick hug.

"You're just ravenous for your new bride. What did she want from the kitchen? Told you a few croissants and mimosas were not enough. Not after what she endured last night. Oh, yes," she stared hard at him. "We heard the culmination. Why?"

Guilt washed through him, "I never meant... Perhaps in time I'll explain. There was nothing to do about it. Can't change anything."

"It is not your fault, and I'm sure she is over what happened. The pleasure is always remembered longer than the pain. Sort of like childbirth, and she'll be cursing you again in a few months. Now that we've put that topic to rest what is it Cas would like?"

"Bacon, lots of bacon as well as coffee. Seems she can't start her day without the black stuff," he said chuckling, appreciating this woman he'd known for his entire life as well as her advice. They were words he needed to hear from someone other than Cas.

"Everything is better with bacon," Cook laughed, smiling at him. "Should have thought of that when you were planning your morning meal. Didn't want to overstep your needs."

"Well, that's what Cas told me too." He supported himself against the counter.

This was heaven to him, this ranch house so far from the tiny town of Cactus Junction. Perhaps Cas would like a home here too, perhaps up on Infinity Cliff. Could be their vacation home, hell, all of the clan could use it when they wished.

"You said Cas wanted coffee too. Would you like to take a pot?" Cook was chuckling, seeming to enjoy this. "You make sure you treat that lady of yours right, or you'll have me to answer for. She's such a tiny delicate little thing. It wouldn't take much to hurt her."

"Good idea or she'll be sending me back to retrieve some for her. I'm sure one cup would not be enough." Indeed, he did know how tiny she was.

"So, she's putting off something." Cook had two frying pans out and the bacon was sizzling. "Care to share or should I keep on guessing?"

"She's teasing me with my own words. Would take them back now if I could but I don't want to give her the win, at least not yet." He stared at the floor for a moment, thinking about everything that happened to him the last week.

"You want to make her work for it then? Whatever it is?" She turned the bacon with a fork, seeming to concentrate on the task in front of her while she waited for an answer from him or confirmation.

"No, not really. Guess it's just part of my nature." With a huge sigh, he ran a hand through his hair. "I'm eager but terrified at the same time. Don't want her to be put off and certainly don't want to scare her."

"You might want to give up on that from time to time. So, what has you out here getting bacon and coffee when all you want is to be in the room with your wife?" She placed a few pieces on the tray, making more room in the frying pan.

"She wants to see me in my cat form." Lord that was what he wanted more than anything and here he was waiting for bacon, which he knew she wasn't going to eat more than a couple of pieces of. He also wanted to see her as a fairy, her little wings fluttering furiously as she hovered.

What seemed like hours later, Cook handed him a platter of bacon as well as a pot of coffee before giving him a quick kiss on his cheek. "You do right by that woman."

"Thanks, and I'm doing my best."

In the time he spent in the kitchen, his family seemed to have disappeared, Kimi too. It seemed she appeared just long enough to ask a few questions. When he walked into the bedroom, Cas was curled up on the bed asleep. He let out a long rush of air. Half expecting this, he wasn't sure right now if he should wake her. He'd already done that once this morning.

"Bacon's here," he spoke loudly, hoping she would wake up and take the decision out of his hands but to no avail. He set the platter on the table, watching her a few more minutes.

Perhaps this was for the best. He smiled, relishing the notion of shifting to his cat then curling up beside her in his bed. When she woke, he would be just as she'd requested, in his cat form.

Quickly he shed his jeans and went through the process of changing. He smiled inwardly when he leapt on the bed, curling next to her, purring contentedly. This was heaven to him. He just prayed she wouldn't scream when she woke and saw a huge black panther lying beside her, hoped too, that she would know it was him.

Closing his eyes, he must have slept. Didn't know how long but when he woke, it was to her hand methodically stroking his back. He arched, enjoying the caress, hoping for more. He didn't dare turn over, yet he needed to see her face, gaze into her eyes.

Minutes ticked by, his contended purr growing louder and to his chagrin more intense. He rose then, standing over her on the bed and looking down. Her eyes wide she tried to push herself away from him, scooting to the other side.

"It was one thing to see your back but this is different. You're huge," she murmured seeming to have second as well as third thoughts about this. "You were right. You are rather intimidating. Perhaps you should shift back to your normal self and we can try this again another time."

He was shaking his head then shaking it again. That wasn't what he wanted to hear. He smiled but it didn't seem to help so he sat down, hoping that was a tiny bit less threatening for her.

She got off the bed, heading for the wardrobe. He wanted her to remain naked so he could admire her. Leaping from his spot on the bed, he landed in front of her once again shaking his head at her, hoping she would understand what he wanted. He wanted to yell at her that he was just Guy, her husband and he could see her naked.

"Really, would it be too hard for you to let me at least wrap a robe around myself until I get used to you?"

He sent out his feelings to her, knowing if she tuned into him, she would read his needs. This was important to him, this fragile introduction to the other part of him. She should feel comfortable with him no matter the form he assumed. This was so much who he was, yet he read the fear and anxiety in her eyes.

Back on the bed she pulled the sheets to cover herself, trying to hide from him. He followed her, and with his teeth he tugged on the covers, pulling them to her waist, winning this first confrontation. Sitting back, he grinned at her again, satisfied he got what he wanted.

"I don't want you looking at me. It doesn't feel right. Perhaps if I'd seen you shift. I feel as if I don't know you." She tried to put the covers back where they'd been a few moments before.

Well, almost what he wanted. He wondered about surprising her this way.

He settled himself on the bed again, rubbing his face against her breast then letting his head rest between them. Once again, he purred softly showing her his contentment. Attempting to demonstration to her he wouldn't hurt her, just needed to enjoy his wife in every way possible. They had so much exploring and discovering to do.

He bent to lick his paws, enjoying the caress of her nipples against him. His tongue touched a nipple as he cleaned his foot.

She gasped, surprised or perhaps shocked by the contact. "That better be an accident, mister," she told him seeming angry, her breaths coming more rapidly, in short pants, most likely from anger. "I don't care if you are my husband, or the fact you claimed me only hours ago. You can't take liberties we haven't discussed."

That wasn't well done of him. It was accidental and he agreed whole-heartedly with her. He tried to get her to rub his head, in the process touching her again and again. Finally, she figured out what he wanted, her fingers caressing him between his ears.

He felt the rise and fall of her breasts as she inhaled and exhaled. Her hand under his chin, his purr grew louder, adoring the contact. Bending toward her fingers he nibbled on them, his claws kneading the covers as his teeth touched her fingers, pulling each one into his mouth as if each was a tender morsel.

This was killing him. He should shift back so he could make love to her. At this point he couldn't stand. His arousal would show and he was certain that would terrify her.

You got yourself in a fine mess.

"Guy, you should shift back now." Her voice was stern yet breathy.

He felt the same way but he couldn't, not until he got himself under control. Closing his eyes, he tried to breathe evenly, everything he could think of to slow his heartbeat as well as his breathing and calm his primal needs as well. The last thing he wanted to show her was how much he craved her.

"This isn't what I thought it would be."

I love you.

The sensation startled him and he didn't know where it came from. Saying the words even in his mind was not where he was mentally. The time was not right, and he wasn't sure about the emotion.

"What? What did you just feel?" On the top of his head her fingers shook. "Guy, say it again."

He would do anything to take the emotion back, not yet ready to say the words to her. He would have to deny them if she confronted him. It was lust he felt not love.

Leaping off the bed, his back to her he quickly shifted back to his human form. "There." He grinned at her, prowling back to the bed still fully aroused, yet at this moment he couldn't hide anything from her.

"Y-you f-frightened me." She pulled the sheets back to cover her again. "I'm not really sure what happened but it wasn't of this world. Look at you. Did I do that to you? Is that the way it's supposed to be with shifters? I don't think I can."

"I'm sorry." He touched her cheek with the back of his hand. "I couldn't resist though. You have no idea what your touch does to me whether I'm human or cat. It steals my breath and makes my heart race with so much pleasure I can barely breathe. No, I would never expect anything like you're thinking. In any case it's not possible."

"You do the same to me, arouse me," she whispered, just before his lips covered hers in a long deep and drugging kiss.

This was his woman and he understood he would have to take his time with her. Shifters were new to her despite her research as well as her dreams. What could she have possibly learned to prepare her for what he just put her through?

Of course she was afraid. He shocked her, brought new untried emotions to the forefront of her mind.

"I smell the bacon now that I'm not terrified," she told him laughing. "You brought enough to feed an army."

To Guy her laughter sounded forced yet the sound was better than the opposite, crying. "I didn't want to return to the kitchen for more if this wasn't enough for you."

Sitting next to her, platter in hand he offered her a piece then took one himself. Closing his eyes, he chewed slowly, savoring the deliciousness as well as the warmth of his wife next to him.

"Tomorrow," he began, "I'll take you to Infinity Cliff."

"What is that?"

"A cliff," he told her, his mouth full.

She punched him on the shoulder. "Wise guy. Why is it special and why does it have that name?"

"Because when one stands on the edge you cannot see the bottom. Sadie slipped and from what my brother would say, she hung precariously until he was able to pull her up. We almost lost her that day even before Brody got a chance to marry her."

"They would have found each other in another time," she told him seeming to understand the meaning of soul mate.

"True, this life would be hell without my mate. I'm sure Brody would have felt the same."

"Once you find your mate, you stop looking." She plucked at the sheets, her gaze focused on her hands. "I never understood the intensity, the complexities or the fact you like to tease mercilessly until I beg for it to cease."

"All of that is true. Maska traveled back in time to find Kimi. You see she died in the future. He knew approximately when. Then, at the top of Infinity cliff, he whisked her away to help save the earth in a totally different century."

"Really?"

To Guy she looked and sounded skeptical. "Sounds farfetched I know, but it's all true."

"Science fiction at its best?" she queried, finally looking at him again. "I didn't know anything like that could happen."

"Probably not the best. There was too much truth in what

happened. With Niagel's help we all teleported through time to find Kimi and Maska. I'll tell you up front, the family had far more doubts about Maska than they ever professed about you."

"Yeah, what's a little fairy dust to complain about?"

Guy set the platter away, "Speaking of fairy dust, it's your turn."

"My turn?" she looked and sounded confused.

"To change to your other form."

"I can now, can't I? Cedric knows where I am, but he's no longer a threat to me. Very well," she tossed the last piece of her bacon in her mouth. "Suppose there is no reason to dress now."

"No reason at all," Guy agreed wriggling his eyes brows at her. "I'm sure you'll look just the same stark naked as a fairy as you do now."

"Only smaller," she said.

"Do you use your fairy dust to change form?"

"Of course, and I use it to fly also." She was sitting cross-legged on the bed, seeming to concentrate.

After several seconds, "I'm waiting," he told her impatiently, reaching out to touch a breast, needing her and growing more impatient by the second. "You're not balking at the idea, are you?"

She scrunched her features, the top of her nose wrinkling. "No, you must have patience. Seems like decades not years since I've been in fairy form or flown. Perhaps I've lost the technique." She paused for a moment seeming to think.

"Well?"

"Maybe I've forgotten, nothing seems to work right."

"Try your magic potion on me," he said. "Tell me to do something I wouldn't normally do?"

"Such as..." It seemed she was at a loss.

"Bark like a dog." He laughed. "I would never do that, you know."

She sucked her bottom lip between her teeth, rubbing her hands together as if that would help her perform. Closing her eyes, she said a few words he didn't understand.

"Well? he asked, "have you used the dust?"

Tears slipping from her eyes, she nodded. "I'm not a fairy any longer. I can't change, can't fly, fairy dust doesn't work. What has happened to me?"

His body shuddered at the thought and the realization he might have done that to her. "I'm sorry. Is this my fault?" He pulled her into his arms. "Did our marriage change you?

"I don't know."

A sudden thick silence swallowed every sound in the bedroom. "How much do you care?"

She sniffed, reaching for a tissue to wipe her nose. "I don't know." Her voice cracked into a thin wail. "It's just that I've been a fairy for my entire life. Who am I if I'm not a fairy?"

"My wife and the mother of my child. Is that enough for you?"

God, he prayed it would be enough but he understood how he would feel if he could no longer shift. It would be as if part of his soul was ripped from him. He looked into her tear drenched silver blue eyes, wishing he could make everything right.

"Maybe. I'm going to have to think about it before I can answer. This is another surprise."

"You could try again. Perhaps the request was so farfetched there would be no way I would ever do it or perhaps a cat is not capable of barking. I could mew but then you wouldn't know if the fairy dust worked or not." He held back the laughter not wanting anything at her expense.

"You're just trying to be nice." She sniffed.

"Humor me, try again and we'll see."

She was shaking her head looking at him with fear in her eyes and there was really no way he could change that if she would try and not succeed.

"Would rather not know for sure," she told him, seeming resigned to the fact she no longer had those special powers. "It's all fine. What it's supposed to be, I suppose."

It was then Destiny flew in the open window settling herself delicately on one of the bedposts. "I planned on staying away. Just poked my nose into the bedroom to see how it was going, you know. Couldn't help but overhear all the woes."

"Not well at all," Cas told her. "I'm no longer a fairy. Nothing works."

"Ninny," Destiny said indignantly. "You need to figure this out. I shouldn't need to tell you."

"What has changed since the last time you were a tiny creature and able to fly?" Guy asked her.

"So many things..." she paused, "No, that's not entirely true."

"Two main things are different."

Guy sat back, grinning a broad male grin, proud of himself of his prowess, understanding the problem would eventually go away. With his thumb he wiped away a tear.

"What? Other than Cedric can no longer have me."

"Perhaps there are three."

"Would you just tell me and stop tormenting me. I can't think and I'm tired." Her hands were clenched and the tears had dried up as well."

"You are married to a shifter who claimed you as his own, and..." he paused.

"And what?"

"Have you forgotten so soon?"

"Guy."

"You are pregnant. Do you think that possibly the fetus might be harmed if there was not enough room for him to grow?"

$$\sim * \sim$$

In his arms, she sighed, nestling close to his hard body while enjoying the play of his muscles as he lightly stroked her. Yesterday had been shocking, amazing, enlightening. She hoped today would prove to be a little bit calmer.

"What would you like to do today," he asked playfully tickling her. "Do you still want to go to Infinity Cliff?"

Cas squirmed in his arms, laughing. "Stop..." She pushed away from him, her hair falling across her face while spilling onto his chest.

"So soft," he murmured, bringing a strand to his lips. "Every part of you is so soft."

"Unlike you." She ran her hands along his chest down the hard abs that seemed to ripple where she touched.

"Unlike me," he agreed, continuing to slowly explore her.

"Are we going to stay in bed all day today too?"

She traced the line of his stubbled jaw enjoying the feel. He was everything she'd ever wanted, and he was hers now. Getting used to his cat form might prove interesting but she was willing to chance it.

"Only if you want to." He nipped kisses up one arm then down the other. "I'll do whatever you like." With a slight pause in his seduction, "Think we should go to Infinity Cliff and stay the night, perhaps watch a sunset. What do you say? Time to see more of McKenna land."

"I'd like that. While I love being here with you, a bit of fresh air would be wonderful." She pushed away from him then, "First, a shower."

"Only if you get there first." He tossed his covers off, racing around the bed to reach the shower before her.

She was quicker and the door to the bathroom was closer to her, but he grabbed her by the waist twirling her around just as she touched the knob.

"Guy, unfair."

"You set the challenge. I won fair and square. You were closer too."

He kissed her ear, sending shivers down her body before following the path of the shudders he sent rolling through her.

"It takes me longer to get ready, hours for my hair to dry." She tried not to pout but couldn't help herself. "Do you want to wait hours?"

"When you put it like that, I suppose no. The shower is yours." He gallantly bowed low, sweeping his arm in front of him.

"Thank you," she told him sauntering into the bathroom and the shower as if she had truly won this round.

Before she'd turned on the water, Guy was behind her, kissing her shoulders and neck. "Did you really think you would get away with the first shower?" He stepped inside with her.

"Yes, because we want to go to Infinity Cliff today, not tomorrow or the next one."

"Can't spend all day making love in the shower?" he queried, his amorous intentions getting him nowhere. "I'll wash your hair and maybe other things also."

"That's not going to help. You can't shave my legs for me," she said in a bit of a huff, irritated by his refusal to admit defeat.

"I'm getting the vibe you don't want me in here." He leaned against the shower wall, his arms crossed over his chest, his gaze fixed on her breasts before traveling lower.

"Pretty astute this morning for a man," she told him, ignoring his avid perusal of her body, yet it seemed he didn't want to give up. With the shampoo already in her hair he began to massage it into her scalp, his fingers roaming lower to her neck and back.

"I'd like to think so," he laughed. "Now that I'm here and soaking wet, I'm not leaving." He used some of the leftover soap to wash his hair.

Turning, her breasts brushing against his chest, she suddenly had second thoughts. "Any other time I would probably like to take a shower with you. Not this morning."

With a huge sigh following her pronouncement, "I see, but not today. I'll hurry up and get out of the way. You can have this all to yourself."

A few minutes later, stepping from the shower, "I'll meet you in the dining room for breakfast."

She closed her eyes thinking she'd hurt him somehow, but she needed some alone time, a few minutes to think. Letting the water wash over her and sooth her nerves seemed to be what she needed. They had been together every waking and sleeping moment since they were wed. By nature, she was a solitary creature. Wasn't used to being in the presence of another all the time.

Guy shocked her when she woke up to find him as a cat nestled close to her, purring softly in her ear. While he didn't do anything untoward, he did tease with the possibilities. At one point she'd been so unnerved, annoyed, dazed, her response was not what she anticipated.

He liked to tease and it was something... well no one had ever joked with her in her entire life. She didn't know how to respond to the gentle teasing.

Finishing with her shower and drying herself off, she found a pair of jeans and a t-shirt to wear for the ride deeper into the Sierra Madres. He would want her to wear a hat, but she couldn't remember what she did with it.

An hour later, her hair dried and makeup applied, she pulled her hair into a ponytail and set off to find him.

"Guy." She looked around the corner into the kitchen, which seemed to be the gathering place of the clan.

"You're finished. Let me pour you a cup of coffee." He rose, sidestepping around Cook to reach the pot and the cups, He poured and brought it to her. "There you go."

"Thank you." She helped herself to a piece of bacon. "See, you remembered what I need in the morning."

From the sink, Cook laughed. "Bacon and coffee. Seems your new hubby has the same inclinations. Scrambled some eggs and toasted a few slices of bread if you'd like more. One can't live on bacon and coffee."

"Bite your tongue," she shot back laughing. "It would suffice for me."

"As long as I'm part of that configuration," Guy said. "I can live on Cas, coffee and bacon."

"Of course." She chewed thoughtfully knowing she would never want to live without him either.

"When you're finished eating, Brody planned a clan meeting. He likes to do that, you know, plan meetings. This one is about your mother." Guy straddled a chair seeming to keep his gaze focused on her. "She's in trouble. We have to do something."

My mother? She turned to him needing to get what happened earlier off her mind before she tacked the subject of her mother. "I'm sorry about the shower. It's just that I needed time to think. You touch me in ways I don't understand and it's not just sexual in nature. Sometimes what you do or say shocks me to my very core, unnerves and sometimes frightens me as well."

"My cat?" he asked, frowning, his brows drawing together. "That was not well done of me. I didn't think it through, just eager for you to see me."

She grimaced, not wishing to lay any burdens on him, but also needing to tell him the truth. "You're cat. I..." She swallowed, tuning her gaze away for a second, felt insecurities assail her. "Truly, I didn't know how to react, what was right or proper. You tested me in too many ways, too soon."

"I'm sorry," he told her, looking remorseful. "I like, no love to tease, love seeing the play of emotions cross your face when you're trying to figure out what to do or say."

"I'm positive I'll get used to you in time." She sighed then, thinking she'd rather that time be sooner than later.

He stood, holding out a hand, "Are you ready to be part of your first clan meeting? Something else I'm sure you are not used to. Your first one was informal. Who knows what this one will be like?"

She let him help her to her feet. "The barbecue when your siblings nearly caught us naked might have, if they didn't make so damn much noise. Was that the first clan meeting?" She laughed and watched the smile grow on Guy's face.

"Am I forgiven?" he asked seemingly contrite.

"Always. Promise I won't ever hold a grudge."

In the living room, the siblings were gathered, leaving a spot for them to sit together. The looks were grim and she wondered what they'd heard. Her mother was the main topic, but she guessed they would consider ways to permanently stop Cedric. She didn't think for a minute the man would let her go this easily. He was sure to have something diabolical in mine.

Brody started, "Kimi has heard things, unnerving things concerning this Cedric. He lied to you about your mother, you know. She's very much alive and she never promised you to him. He's been keeping her chained in a small cubicle in his home."

"Alive? Chained?" Her heart nearly stopped, her hand going to her chest. Guy pulled her close, seeming to understand the desperation assailing her. "When Guy told me this was about her, I didn't think it was because she was alive."

"That's good news," he said, giving her shoulder a squeeze. "We will have to rescue her, bring her back for you."

"She never promised you to Cedric. The man lied to you all this time about pretty much everything," Kimi said. "She's been a prisoner of his all these years. It's about time that changed."

Cas shrugged from Guy's arms, standing, swaying for a moment before she began to walk around the room. Her thoughts swirled in confusion, her mind reeling with possible scenarios. Tears welled in her eyes. Her mother reached out to her on their wedding night, but she had no idea the hell Etain had been put through.

"Does Cedric still have her locked away?"

Turning, Cas focused her question on Kimi.

"Yes," Kimi said. "He's hoping to lure you away from us so he can capture you and keep you with your mother. He no longer wants you for his wife though."

Cas inhaled a swift deep breath of air, "No."

Guy was beside her then, once more pulling her close. "We won't let that happen."

"We plan on rescuing your mother and not allowing anything to happen to you in the process," Margo told them. "Together we have a lot of power, some unique. Cedric will be surprised and displeased with the outcome if he persists."

"Indeed," Lyn said as if she harbored her own secret.

"I will reach out to him mentally. Try to convince him his best course of action would be to let Etain leave with us when we come to pick her up," Kimi said.

"When do we start?"

Cas was eager to end this. She had a new life, one she wanted to live without fears surrounding her. Leaning into Guy, she placed a hand on his chest.

"Not we, us," Carr said sweeping his hand around the room.

"Wouldn't Cas be in more danger if she's left here alone?" Guy was frowning now, clearly concerned about this plan his family was concocting.

To Cas this seemed like a strategy with flaws before they even started. "I don't like the way that sounds. If Cedric were to discover me here..." She was shaking her head, terror spinning within her.

"You're not going to be alone," Brody said. "Guy and Niagel will be here with you as well as Cook. When we leave, Maska will create a protective bubble around the ranch house. You will have adequate protection for the time we are gone. Afterward, if all goes as planned you won't need it."

"So, you don't want me to go."

She was trying to get her thoughts organized. Of course they didn't want her. She had no powers and even her fairy dust was useless now that she was with child.

"You will stay with your mate and protect her. Cas would be too much of a liability if she were to go with us. We can't have that. We don't want to have to protect her while we are trying to rescue Etain."

"I'm torn between the need to seek revenge against the wrongs done to Cas and my need to stay by her side." Guy's fists were clenched at his sides as he stood in front of the window staring at the Sierra Madre landscape. "I don't like feeling useless."

"You have no choice," Brody spoke up, the steel blue of his eyes gleaming fiercely. "As her mate you must stay with her. That fact does not make you useless."

To the rest of the clan, "We will spend the next few days planning and practicing our skills. It's been a few years since we have used them."

"Practice?" Lyn sent the cup Brody held in his hand spinning toward the opposite wall, Carr ducking before it hit his head, coffee spilling across the floor." Brushing her hands together she looked at Brody with a self-satisfied grin.

"She doesn't, just as I don't need to train." Margo concentrated on a spot in the back of the kitchen, a few napkins erupting in flames before walking to the door staring onto the dessert landscape, a cactus flamed in front of them the fire sizzling skyward. "I think I've made my point."

"In any case we will practice our skills together and decide if we wish the girls to stay in human form. Kimi can learn as much as possible about Cedric and where he lives. It is likely they will do more` good that way than as cats," Brody continued with his carefully thought out lecture.

"If all of you believe it's safe, Cas and I will go to Infinity Cliff today and stay the night. I'd like to watch the sun dip below the horizon with her. Cook, hopefully, has a basket of food packed for us. I promised Cas and I know she wants nothing more than to ride a horse again. I can create a barrier that will keep Cedric out."

Cas shot him a glare of frustration. "We could take the helicopter or... if," she waved her hand in the air. If she wasn't pregnant, she could fly. "I'd like nothing more than to ride Sheba again." She slanted him a wicked grin, knowing he would never believe her. "We hit it off so very well as you know. She understands me."

"Good, then let's see if the food is ready then make our way to the stable." Guy wrapped an arm around her, drawing her close.

"I'm ready." She shrugged her shoulders, "If you are."

"Always ready to be alone with you."

She wasn't sure what to say. Needing to say something outrageous back at him, she couldn't think of a thing.

When they stepped outside, his gaze was on the horizon, a grim expression replacing the broad smile. "Clouds are building. Think we should take some extra supplies, a packhorse. Thunderstorms can come up quickly. Don't want to be caught unprepared in the mountains."

She shivered, remembering the flashflood they'd been caught in not too long ago. "Should we go?"

"Might be sunshine and blue skies the entire time. In any case, it will be nice to watch the sunset and stay the night, a different scene than the one we've been enjoying, not that I'm complaining. The rest of the clan will be busy and a tent and sleeping bag will be a nice change from our bedroom."

"So you say," she murmured, skeptical of spending the evening in the outdoors again. "What if Cedric decides to come calling."

"He won't, not if he's planning to lure us to his fortress, but I will set up the shield."

"You have an answer for everything."

"Try to." He lifted his broad shoulder in silent confirmation.

A half hour later after Guy secured the supplies they would need, they set off. For Cas, the ride was much easier than the first time, the sun not too hot as they rode into the middle of the day. The clouds on the horizon continued to grow, at times shielding the sun and creating cooling shadows. This time she was sure his brothers or sisters didn't accompany them in their cat form.

"How far is it?" Cas asked, laughing. "Know that I'm not in a hurry to get there. I'm just curious. I enjoy watching you ride."

Over his shoulder he looked at her, turning slightly in the saddle, his grin running from ear to ear. "What is it you like to watch?"

She smiled, tipping her head flirtatiously having no intention of telling him. She slowly lowered her lashes for a second then, "Just you."

"Perhaps you should ride a little in front of me enough so I can watch the sway of your breasts. Yes, I do believe I would like that. They move sweetly beneath your t-shirt."

"If I do that, we might not get to this Infinity Cliff this afternoon, might not get there in time to see the sunset you so want to show me." She smiled sweetly, thinking they could have stayed at home for what would probably happen next. No, she wanted to see this special spot of his, of his clans.

"I will control myself," he said, his eye gleaming with desire. "But it won't be easy."

"Control is always good," she agreed as she sent her gaze toward him. "Tell me what you like and what you don't like? We've been together such a short time," she paused then. "It's the little things I want to know about you now."

"Not the big things? I thought you were talking about sex."

She laughed, "You've already taught me about the big things."

"So, then, what are these little things you want to know?" He let her catch up to him so they rode side-by-side, silence encompassing them for a few minutes.

"Let me see," she turned to him, studying him. "Your favorite food."

"Love all food, well most. Can't say I've a favorite? Yours?" He turned the question back to her.

With no hesitation, "Ice cream, strawberry cheesecake to be exact. Did you go to college?"

"I did and I graduated in microbiology."

"Microbiology, I would have never guessed, and you run the saloon in Cactus Junction. Seems a waste to me."

"Along with my brothers and sisters. And," he paused, "I work independently."

"You know all about my college then..." she paused, thinking about what he just told her and everything that came before. "I want to know..." Her silence lasted too long for Guy's patience.

"Well," he grinned even wider than before.

"Well what?" She kicked her horse, urging Sheba to a faster pace, not too sure she really wanted to ask the question prevalent in her head.

It seemed he didn't want her to get away without answering. Suddenly, his horse was by her side, and he pulled it to a stop. Leaning forward, he scooped her from her saddle, settling her on his lap.

"Guy!" She pounded on his shoulders, protesting.

He wasn't going to let her go no matter her objection.

He shocked her yet she rode on his lap that night they first met. He was a man who would do what he wanted when he wanted. His lips found hers and they were sweet and warm, so very gentle. She liked kissing, enjoyed it more than she wanted to admit. He was teasing her again, trying to persuade her to tell him what she was meaning to ask only a few minutes ago. She decided he would have to work harder if he was going to succeed.

After he thoroughly ravished her with kisses, he drew away, looking at her differently than before. "Well?"

"I changed my mind, perhaps we should move to a safer subject."

She couldn't remember what she was going to ask. Perhaps that was a good thing.

"You can try. What is safer?"

"So, you won't let this go even though your wife of only two days would ask it as a favor." She tried to make him feel guilty but quickly realized that just wasn't possible.

"Female ploys won't work here. I would give you the moon and the stars if possible, but I need to know the question. Want to see the blush on your cheeks when you ask."

She ignored his subtle innuendo that he had an idea what her question was about. "But not this one little concession?"

She still tried, still wished she'd never thought the question. The words escaped her mouth before she had the chance to think it over.

He kissed her again and again, his hand finding the skin beneath her shirt before nimbly unfastening her bra. "Ah, sweetheart, you unman me. Do you think it's possible to make love on a horse?" He turned her so she sat astride him.

She felt him then, hard against her core and he was heavily aroused, needing her and his groan touched her heart. "I don't think so. At least I don't want to try. We'd fall off, best case scenario."

"Perhaps it's time for a rest." He traced the shell of her ear with his tongue before letting his teeth close gently on the sensitive flesh.

"Perhaps it is." She thought perhaps he would now forget her unasked question.

He let her slide to the ground first before swinging both legs over the saddle and landing on the ground beside her.

"This is still our honeymoon." He pulled her t-shirt over her head along with her bra. "It seems I just can't get enough of you."

"Aren't you afraid someone will see us?" She shivered thinking of the possibilities.

"Out here?" He sounded incredulous. "No way in hell."

He left her standing beside his horse to retrieve a blanket from the packhorse. In only a few seconds the blanket was on the ground and they were naked. He was inside her, her breasts filling his hands, while she moved with him. Her climax sent him over the edge, pumping wildly into her until he cried out her name.

He was braced on his forearms, grinning at her. "Well?" he asked, still deep inside her, touching her still.

"Well what?" She wasn't sure right now what he spoke of.

"What were you going to ask me?" His lips closed over one nipple, sucking it deep into his mouth, drawing on it until her hips moved against him again.

"I-I can't think, damn you." She hit him on the shoulder, wishing he'd forget something. He remembered everything. She would have to be more careful in the future.

"That's no excuse." He shifted his attention, exploring more of Cas.

~ * ~

The siblings set up a mini training area. Brody, as the oldest was in charge, accepted all responsibility and Carr played second in command. During the following hours, boulders flew through the air as missiles directed at standing cacti. While any wayward bush burst into flames.

The two-acre plot looked bombed or nuked by the time the siblings and their wives finished. Everything had been laid flat by the two women.

Maska worked on spells that would open or close locked doors as well as cloaking spells for the clan.

Sadie watched from the bay window in Niagel's living room, the doors of the house banging shut every few seconds before they opened again.

Kimi on the other hand, concentrated on discovering all the hiding places in Cedric's fortress while also figuring out exactly where this place was located. She wavered, frown lines creasing her forehead before she suddenly collapsed.

Carr and Brody raced to her side, kneeling beside her. Brody touched her pulse, which still beat strongly.

"She is steady and strong but she needs more work. We can't have her swooning from the energy drain this takes.

Maska, at her side, scooped her into his arms, heading for the house. Without turning, "Kimi needs to rest. It's obvious she has worked too hard this afternoon. This evening at dinner she can tell you all what she has learned. Until then no one is to interrupt us."

"Take care of our sister," Brody called out to Mak's retreating back. He'd given little thought to Mak's role in this, but he might very likely prove useful in getting all of them to Cedric's fortress without anyone knowing. Mak also had the ability to get into people's heads, but his skill wasn't as strong as his wife's.

Mak didn't turn around, with Brody's words. He marched steadily to the house.

Sadie stepped from the ranch, leaving the door open for Mak and Kimi, striding steadily to meet Brody. He understood she would have something to say in this even though she was only a spectator.

"Is all this necessary?" she questioned. She was lifting her delicate shoulders all the while shaking her head. "Cedric would be a fool to try anything against this clan."

"He is a fool," Brody sat down beside his wife enfolding her in his arms before kissing her. "He should have never taken his plans as far as he did. Now he will have to pay for his crimes."

"You mean Etain?"

Nodding slowly, appreciating his wife more than she knew, "Etain's kidnapping and following Cas here, not accepting her wishes when she made it clear she wanted nothing to do with him."

"I understand he didn't want to give up on Cas. From what I understand he's coveted her for many years," Sadie said, "Just as you never gave up on me. What would have happened between us if you just said fine and let me walk out of your life?"

He growled low in his throat, remembering that time when she left him, and he followed her. "I would never let you leave."

She shrugged from his arms to stand in front of him, "Isn't this the same? How is it different?"

"No, Cedric doesn't love Casidhe. He just wants her as his possession. She is very beautiful. She was to be a conquest, nothing more. You on the other hand are my mate. I could no more let you walk out of my life than stop my heart from beating."

"I suppose that's true."

She sat beside him again, leaning into him.

He set his chin lightly on the top of her head. "It is the same for the rest of our family. That is why we will do everything in our power to help Cas and Guy through this. To make sure they don't have to look over their shoulders for the rest of their lives."

Brody stood then, clapping his hands together. "Time for all to take a rest. We'll resume training tomorrow morning and hopefully the next day. After Guy and Cas return, we will see to Cedric."

A cheer of approval at this new directive rang around him as his clan gathered together, laughing and chatting. "You still believe we need to practice?" Lyn asked. "We didn't do a good enough job today?"

"You were all excellent. Tomorrow we will make sure Mak can

transport us through space to the fortification that Kimi hopefully has located," Carr told them. "That doesn't mean we don't need the practice or the planning.

"Go now, we'll gather for dinner at six. After that only time to yourselves and spouses," Brody said. "All of you did very well today. I'm proud of you."

"Would like to know though what Guy and Cas are up to," Sadie laughed.

"Just what we are going to be up to after dinner," Brody kissed her soundly, thinking of the outings they'd taken to Infinity Cliff after they were married as well as the sunsets they watched. Their second child was fathered there.

"Find out what you were going to ask me?"

Chapter Eight

Guy and Cas stood at the brink of Infinity Cliff, gazing over the vast, endless space. The sun was about an hour from setting. A tent had been raised and a small fire crackled a few hundred yards from the edge of the cliff.

"It is beautiful and I would truly like to walk to the edge and look over," Cas said attempting to step closer.

Guy tightened his grip on her waist. "Not a chance."

"Perhaps you'll be more lenient when I get my fairy back and can fly," she told him, leaning into him as his hands caressed her. "I would like to know if one can or cannot see to the bottom."

"Perhaps, but don't count on that ever happening." His inner cat growled his disproval. "What would happen if you were hovering over the edge and a wing gave out?"

She looked at him askance. "Wings just don't give out. I want to know now. Don't want to wait. I could lie down on my stomach and crawl to the edge so I can look over. Have you ever looked over?"

"One cannot see the bottom, nothing, nada. Do you understand it is not something I want you to do? Trust me." More than anything he needed her to trust him with everything.

"Trust goes both ways," she reminded him tartly.

With his arm still around her waist, he turned her toward the campfire. "For now, we are going to eat some of the wonderful stew cook made for us as well as pull out one of the bottles of Chateau De Fleur sparkling wine. We are going to watch the sun go down. See." He pointed toward the horizon. Colors are already beginning to paint the sky. "You are going to remember what you thought to ask earlier."

184

"It will embarrass me."

"Then I will have to ply you with wine so you will forget about your inhibitions and talk to me, truly tell me what's on your mind. What you didn't say but was curious enough to think about it."

She sighed deeply, "Remember, it's non alcoholic. There won't be much plying. I suppose you're right but you have to promise not to laugh at me."

"I would never do that," he told her, knowing the truth. He would only laugh with her.

"Yes, you would." She sounded adamant.

The sincerity of her statement struck a chord within. "Have I done that? Laughed at you?"

She skipped ahead, affectively ending this conversation. At the campfire she poured them both a glass of wine before sitting on the makeshift bench someone made long ago. "Who's putting the stew on to warm?" She handed him his wine.

"Can you cook on an open fire? Can you cook at all?" He grinned at her, knowing he'd wheedle the important questions from her before the night ended.

She lifted her shoulders slightly, smiling at him. "Could always try if you don't mind burnt or undercooked food."

"Won't be undercooked but I suppose it would always be possible to burn it. Think I'll do the cooking tonight." He rose, sauntering to the packhorse, whistling. "Don't want you to work on our honeymoon."

"You shouldn't have to either." She leaned back sipping her wine as she watched the sun as well as the colors painting the sky. "It's beautiful you know. Mother nature never fails to impress, one way or the other."

He smiled at her, pleased she seemed content and eager for the issue of Cedric and his obsession with her to be taken care of. "How hot do you want this?" He was stirring the pot, watching her, remembering the sweet interlude they shared on the way here. It would be like that tonight too. Hot and sweet.

"Any way you cook it, I'll love it. I'm famished."

His eyebrows rose and a cat like grin swept across his face. "For me?"

"Always."

She walked toward him, her breasts swaying provocatively beneath the t-shirt.

Sometime when he wasn't looking, she had taken her bra off. "You're playing with fire, little imp." He wouldn't have it any other way.

She ran her hand along his back, letting her fingers rest inside his back pocket. "You're wearing too many clothes." When he turned toward her, she slowly unfastened the buttons on his shirt, slipping it off his shoulders when she finished then running her hands along his arms.

"I'm not wearing more than you are." He dished stew into each bowl, handing her one.

She was powerless now, holding something in each hand. He meant to tease and seduce until she could wait no longer for him. Kissing her lightly on the lips and letting his fingers tantalize her, he continued for a few seconds, "Then we should eat. Do you have your phone?"

The tiny sound of pleasure rippling from her gave him reason to smile. He could barely hold himself in check. Seducing her created a raging desire in him. He ignored it. There would be time for sexual play.

"Why?" she asked quickly stepping away, distancing herself from him.

"Pictures. The photos tonight will be beautiful, almost as beautiful as you."

"In my pocket." She reached behind to check.

The tight buds of her breasts pushing provocatively against her shirt. "Good, keep doing that and we won't get dinner."

"I know. I can't help myself when I look at you. Promise, I won't do anything else. I want to eat. Do you want me to put my bra on?" She grinned as if she knew the answer.

"And forego looking at you and anticipating things that will happen later this evening?" He sat down beside her, handing her a spoon.

Beside the bench there was a small wooden table on each side. "Someone thought of everything." She set her glass on her table while she ate.

"Mother and father."

His feelings turned inward. While he didn't want to exclude Cas, he also didn't want to talk about his parents. He felt as if he'd lost them every time he thought about the people who sired him, raised him with solid values then disappeared from his life. The impact on him had been substantial. He was the youngest. Brody and Carr took their departure in stride and the twins had each other.

He had always felt alone, until now, until Cas.

"I haven't met them."

She reached out touching his arm. "They are alive? I don't even know who my father is."

He guessed he shouldn't feel sorry for himself. Her mother had been taken from Cas when she was a small girl, and she didn't even know who her father was. "My parents left when they thought we were all grown up and could take care of ourselves. They had adventures that needed sharing, they told us."

"Just left you?" She held his hand in both of hers. "I'm sorry. I suppose it's different when you lose someone you've come to love. I loved mother until Cedric poisoned me to her with his lies. Father just wasn't ever there."

"Rather than never really knowing your parents?"

His bitterness surprised him. He wanted to kick himself. His sudden change of mood was not her fault. He had been the lucky one in this. At least he knew his parents, understood their love for him.

"I didn't mean to bring up something you feel so strongly about." She tugged on his hand. "The sun is setting now. Pour me more wine then..."

"You couldn't have known."

"Which is why we've a lot to learn about each other."

He picked up a quilt and poured the wine before following her to the spot he picked out earlier. A large boulder was strategically placed to lean on and earlier he spread a blanket on the ground.

They sat and he pulled the quilt over them. For the longest time they didn't speak. The sun slowly descended, brilliant colors spreading across the sky. The weather this evening cooperated. Cumulus clouds of the early afternoon threatening to become thunderheads never materialized.

Cas snapped pictures about two minutes apart until the last of the sun vanished. He kissed her then, pulling her into his arms, longing for a life filled with happiness and lots of children.

"Are you always this romantic?" she asked, gazing into his eyes.

"No, only with you," he told her, seeing the expression on her face change before she looked away.

She snuggled against him, sighing deeply. Then, "That was kind of my question, you know."

"You still have me guessing."

His hands rested beneath her breasts. One turn of his hands and they would fill his, and they wouldn't come up for air or talk the rest of the night.

She leaned her head against his chest, closing her eyes, seeming to enjoy the moment, "I've never ever kissed another man or boy."

"That wasn't your question. As for my answer, I don't how many women I've kissed, slept with. Never thought it important to keep a count. Never thought anyone would ask."

"Why? Don't you want to remember them?"

"Until you, no one meant anything to me. They were just women I had sex with." His words sounded callous even to him but he gave them pleasure, never lied to anyone how he felt.

"What about you? Were there any men you wanted to kiss you? Did you date, go to a movie or grab a cup of coffee with a man?" This was something he didn't care too much about yet her lack of experience influenced her, perhaps even made his conquest of her easier.

"No one. I stayed away from people. Always worried Cedric had spies out looking for me, not that I wanted to meet anyone." She sipped her drink. "I studied and went to class and the library. That's about sums up my life after I left Cedric."

He felt her relax against him. "When was your first dream, the one where you saw me shift?"

She was so relaxed he was sure she fell asleep. He touched her chin turning her so he could see her eyes. She opened for him. When she moistened her lips with her tongue, he leaned forward and kissed her lightly, brushing his lips across her yet unwilling to deepen the kiss, which would effectively end their conversation until morning.

Their discussion needed to continue before they found their way inside the tent and another night of making love, mad sex or whatever one wanted to call the passion that ignited between them.

"I think I was about ten," she answered after he pulled away.

"Ten," he repeated, his voice husky with the passion building inside wondering just how long she'd been dreaming about him. "You saw me naked when you were just ten."

"No, for some reason I only saw you with clothes on then your cat form. Never really saw your face. Never saw you without clothing until I was an adult."

"You did see me naked." Suddenly he thought that fact unfair. In his youth or even the recent past, he never had dreams where he saw his mate without clothing.

"Yes."

She looked down as if the fact embarrassed her.

He placed a finger under her chin, lifting so he would see into her eyes but it was too dark. "I would have given anything to see you before we met. I would have known."

"I thought you did know when you saw me."

"Did I really come across that confidant?"

"Arrogant, self-assured, I only went with you because I understood the power you held over me as well as the fact you might have more power than Cedric. You recall I traveled to Cactus Junction because I needed you to help me."

"Let's go back to the fire. You're shivering." He lifted her carrying her back to the bench where they'd been sitting before he returned for the glasses.

"Who's going to do the dishes?"

"They'll wait until morning." Yet he rose, tossing the paper plates into the fire and putting the leftover stew in a container. "Stay close to the fire and yell if you see anything besides me. I'm going to rinse all this stuff in the creek we crossed before we got here. I'll be right back."

"I'll yell real loud."

He left, humming and thinking of the rest of the evening, which he didn't want to spend in question and answer mode. Learning everything about each other didn't need to happen all at once.

When he returned, the stew pot was effectively cleaned out as well as filled with water and ready for the next round the following day. The spoons were inside the pot, which he set on the fire to bring it to a simmer.

He sat down next to her. "Do you have any regrets?"

She looked up suddenly. "Why would you ask something like that, Guy? Of course I don't have regrets. This is exactly what I wanted although I didn't expect you to go as far as marry me."

He laughed then, a soft laugh one filled with love and caring. "Not even the loss of your fairy?" He was hoping she would say no because he was afraid she would never get it back, feared that when he marked her as his, her wings had been sheared.

"I've thought about that but haven't been able to decide. It's not a part of me now. I don't need to make myself small and fly places. The last several years have been spent hiding the fact I have special powers, I'm different from most."

"You will always be unique, Casidhe, and special, very special. I've a feeling you might not ever be able to fly again. Would that be so bad?"

There he said the words. The fact was out there for her to think about. If the statement was true, she would have to come to terms with the truth.

"Why?"

"Why unique and special or why not be able to fly?" Avoiding the truth and confusing the issue as well was not well done of him. He cleared his throat, hesitating, searching for the right words.

"Fly. Why do you think that?" She had turned to him, was staring at him as if he gone quite crazy. "We decided both of us, Destiny too, my inability to hover off the ground was because of the pregnancy."

This had to be the end of the conversation. In any case it was all speculation and didn't deserve further thought. "Come, finish your wine then let's go to bed. I'm eager to pick up where we left off this afternoon."

"No," she said pointedly, her tiny fists clenched desperately at her sides. "Not until you answer my questions. I won't just hop into bed with you and be your sex slave anytime you snap your fingers."

The breath he inhaled seemed to stick in his throat. For the time being he would ignore the part about being a sex slave, unsure if he liked the notion or abhorred it. "I'm afraid I might have done something to your wings when I claimed you on our wedding night."

He felt guilty as hell but at the time he thought of nothing but himself, his pleasure and needs. Well he had also thought about her pleasure but knew the claiming would cause her some pain, nothing like what she experienced.

"Is that why it hurt so much? You cut my wings?" She blinked a few times, downing the rest of her drink in a gulp. "I never thought about my wings. Your marks were on my shoulders and arms, not my back."

"I was afraid." He pulled her into his arms. "I was afraid for you and now I'm terrified of what I might have done to you."

"We won't know until after the child is born. There is no reason to worry about it now. You didn't cut my wings when you claimed me. There is no way that could have happened. I'm sure of it."

"You are? You are sure?"

He felt relieved even though he still had a few doubts. They would wait and all would be fine. She was sure even though he was not, but what did he know about fairies?

Sometime in the middle of the night, raindrops began to pound the tent. The soft pattering was nice, the sound of the water falling soothing his nerves that were ragged with the notion he'd hurt Cas.

It was a large tent with plenty of room to stand if that was what one wanted to do. All Guy wanted was to pull the sleeping bag around them and make love to his wife. He should do that.

As soon as she would allow it.

~ * ~

She admitted to herself it was nice to think about something other than losing her wings even though his explanation failed to make sense to her. Closing her eyes, she snuggled into his hard body, trailing a finger down the middle of his chest, his abs. She would have to think more on what he told her. It did seem plausible.

"You're not asleep, are you?" she asked wondering where his thoughts were as she stroked his arm, enjoying the play of muscles against her fingertips. "Care to tell me why?"

"Worried."

"Yes, I am too. Don't want anyone hurt because of me and my problems with Cedric, especially your clan. Wish Cedric would just go away and forget about me."

"Kimi reached out to me. That's one reason I'm awake. They have found the fortress where he lives with his extended family, I suppose. Don't know much about fairies. Is this place so tiny humans cannot walk inside or do they live in their human form?"

"Why didn't Kimi ask me? I would have told her where they were. The fortress is tiny. Your clan would never have access to the inside." She rolled over, watching his face. It was still dark. She couldn't tell much, couldn't see if the lines in his forehead were furrowed or if he was calm. "What are the other reasons you're awake?"

"Brody sent Balor up here to guard us. Promised me the sea demon would keep his distance. Don't like the idea we need protection. The only reason we are at Infinity Cliff is because we thought this place to be safe for us."

"I don't think that's the only reason."

She knew he wanted to show her the land, his clan's land, his heritage.

"No, you're right. With Balor here I forgot about the other, an extension of our honeymoon as well as some of my history. It was to be a learning experience for both of us."

"Balor? Did I meet him then forget who he was?" she asked, caressing his lips, thinking about making love again.

Sometimes she thought that was all she could ever think about when he was around, even when he was not. She smiled, staring at his mouth.

"If you want to talk, you should really stop staring at my mouth," he told her with a soft chuckle. "If you don't, I won't be responsible for what happens next.

"Maybe we can do both."

He heaved a long drawn out sigh, seeming to think about her comment before proceeding, "When Great Grandfather has company, Balor usually makes himself scarce. He really only likes and trusts Lyn and Deacon. You should stop staring at me. I can't think."

"So, why don't you think Kimi asked me."

She didn't want to change the focus of her thoughts, but she exhaled slowly and looked at the ceiling of the tent. Kimi should put her trust in someone who could answer her questions, not a man who knew next to nothing about faeries and how they live.

"I don't have an answer for that."

He bent close, kissed the tip of her nose then her forehead.

"Make something up," she laughed softly, listening to the raindrops, patter on the tent. "Do you think there will be another flood?"

"No. Perhaps Kimi didn't want to bother you or maybe she wanted to see if she still had the skill to ferret out the information from Cedric's head. They were supposed to be practicing their skills yesterday."

"That's why we should have stayed and helped."

He drew her into his arms, her head to his chest.

"This is our battle not theirs. Do like being secluded from the rest of your family though? We don't have to listen to make sure they aren't intruding on something private."

"No, but I would never disobey either of my brothers. They are the leaders of our clan. By that fact alone they make all the decisions. I'm the youngest in the family and while they sometimes listen to me, they rarely take my advice unless it coincides with theirs."

Once more, Guy tenderly kissed her forehead, her cheeks and the tip of her nose. He too rolled to his back and stared at the ceiling. "What is so fascinating up there?"

"Is the honeymoon over?" Cas asked, feeling as if he ignored her. "You know nothing is intriguing or captivating on the ceiling of the tent. It's just that you told me not to stare at your mouth. I was doing my best not to look."

"No again, and I hope the honeymoon is never over for us, but

I've seen Balor's shadow hovering, and I don't like the idea of him being so close when I make love to my wife."

She sat up, the sleeping bag falling to her waist, turning toward him. Cas knew if he could see her clearly, not just the outline of her body, she would tempt him, but in the darkness, she didn't think... "Well, why did they send Balor here? There was no concern when we left yesterday. Either you're not telling me something or..."

"Kimi is not telling me," he interrupted.

His voice sounded worried, concerned and she suddenly didn't like that thought very well. If he was anxious about her, about them, she wanted to share the burden with him. "Something has happened. You must reach out to her and find out what she has discovered. I have to know."

"I've tried. She obviously doesn't want to tell us anything or she would have already. Kimi isn't answering my requests." Cas inhaled swiftly and deeply, thinking. "We should get up now. In any case, I doubt if I can go back to sleep with all these thoughts rambling around in my brain, and if you won't make love to me because someone is watching the tent, I don't see a reason to put off coffee and bacon."

Guy reached out, holding her wrist before tugging her to him, her breast pushed against his chest. She still loved the way he felt against her, so different. "I'm not hungry for coffee or bacon. Besides it's not yet time to rise. Still dark out there."

His voice was low and husky, tempting her, reaching out to her. His passion was always so strong and intense.

"Unfortunately, neither am I. It seems the sun must be up for me to want breakfast of any sort. What should we do now?"

"Reach out to Kimi like you said. She will either ignore me or tell me what she knows. I'll try one more time."

He closed his eyes, and she watched him, as he seemed to strain with the effort.

"Anything?" she asked when he opened his eyes.

"Perhaps it was an oversight and she really wants to enlighten us as to what is going on. Maybe for some unknown reason she can't reach us up here. Truth is I don't have any idea, and that bothers me even more than watching Balor's shadow around the tent. It's as if we're about to be attacked and there's a damn protective bubble around us."

"Perhaps there is no cell tower where they are," he laughed, running his hands along her back until they reached her butt. "There are too many plausible stories. Let's forget about Kimi and Balor as well."

"Cell tower?" she queried, wondering what the devil he was talking about. "I don't understand."

"When we traveled into the future to save the world, the people lived underground. It was difficult to reach each other. Sometimes we did, sometimes not, It all depended on where they were."

"What does this have to do with Kimi?" She still didn't understand what he was trying to tell her.

"You may sit on me," he told her, whispering softly. "Then we can continue this discussion if you like."

"You want me to sit on you now?" She blinked several times. "Just because you don't want to explain yourself, I gather."

"Yes, to both."

"Very well, if that's what you would like. Can't see that I have any objections. She straddled him then came down on top of him, heard his masculine groan of pleasure. Funny how he'd barely touched her, not even kissed her and just thinking about this, she was ready to take him inside. No, she'd been thinking about him inside her since he asked her to stop staring at his mouth.

"Are you happy, Cas?"

"In the morning you can show me your cat again and maybe go for a walk. I'd like to meet this man who is even now planning on being our guard. We don't need someone unless Cedric is planning on attacking us. Would Cedric do that?" She paused for another breath of air. "Of course I'm happy."

"Where you are concerned, Cedric seems a bit deranged, obsessed, possessive of you when he has no reason to be. You are not his. You are mine." Guy spread his hands across her belly then upward to finally cup her breasts. He was grinning now, and she was very glad the sky was beginning to lighten.

She liked seeing him smile. "In any case, tell me about Balor. I'd like to know how this demon came to be a trusted part of your family. A man who would drop whatever he is doing to come here to guard someone he doesn't know."

She rose slowly on him before settling against him, setting a slow erotic rhythm. His groan of pleasure delighted her to no end.

"Do you also want to learn about all the other monsters we've defeated?" he asked, his voice shaking but he was still smiling at her, his eyes gleaming with passion and desire. The primal lust was potent, strong in the early morning light.

Dawn must be closing in on them, because she could see his face more clearly with each passing second, his eyes as well. "I would like that but Balor first, because I'm going to have to deal with the monster. If Cedric is foolish enough to come for me, I will have to know that I can trust the man as well as his skills. He does have magical talents, doesn't he?"

"My word that he is loyal and trustworthy is not good enough?"

He stroked her then, her back, her thighs then the intimate folds between her legs.

She couldn't hold back the tiny sounds coming from her although she tried. God knows she tried. She needed to prolong this, take it as slow as possible. He wasn't going to let her though. She sat perfectly still, refusing to move on him, but he wouldn't give in to her ploy as he continued to tease and stroke, bringing her ever closer to her release.

Spasms slowly built within her. It seemed he controlled everything again, the pace and the depth as well as when she would climax. She spun out of control, crying out his name as the ripples of her passion built to such a level she succumbed to them even though she tried to stop them. She cried out, her head thrown back while he pushed himself deeper, all the way to her womb.

"Guy." She lay on top of him, exhausted yet satisfied. He remained deep inside, hard and pulsing. She could still feel him as he seemed to grow even larger. "I'll never get tired of you or this."

He laughed soundly, rubbing her back, easing her to a calm before he flipped her over, driving deeper inside her once more, again and again until she reached the shattering pinnacle of her release, hearing him cry out her name then groan with what sounded like pleasure and pain. He remained still for a moment. Now he rested his forearms braced on either side of her. Their bodies were sweat sheened, still pressed against each other and he grinned looking down at her.

"Do you want to do that again or would you like to hear about Balor?" He ran his fingertip across her eyebrows.

"Both," she told him, placing a kiss on the tip of his nose.

"I'll do my best but I'm not sure I can do both. No, I've decided we will do one at a time. Is that to your liking?"

He laughed then, appearing worldly as well as in command. She wouldn't allow him to command her, yet he would always try and she supposed she'd let him once in a great while.

"Suppose it has to be," she sighed, stroking his chest.

He rolled off her, still holding her close. "Balor, let me see. I will start at the beginning, the legend that is Balor anyone can look up if they have the inclination."

"Are you telling me I should ride back to the house, pull out my computer and Google him? You could make this easy for me and just tell me what you know about him. Maybe you don't know anything."

She understood his need to tease but she was really tired at the moment, wanting more than anything to learn a few things so she could make reasonable decisions. This was her life, their life after all.

"No, but you could most assuredly do the same on your phone." He kissed her lightly on the lips as if he once more wanted to distract her.

She punched him hard but smiled at him too. This attempt to sidetrack her wasn't going to work. "I will close my eyes and listen to your story. Then you can tell me about Jokul."

"Balor first, seems his son killed him. Now that seems strange, doesn't it? So, why is he alive and kicking?"

"Not in this family, nothing strange where the McKenna clan is concerned. Go on."

She watched him, squinting his eyes as if trying to think of what to say next. She knew it was another ploy but enjoyed it immensely.

She could wait.

"He didn't want to be dead so he made a deal with these people called the Fomori who had the power of life and death. Nothing comes for free, and it seemed Balor got in over his head."

"A deal you say and it involved your sister somehow. I read about those people when I was researching shifters." She couldn't remember anything about them though. At the time she wasn't interested.

Slowly he traced the line of her jaw, still smiling, still seeming to enjoy each moment with her. "The Fomori wanted a sacrifice in order for them to restore his life."

"They wanted Lyn." She came to the conclusion with little thought. "Lyn of course didn't want to go, didn't want to be a virgin sacrifice."

"Who would?"

"No one, but they weren't asking."

"In any case he tried very hard. He did want to become immortal but when Lyn saved his life, he turned on the people who gave him a second chance to live. I don't know why they let him go."

"Balor fell in love with Lyn then?" She really didn't have to ask. She knew the answer. "What about Jokul? Was he after Margo?"

"He was. The demon followed her through time, and Margo had no idea she was a firestarter. Carr discovered the strange fact accidentally. Once they knew they had to go to great lengths to keep her out of Jokul's icy hands."

"How do you folks attract these characters? At least Cedric is not some strange demon who no one knows anything about?"

She shuddered at the thought. In his own way Cedric was a demon. He kept her and her mother captive for years.

"A demonic fairy," she giggled.

"He is also ruthless and domineering. You shamed him by running away and eluding him for so many years, and that is part of the problem. He's a man and he won't allow a woman to best him. Can't come to terms with the fact that is exactly what you did."

"Cedric's touch sent vile shivers down my spine. I could not bear to be in the same room with him let alone marry him. I would never have been intimate with him. I'm glad to know mother had naught to do with promising me to that man." Her body shook with the thought.

"No, it would not have been good of her to do such a thing. I'm truly sorry she spent so many years imprisoned."

"The clan will release her. She will be with us soon," Guy tried to reassure. "There is nothing to do but wait and stay vigilant."

"The sun is finally up and my stomach is growling. Should we get coffee and bacon?"

"Sounds like a good idea then I can shift. We can go for a walk together while listening to the world wake up. Would you like that? The sunrise was probably gorgeous this morning and we missed it."

"Sunrises herald the beginning of the day, of new life. If we're still here tomorrow morning, we should watch the sunrise."

She grabbed for her clothes, hoping to dress in the warmth of the sleeping bag, shivering as she tried to stay beneath the cover.

Guy stood, pulling on his jeans, "I'll get the fire started."

She could look at him forever. "To bad you can't just point your hands at it and have flames. That would be nice."

"My hands would not get cold."

He stepped outside then poked his head back into the tent. "Seems Balor must have started it, either that or he kept it going all night. The coffee is on and I'm surprised we didn't smell the bacon sizzling. Everything is ready for us whenever you are."

She hurried then needing privacy, she didn't stop at the campfire, merely nodded at Balor as she walked by. Her muscles sore from yesterday's ride, she hobbled for a few steps as she tried to get the kinks out.

No more than a few minutes passed before she was back in their midst. She had no idea Balor had one eye, right in the middle of his forehead. She had not seen him yesterday. Guy did not tell her. "Good morning," she said a bit too formally for the situation. "Thank you for cooking and making the coffee. For guarding us even though we shouldn't need protecting."

Balor didn't reply, simply nodded his head to let her know he heard.

Guy had set a plate and a cup on a table by the bench. "That's yours. Is that enough bacon for you?"

"Sure." She lifted her shoulders slightly, suddenly not so very hungry.

The silence seemed to go on and on. She didn't have words so she kept her mouth closed, wishing someone would say something. Balor finally broke the silence.

"I'll be close by for the rest of the day. We should hear from the clan soon. I don't think it will take long to retrieve your mother. I know I'm a third wheel here. So, I hope you don't have to see me," he said starting to walk away.

"Wait," she stood suddenly. "Why do you have to be here? We are in no danger." She hoped it was just a precaution, but something deep in her gut told her it wasn't.

He turned a grim expression on his face, "Can't say. Just did what Lyn asked. Always do what she asks. She seems to know, but it's Kimi of course who knows those things."

"And you never ask why?"

"No."

~ * ~

Destiny flew frantically after Cedric. He was making a huge mistake, and she had to figure out how to stop him. She'd been in love with the damn man most of her life. Now she wanted to cosh him over the head as if that would knock some sense into him. Others warned her against him, telling her he was a bad man, that he would take advantage of her, hurt her terribly.

She refused to believe that nonsense, even lying to her best friend about an imaginary boy friend. Destiny didn't understand her feelings for Cedric, but what she did understand was that she loved him, always had.

Cedric was just stubborn and used to getting everything thing he wanted. He wanted Casidhe and was furious she wasn't as enamored of him as he was of her. True, he used his servants for sex, but not one that she knew of had spoken harshly about him.

"You shouldn't be doing this." She finally caught up with him. "It's not going to end well. You know very well you don't have the power to defeat a shifter. You need your army. Don't know if you noticed. They are not here."

"None of your business, Destiny. Don't be stickin' your nose in business that isn't yours. I plan on getting Casidhe back and killing the shifter." His wings beat faster trying to distance himself from her and all her demands.

"Cas is my friend, so I'm making this my concern. She's married. You can't have her so you need to come to terms with that notion." Frustration, irritation, building to anger simmered deep inside threatening to spill over. She had to stop him before he got hurt. She couldn't bare that.

"She's mine. I was promised her." He stopped, turning to face Destiny. "Don't need a woman's protection so stop hovering over me as if you can save me from myself."

"You know as well as I that it's not true. Her mother did not promise her. No one ever promised her to you. Cas is not yours and never will be. Her heart is with the shifter." Her hands were on her hips as her wings beat furiously.

He settled on a rock. "Your jealous?" One eyebrow lifted knowingly, "Even with my reputation with the ladies. I could have you right now if I wanted, but I don't."

"I know what you do to the women you summon to your room. It's no secret that you have sex with them, but I guess I don't care. You've never treated me badly, always with respect."

"It's because I don't care about you, Destiny. I don't want you beneath me. You don't make me hard with lust," he taunted her, seeming to enjoy the change of expressions flitting across her face.

She couldn't help feeling the verbal slap in the face, but she had to try to ignore the words. "You're lying, Cedric, and you know it. You just do those things so you can frighten people into doing your bidding. Heaven knows why but you only want the reputation."

"You can believe that if you wish. Do you want me to take you right here on this rock?" he repeated as if he still wanted to hurt her. "For everyone to watch. What if Casidhe saw us?"

Her heart leapt beneath her ribs. "No, but I wouldn't mind if you made love to me or kissed me in privacy. I'd like you to kiss me. Yes, that would be very nice. I think but not here." She was taking chances she shouldn't they both knew it. In her mind the rumors surrounding Cedric were just that rumors.

"Ah, sweet Destiny. Your faith in my character is overwhelming but all wrong. I'm a bad man." He traced her eyebrow with a fingertip, moistening his lips as if planning to kiss her. "I've never turned down a willing woman though."

She sucked her bottom lip into her mouth. Now that he was willing, she wasn't sure she wanted to go through with this, even if it was just a kiss, "I..."

"Second thoughts, darling? Ach, lassie, you want to keep me away from Casidhe. So, this is a ploy."

"No, I haven't lied. It's just that now that..." She stiffened her back. "I've never been kissed and you, while I want you, you do frighten me. Even kissing frightens me because I don't know what kissing entails."

She found she was staring at him, enjoying the smile on his face and wondering now about the rumors.

"Take care lest you get what you ask for. All the rumors are true. I take what I want including women who aren't all that willing. I don't see to their pleasure, only mine. If you're wise you should stay far away from me. I don't have the time or the inclination to give a woman her pleasure and if for some reason I take her before she is ready, it doesn't make a bit of difference to me."

Her wings fluttered behind her, her breathing faster, agitated as he spoke. "I always take care." She waved her hand in the air. "I've seen this day in my dreams when I close my eyes. You'll rue the day you confront the shifter. Go home lest this ends in a bad way."

For a moment he turned away. When he looked at her again, his features had changed. He was angry now, if what she saw in his expression was true, furiously so.

"You knew where Casidhe was before you finally told me. I understand now. Your intentions are not for me but to protect the little fairy, your friend." He flew high and with great speed before he raced back to the rock.

"Yes, yes, I did want to protect Cas. After all she's my friend, but even more than that I needed to keep you away from the McKennas. They have so much power and magic at their disposal. You will not survive this day if you go through with your plans."

"I know but as you see, I've taken precautions. I'm not where they expect me to be." He laughed then. Threw his head back and roared with laughter.

Shivers swept up her spine. He was wrong and he had to listen to her, heed her warnings. "Where is that?" Destiny wasn't at all sure she understood what he was talking about.

"My other seers proved to be much more useful than you. They saw the clan and they were on their way to the fortress."

"That's nonsense. They are too big to do any damage. If you would have just stayed put inside, you would be safe." She didn't understand anything he was saying.

"You yourself told me the clan wielded great power and magic."

"I did." She didn't know where this was going.

"You don't think they could make themselves tiny and find their way into the fortress? They will find Etain but not me. I'm going to kill the shifter and take what is mine."

Chapter Nine

After the evening and early morning rain the day was cool. The sky was clear and very blue, a few white clouds floating along the horizon. When they finished breakfast to move into the tent, the shifting room Guy thought, he had plans with his wife.

She would become more comfortable with his cat form.

They stood in the middle of the roomy tent. His head just touched the ceiling. She was watching him, staring at him, her smile innocent and intriguing. He liked the way her eyes focused on his eyes then glided lower.

"Are you going to shift or just stand there looking at me?" she asked him, her hands on her hips. "I'm waiting, rather impatiently if I do say so myself. I want to see everything I missed the other day."

"Don't let me keep you waiting then." Quickly, he shrugged out of his shirt, his hands on the fastening to his jeans.

"May I?"

Before he could say no, she was kneeling in front of him, her fingers on the zipper, her sweet soft lips so close to his arousal. He inhaled a swift breath of air, wishing she would put her mouth on him. If she did, there would be no shifting for the next few hours. "You should stand back, that is, if you want to see my cat form. Right now, I've so little control I don't give this much of a chance if you remain where you are."

She moved back, sitting cross-legged on their sleeping bag, watching intently, grinning as if she knew exactly how she made him feel, knew his need for her. In a few seconds he stood before her naked and fully aroused. He didn't want it this way but it seemed he had no choice.

Then, he was a cat. He sat on his haunches grinning at her, waiting

204

for her to come to him. She didn't move. She didn't say anything. He decided he would have more patience.

"You are imposing," she finally said. "Powerful."

He blinked a few times trying to agree with her. It was disconcerting when he couldn't talk to her yet he could still read the passion and desire written in her expression. Before he'd always liked this part, the silence and solitude. She reached inside his head though, elicited his feeling. So he grinned at her.

"I'm not going to let you frighten me today," she murmured as she moved closer, stroking his back before moving to the spot behind his ears. "Do you like your stomach rubbed? Most cats do not."

He purred, nodding his head, wishing she would do what she asked.

"You like that, don't you? I've always liked cats. Guess that's a good thing isn't it," she murmured as she idly stroked him.

He rubbed against her, walking around her. *You should take all your clothes off and I can lie down beside you. My fur is soft.*

"Naughty cat, if you're going to do that you have to shift back. I never thought I could understand what you're thinking, just your feelings." She shook her head then one more time. "Is that a thought or a feeling? Never mind. No liberties while you're in your cat form."

He smiled, rubbing his head on her neck, his tongue touching quickly before retreating. He would never take liberties but he did want to feel her next to him, know she could handle the differences.

"Very well, if you're going to make a menace of yourself, it's time for that walk. You can show me what you can do."

I'd rather stay here.

"No, you wouldn't." She stepped outside, holding the tent flap open for him as he followed. "You want to do this as much as I want to see."

He realized suddenly that he loved her. Had loved her since the moment he saw her in the saloon. He loved his mate. He supposed he should tell her sooner than later.

"Which way do you want to go?"

She looked at him as if he would answer. He didn't care. Yet she didn't look as if she was going to move an inch until he decided.

He started out at an easy lope, distancing himself quickly from her. Turning and sitting he waited for her, thinking about the danger and intending to stay close to camp. They could roam farther afield when the danger wasn't present. When Cedric was taken care of.

She sat down on the sand, waving her hand at him. "Run, I want to see how fast you are."

Panthers were sprinters not distance runners. Stamina was not his strength. He obliged her, racing across the plateau then turning to return to her at an easy lope. When he returned, he rested by the rock, his chin on his paws, attempting to smile at her.

"You are really magnificent." She sat down beside him, stroking his back again. "Just as magnificent as when you are a man."

Magnificent, he liked that notion.

He reached out to Kimi, still nothing and he didn't like it very much, needing to hear from her. The need to shift back to human form assailed him but he shook it off. He would be more powerful in a fight against Cedric if he stayed as a panther.

"You're worried."

He stared at her then, slowly nodding his head, agreeing with her.

"Maybe we should go back. I'm not feeling right about this. We should stay at camp so Balor can reach us."

The sun warmed his back, but even if the problems confronting them weren't an ever-present danger, he wouldn't want to stay in his cat. Yet if there was trouble, he was of more use to her this way. He could run, fight, defend her more thoroughly in this form.

Still, despite her request, he remained, listening to the wind, testing the air for lingering and new scents. Balor was downwind a hundred yards or so. No one else was close by. He wondered what the fairy's scent would tell him.

Then Kimi's voice pounded in his head. She sounded frantic with worry, but she wasn't telling him anything. All he heard were noises and grunts. The word Etain filtered through all the chaos to him.

They were in a fight. Kimi had few powers. Unless she was in her cat form, she'd be in trouble. His tail twitched while the hair down his back rose. He wanted to be there, to fight alongside them.

"What's wrong?" Cas held his head with both hands, staring into his eyes, searching for an answer. "I don't like this. Don't like not being able to talk to you, have you answer my questions.

He reached out to her, speaking of the ensuing fight as well as his fears about Kimi. He was closest to her, simply because she understood his youngest sibling status better than anyone else.

"We should go back to camp and I should call for Balor." She rose, walking quickly, following Guy.

"Good," Balor walked beside her. "You are returning."

She jumped, startled at his sudden appearance. "You scared me."

"Sorry, didn't mean to. Well, there is an urgency in the air, words not said by Kimi but a fear for your life nonetheless."

Silence filled the morning, an eerie silence. It seemed even the dessert sounds were nonexistent. Guy trotted beside Cas now as they headed back to camp, alert to anything unusual.

The only thing abnormal was the silence. The calm before the storm he mused, thinking the fight might well be here not there. In his head he saw the clan leaving the fortress, heading this way.

"Isn't it strange that I don't hear anything. I think I'd even like to hear the screech of another panther trying to frighten me away. Your brothers did that, didn't they? I should laugh at how gullible I am but I won't, at least not today. Today I'm going to try to be useful." She wrapped her arms around herself. Bent over slightly as if trying to protect herself.

"I'll make lunch," Balor said. "You both need to keep up your strength." He then strode ahead of them.

"Well, that was interesting. He's worried about Lyn but is going to make lunch. What do you think he knows?" She looked at him, her lips thinned.

Balor is always worried about Lyn. He loves her.

"Well, that is an interesting thought. Not the love part, you told me that earlier. He is very fond of her and that's a good thing for us." She stuck her hands in her pockets and finished the distance to their campsite, her hips swaying provocatively.

"What's for lunch?"

Balor grunted.

He won't talk to anyone but Lyn, at least not until he has to.

"That's always nice to know. I'm sitting next to a beautiful black panther entertaining someone who doesn't like to talk. How could things get better?"

You think I'm beautiful.

If she didn't know better, she would swear he was preening. "I've never been close to a black panther before," she shrugged, "What do I know?"

He growled and he almost laughed at her smile. *You're lying.*

"Would never admit to the lie if I am." She danced off, reaching camp and the sight of Balor hunkered over the fire.

The sound of wings surprised him. He turned, listening. High overhead a small object moved quickly toward them.

"Cedric," she gasped.

Get to the tent.

Balor lifted the pan from the fire, turning his attention to the sky. Cedric was headed straight to him. He tensed ready for the ensuing battle. It would be to the finish.

"Stop, Cedric." Destiny flew behind the fairy who didn't heed her words.

Cedric flew directly at Guy. Guy swiped at him, hitting him and sending him reeling backward. The fairy landed on the ground a great distance away.

Guy inhaled sharply as he watched Cedric slowly pick himself off the ground. The fairy squared his shoulders.

"You won't have her."

Once again, he spun toward him, his wings beating furiously.

And once again, Guy sent Cedric whirling away. Really, he should stop.

Destiny hovered beside Guy. "You must leave him alone. Can't you see he's hurt?"

Tell him to stop attacking me.

"I can't convince him. Truly, I've tried. He thinks Cas is his. He's just not used to losing." Destiny fluttered around him as if trying to distract him.

To some degree her ploy worked. Cedric was upon him again and he was almost caught unaware. This time when he batted him away, he sent the fairy straight toward infinity cliff.

"His wings aren't working." Destiny flew toward him, but he was falling downward.

He disappeared below the edge of the cliff.

"No," Destiny cried out following him.

She, too, disappeared.

As battles went, there was not much about this one. They were not matched opponents. Guy watched for a few seconds before turning to lope to the tent. He needed to shift and talk to Cas. He wanted to hold her in his arms.

Inside the tent, he changed form and quickly dressed. "I'm fine." He wrapped Cas in his arms. Felt the cadence of her breathing, and knew she was terrified.

"What happened out there?" Her voice shook with her fear.

He didn't like her terror. "Wait."

She nestled against his chest, her cheek resting there. "Guy, really."

"I'm hearing from Kimi. We don't have much time. The best I can tell, Cedric is gone. I either knocked him unconscious or tore a wing. He fell over Infinity Cliff and Destiny went after him."

"Destiny?"

He was shaking his head, one large hand holding her against him while he stroked her back with the other. "That's all I know. Everything else would be guesses. Our family is on their way. I'm sure they'll investigate, but there is nothing to see."

"I don't like this, the not knowing."

"Neither do I." His heart raced, needing to join with Cas, feel her naked against him. Their joining would have to wait.

"This way there is no closure."

He wanted to kiss her. Lifting her chin, he paused. She was staring at his lips. Nothing had changed. The passing of those few minutes, nothing was different and yet everything was.

Even though they stood inside the tent, the wind seemed to shift. Slowly he bent to take her lips in his. She gave him her tongue. For a moment he forgot the terror and fear. Cedric was gone, and he prayed Destiny didn't meet the same fate.

When the kiss ended, "We need to meet our family. I can hear their collective noisy voices in my head. I believe your mother is with them."

"My mother, yes."

He watched her eyes darken.

"Do you know what you will say to her?"

He held her around the waist as they stepped through the tent flap.

"No, no idea." She held her bottom lip between her teeth. "Stay by my side. Please."

He nodded, watching the horizon. Balor stood at the edge of the cliff. As he turned, he seemed to study them.

"Do you know what happened to Cedric?" Guy asked.

"The little fairy carried him. It seems he couldn't fly by himself."

"He won't be back," Kimi said.

The clan gathered around them as Kimi continued. "You ripped one of his wings. He will be forever grounded. In any case, perhaps your friend, Destiny, will help him forget about you."

"How?"

"She fancies herself in love with the big oaf," Lyn said, striding to Balor before gently touching him on the back. "Thank you."

The man nodded then left, trotting easily in the direction of the ranch.

Margo held an older woman's hand, slowly walking toward them. It had taken them longer to reach the campsite. "This is your mother, Etain," Margo said, stepping back, staring at her with an expectant smile.

It didn't seem as if Cas knew what to do. She stood, unmoving by his side. He bent to whisper, "Etain appears terrified. You should say something."

"As am I," but Cas stepped forward, unsure if she should hug her mother or simply introduce herself.

"I've loved you all these years and was also terrified Cedric would succeed with his evil plan," Etain said, standing stiffly with her arms at her sides. "I'll understand if you never want to see me again."

Cas rushed forward, hugging her mother, the decision seemingly being made for her. "I knew you would never condemn me to a life with him, but I never quite understood any of it until I met this man."

"Your husband? A shifter?" Etain smiled, her words to her daughter soft.

"It is unusual, I suppose. Come sit by the fire. Perhaps we can get to know each other."

"There is little to know about me. I've spent the years in a small room, imagining what you looked like as you grew to be a woman."

"Unfortunately, I spent the years hating you for something you didn't do. I apologize. You can make your home with Guy and me." She shifted her gaze to see if he agreed.

He nodded, "We have a large home, plenty of room for a mother-in-law."

"No, but thank you. I don't want to impose on either of you. My home is with the fairies."

"You can't go back there." Cas was quick to protest. "What is there for you?"

"I'm a fairy, remember. That is my home and even though I was imprisoned, I've friends."

"You can visit anytime you like." Guy stepped in.

"When the baby is born, I'll come. I'd like to see my grandson and be part of his life." Etain was smiling now.

"It's a plan then," Cas hugged her mother again. "I'll make sure you know. If Destiny has not turned on me, then she can bring you the news."

Maska took Etain by the hand and a few seconds later they disappeared.

"Don't worry, you will see your mother. What you don't know is that one of her friends is a man. She is not that old. Perhaps she will find a love for herself."

After the clan was fed and stories shared, they left. Guy and Cas stood side by side watching them board the helicopter. The sun was going to set on another day.

"Did you mean it when you said we should get up to watch the sunrise?" Cas asked.

"A sunset and a sunrise at Infinity Cliff. What more do we need to start our new life together?"

Cas laughed softly. "Does that mean our honeymoon is over."

"I suppose it does," Guy whispered.

"Then we should make the most of it. I know all my future dreams of you shifting will be all the sweeter now."

"Sweet dreams," Guy murmured, touching the delicate shell of her ear with his tongue. "My sweet dreams. I love you."

She stared at him her eyes wide with surprise, "You love me? Then you've answered all my dreams. As you know, I've loved you forever."

Coming Soon
by
Christine Young
at
Rogue Phoenix Press

In Ryan's Arms

Chapter One

Scottish Highlands 1747

The last two years following the battle of Culloden had been turbulent ones. Connal McKenna as head of the clan Chattan somehow managed to maintain neutrality between the combatant Jacobites and the English. As a clan they united in choosing neither side. A few individuals chose to fight with the Jacobites, but there were not enough for the English to turn their hatred and vengeance against the entire clan. Still, the English patrolled the area searching for any man who might have fought against them.

Rumors abounded about a group of men who helped the wanted Jacobites escape Scotland to sail to America where they could live in relative freedom.

Brady McKenna, the oldest son of Connal and Wynnie, sat in a room adjoining the kitchen sipping a glass of ale. Relaxed and in his prime he searched for diversions. His gaze was focused through the doorway on a newcomer, her hands deep in bread dough, flour smudged on her cheeks and the tip of her nose. Her eyes were the clearest softest blue, her cheeks pink from exertion and the excessive heat of the kitchen. Her golden-reddish hair was piled high on top of her head, a scarf wrapped and tied to keep the strands from falling into her face. He wondered what her hair would look like, how it would feel against his naked flesh or if he threaded his fingers in the silken mass. She was tall for a woman, slender, almost too much to be attractive to Brady. Her pale gray dress did little to reveal but was adept at concealing what curves she might possess. The apron she wore, however, hinted of a tiny waist. Still there was a certain striking quality surrounding her, a haughty air that belied her status as a serving wench.

She was a puzzle to be figured out, he decided.

Until recently the clan accepted newcomers into their midst on a trial basis. Now, after the battle that left much of Scotland impoverished, Connal, the laird, was reluctant to even allow a wide-eyed innocent lass to gain access to the castle and the lands. So, how did she manage to secure a position inside the security of the castle walls no less?

Robby, his brother, sat down beside him, a grin on his starkly handsome face. His dark hair too long, he swiped away several strands that had fallen into his eyes. With a nod he began, "You seem distant. What's got you staring into the kitchen with that look on your face? It appears you mean to devour that sweet lass. She looks to be a tender morsel, too innocent for you or me for that matter."

"What look?" Brady grinned, lowering his lashes in an attempt to keep at least a few of his seething emotions private.

"That besotted expression you always get when you've seen a new conquest. Doubt if the lady stands a chance against you when you've set your sights on her," Robby said following the line of Brady's sight. Then with a bland tone belying the light in his gray eyes, "She doesn't look like one of your normal ladies."

"And what would that be?" Brady's voice was flat as the thought that Robby was right in his assessment. Nor, at this moment was she readily available. His father frowned on dalliances with the hired help. Discretion would be the word if he decided to pursue the woman. Ah, but if he first installed her as his mistress then his father would have no problems with what would be a short-lived infatuation.

"Well," Robby leaned back, stretching his legs out, one arm negligently propped on the chair next to him, looking much the same as his older brother, thoughtfully stroking his chin, "short, lots of curves and blond."

A frown marred Brady's face, his eyes narrowing as he looked at the chit again. Hell, she was nothing like the women he usually preferred. So, what was it about her that drew his interest? Fascinated him? He grinned when she made a face, her nose crinkling, her lips parting slightly.

She turned her head just then, sneezing. Most likely from the flour on the end of her nose. With the back of her hand, she wiped her forehead, more flour arrived on her tiny, perfectly shaped face.

He chuckled, amused by the scene.

"What's her name? Do you ken it?" Brady asked, turning to his brother in an attempt to put the lady out of his sight if not out of his mind at least until he discovered more about her. It wouldn't do for him to claim his feelings just yet.

"You really that interested?" Robby sounded surprised then in an ordinary tone. "Lillian Townsend."

"Sassenach."

"True, still she is striking in looks; too bad she is English. Father told me she's living in the Fraser cottage." At his quick look of surprise and a shrug of his shoulders, "She says she's a Fraser? The family hasn't been around in years. Heard tell one of them fought for the Jacobites. Father wouldn't want any of the clan settling into this area. Only bring trouble. So, what do you think he is doing?"

"She's lying." Brady was suddenly determined to discover what else the lady was not saying. Even though she intrigued and captivated him, he didn't trust her. Lust was never a reason to put oneself in danger. There was something else going on here. By the way she kneaded the dough, she didn't ken how to do it.

"Suppose she probably is," Robby agreed with a smirk on his face. "Suppose you're going to make it your mission to find out what she hasn't told the laird. This should be entertaining to watch."

"That is a distinct possibility." Brady rose from the table. Without looking back his long strides took him outside the castle walls. Curiosity driving him, he headed in the direction of the Fraser cottage eager to add to his knowledge about Miss Lillian Townsend. No one had lived there for almost fifteen years. The place should be rundown and dirty, uninhabitable. If she was destitute and had to work in the kitchen, why wouldn't she live within the castle where it was safer? There were rooms available for the servants. A woman shouldn't be alone, shouldn't be walking the narrow dark paths at night. His fists clenched.

Fifteen minutes later he strolled around the small home, stroking his chin as different thoughts filled his head. First, he walked the perimeter then knocked on the door. A polite reflex, he chuckled since she was at work. When no one answered, he pushed open the unlocked door, discovering the door had no lock. Neither did it have a bar to place over the opening to keep unwanted intruders from entering when she was at home, presumably alone.

Blood pounding furiously at her ignorance or nonchalance about her safety for a few seconds he stared around the room. The Frasers must have left everything behind when they moved. The place was clean, the furniture old and worn. He strode into the kitchen, opening cupboards and drawers to find utensils, plates and cups for two.

For two people? Robby said nothing about a second person. His annoyance as well as his curiosity blindsided him.

A broom. She had a broom. Well, the floor was clean and tidy.

He strolled into the bedroom. There was a large bed with warm quilts and pillows. The sight caused carnal thoughts to flow through his head. When he closed his eyes he could see her, entangled within his arms, her thick hair flowing down her back, wrapped sinuously around him. In the far corner a massive trunk sat. When he lifted the lid, he saw it was filled with gowns. Gowns in silk, satin and velvet. He delved deeper. There were all sorts of frilly frothy underclothing, corsets too. When he stared at her earlier, he would have sworn she wore only a chemise beneath her worn and very serviceable gray gown.

He sat on the bed, running his hands through his hair, thinking, wondering at what he discovered.

Still deep in thought, Brady wandered back to the main room. In the fireplace a stew simmered in a huge pot. Picking up a ladle, he stirred and tasted, examined the meat. Rabbit. When the hell did she have time to hunt and snare food to eat?

Obviously, she wasn't alone. A husband? A lover? His gut clenched at the thought of another man sharing her life.

A month earlier about ten red coats rode through here, searching.

It seemed they never quit looking for Jacobites. They found no one. Brady knew there were rumors though, gossip that a handful of traitors were living near here in the woods. The last thing his family wanted were English soldiers traipsing over their land, enslaving people of the clan, discovering just how different they were. If that happened there would be no privacy, no way to shift and run wild over the heather throughout the ragged hills and cliffs. They would all be prisoners within their homes.

He was shaking his head as he turned toward the castle when a movement caught his eye. Stopping, he waited holding his breath, sensing that whoever he thought he saw was doing the same.

For a moment his breath caught in his throat his heart stopping. "Robby."

His brother grinned at him. "Thought I'd keep you out of trouble. Didn't like the way you looked when you headed out the door. Sure does look deserted doesn't it? What did you discover?"

"Thought you'd never ask," Brady said dryly, watching, hoping he would find the second person in this scenario. Wishing there was no one else. From what he'd seen of her so far, her entire life was a lie.

"Well, you don't have be sarcastic." Robby stuck his hands in the pockets of his jacket as he fell into stride beside him.

"Lillian does not live here by herself. She has a man with her if the rabbit simmering in the pot is any indication."

"Nay, you've got that piece of information wrong. Heard father saying he sent her the rabbit with his blessings and would help her with food until she was able to fend for herself."

Brady wasn't sure why he felt a small lift to his heart. He didn't like to think of her sleeping with someone or hiding someone either. The only person she was going to sleep with in the near future was him. If she was hiding someone, when caught the soldiers would imprison her just as quickly calling her a traitor as they would a man. Even though she was English through and through, they wouldn't care. They meant to make sure the rebellion was completely squashed.

By the time he reached the kitchen again, she was nowhere to be seen. It was just as well. His emotions were in turmoil. He wasn't at all sure what he would say to her when he did get the chance to speak with her and he would. There was no question in his mind that he would talk to her, the only question was when.

When he walked into the main room, his uncle Alistair was with his father deep in discussion. He sat down beside them, listening. Much of their conversation was the same. Now their conversations were always about when they would have their first grandson or daughter. Who would be first? None of their children were married yet. Not even his sister who was of age. Problem was she needed to find her mate. Perhaps their father should send her to Glasgow or Edinburgh for a period.

Brady sat next to his father, unwilling to waste time listening to their idle chat. He blurted, impolitely interrupting, "What do you know about Lillian Townsend? Why is she here?"

Connal slowly turned his gaze to his oldest son, his brows drawn together, clearly displeased with the untimely interruption. "I don't believe that is any of your business, son. Unless she wishes to say anything it is not my place to tell tales. I gave her permission to live in the Fraser cottage for as long as she needs to do so."

Brady heard the ice in his father's voice, giving him even more reason to seek out Lillian's truths as well as her lies. She was purposely hiding something from the laird, putting everyone in danger.

"Come, let's eat." Together they walked to the table designated for the laird and his family. Wynnie was nearly finished with her meal. Brady didn't believe he should engage his mother in questions about the woman who seemed to be occupying his head. She would see right through him.

He found himself leaning back in his chair, staring at the opposite end of the room. The food was unappealing tonight. He found he wanted to sample a bit of the rabbit stew with Lillian in her cottage.

"Is there something wrong with the food?"

The sweet sultry voice next to him shook him out of his melancholy musings. He looked up into the soft blue eyes he noticed earlier. She smelled of vanilla. He reached up and swiped away the flour on her nose.

She inhaled a sharp breath, stepping back so quickly she lost her balance for a moment. Brady reached out, stopping her fall. "My apologies. I only meant to rid your nose of the flour left from your baking today," he said with mocking disdain, still wondering about her as well as her intentions. "You don't ken much about cooking, do you?"

Lillian touched her nose, staring at him as if she thought he'd lost his mind. She was a skittish little thing, almost as if she wasn't used to men. He decided she was a good little actress. She had the emotions correct right down to the hand at her throat and the widening of her eyes, a deceitful little thing. Amused he slanted her a mocking grin. Unraveling her would be interesting.

"You had no right to touch me," she blurted suddenly, her eyes fixed on Robby as if she couldn't bear to look at him or she saw something she disliked.

"I was just trying to help," he growled, his gaze riveted on his brother who was grinning, clearly enjoying this encounter. His brother knew how he felt about the girl and was using this opportunity to mock him.

"Then I beg of you, don't help again. I'm quite capable of getting the flour dust off my own nose." She stuck her chin in the air. The regal tilt, the stiffness of her shoulders spoke of nobility.

Not a common serving wench. His thoughts returned to the silks and satins he saw in the trunk.

Another piece of the puzzle that was Lillian Townsend.

Then she cleared her throat, looked at him with an imperious glare in those soft blue eyes, repeating her earlier question. "Is there anything I can get for you, sir?" she stood back, waiting.

He reached out, confronting her earlier statement that he had no right to touch her as he placed his hand around her wrist, closing over her wrist, tugging her closer. "I want you," he said, his voice assuming a husky gentle timber.

The gasp of air, the sucked in breath was another good ploy. "Food, drink anything of that nature." She tugged on her wrist, seeming to ignore his statement. She would not ignore him forever.

"Tonight, when you are through working. Wait for me in the kitchen. I'll walk you home. Shouldn't be out there by yourself in the dark. 'Tis not safe for a pretty lady." He knew she would not, at least he knew she would try to leave without him seeing her. She would not succeed.

"No."

"Yes, I believe you will. We've matters to talk over. You can't deceive me like you have my father." He watched her eyes narrow. The soft blue turned to silver ice as she stared at him, never turning her gaze from his. She provoked him.

"I've not deceived anyone." She tugged again, her lips thinning into a straight line.

This time he let her go, hearing Robby clear his throat behind him. Something else was happening in the hall. His guess was that he had the attention of his father. "Tonight. That's a promise."

Without confirming his request, she fled the room, her skirts swaying gracefully around her feet her back stiff as a board. He placed his hands on his belly, watching, anticipating what was yet to come. He meant to discover her secrets as well as enjoy anything else that might come from their association.

"You're playing with fire, big brother. If father discovers what you're about, he'll be displeased."

Connal sat down, his hands folded on the table. "She is not what she seems. For your own good, leave her be."

In a dry tone, "I've figured that out by myself. This has nothing to do with my own good, rather hers."

"You should leave her be. She is not your mate." There was a tinge of anger in Connal's voice.

"It seems, I can't leave her be," Brady said in all honesty, his voice cold and hard, wondering why he felt so intensely when it came to Lillian Townsend. He thought on his father's words. 'She is not your mate.' How the bloody hell did one know if a woman was his mate? Ah, he brushed the thought aside. If he had to wonder, she most assuredly was not his throughout all eternity.

Thinking about that he decided it would not be unpleasant to have her for a few months.

She walked back into the hall, a tray of drinks and food in her hands. She was graceful when she moved. He liked everything about her except the deception and the lies. Lillian would be his, at least until he grew tired of her. He would begin the subtle coaxing he was known for this very evening when he accompanied her home.

He turned to his father, "Did you snare a rabbit for her?"

His question seemed to surprise Connal. "What if I did?"

Brady lifted his shoulders in a slow dramatic shrug, more questions coming to mind. "Something you don't do for the crofters. Is she more than just a tenant on McKenna land? Is she really a Fraser?"

"Leave it be," the laird said harshly, rising. He held out his hand for his wife. Together they exited the room, Wynnie looking over her shoulder, her eyes seeming to plead with him to do as his father asked.

He could not.

Normally, he would have given in to his father's wishes in a heartbeat. Something about this woman stirred his senses, provoking every masculine part of him; intrigued, fascinated, leaving him spellbound and needing more. He sought to kiss her senseless, possess her soft lips until she told him everything he wanted to know, until she gave him all of herself.

"I cannot," he whispered as Lillian whirled passed him another tray in her hand. The breath he inhaled was long and deep. The scent of vanilla floated around her. "God help me, but I cannot."

The seconds and minutes seemed to tick by more slowly than they ever had in his entire life. The great hall slowly began to empty. The servers were few and far between. When he watched Lillian slide passed him into the kitchen, he rose, following behind her.

Brady leaned against the doorjamb, arms crossed in front of him as he watched Lillian go through the process of leaving. If she realized he was there, she gave no indication as she wrapped her threadbare cloak around her. When she became his, he would make sure she dressed in the silks and satins she already owned, no more pretense. What she presented here was a complete fabrication of her life.

As she left, the room he pushed away, stepping at her pace until she was out the door. The darkness seemed to swallow her whole. Under his breath he cursed, wondering how many times she made the fifteen-minute walk to the cottage she was calling home alone by herself.

Anger simmered, annoyance at her flagrant abuse of her life flared deep in his soul. Did she truly think it safe for her to walk that distance by herself? After tonight, no longer would she put herself at risk. This was untenable. Furious strides ate up the ground between them until she noticed he was behind her.

"I told you to wait for me." His voice was cold with rage. He held on to her arm, turning her to look at him, needing to tell her that she would obey his commands.

She tried to wrench her elbow from him, her eyes darkening with her own anger as she stared at him, realizing she was helpless to resist. "I don't take orders from you, sir. Unhand me," she grit out between clenched teeth, her resentment with him simmering as hotly as his own.

"No?"

"No!" She swung at him.

He wasn't expecting her to retaliate. She moved like lightning. Her hand connected with his face so hard his head jerked back. He felt the fire on his face where she slapped him. He could even feel the imprint of her fingers forming on his cheek. Awe at her audacity filled him. Irritation at her inability to see the danger in the situation gave new meaning to his need to see this through to whatever end awaited them.

"You are an audacious piece of baggage." He held both her hands, tugging them behind her back, bringing her against him, her breasts pushing against his chest. He heard each breath as she labored to draw in air, felt the heat of her body pressed so near to his, felt the lush curves he had not seen beneath her serviceable gown. She lowered her lashes, another ploy he thought to get the better of him. If anything, she was a consummate actress.

Then she looked up. "Bastard!" she spat out. "Let me go."

His smile hinted at mocking amusement. "You, madam, are in no position to make demands. Perhaps it would be more prudent on your part to yield to my requests and humor me." He changed tactics. Request seemed much more biddable than the words demand or command.

"Jackal! Swine!"

"Sassenach." He spoke plainly.

She turned her head, seeming to school her features. "I'm a Fraser."

"Townsend."

He released her elbow. She continued walking as if he didn't match her step for step. The silence permeated his thoughts, soaking into every pore of his body. Her back was stiff, her strides long for a woman while her fists were clenched tightly at her sides. An apparition of frustration and fury, if he didn't miss his guess.

If she were a man, she would be a worthy opponent. As a woman, she would fall nicely into his plans. He was confident to believe all he needed to do to make her his was meet her lips with his own.

Soon.

Rain began to fall, a few drops at first then turning into a deluge with gusting winds. She pulled the hood of her cloak over her head, pretending he wasn't there or perhaps hoping he would disappear. He was sure the hood would blind her to him. A grin nestled in his heart sending signals of delight all the way to his toes. He didn't want to but he appreciated her stubborn infuriating courage. Still, she sought to win this game she was playing with him. Not by ignoring him she wouldn't.

A deer bounded across the path. She cried out, turning to him before realizing what she was doing. He pulled her close.

"'Tis nothing to be afraid of this time, Lilly. Next time the animal might be of human form," he murmured, his breath touching her face, his knuckles tenderly stroking her cheek. "Much more dangerous."

Placing both hands on his chest, she pushed on him. He didn't move as he turned her. When she looked up, his mouth was so close to her own, he could feel her rapid breaths against his lips. He watched her small tongue run across her full bottom lip that he knew would be soft and wet for him when he chose to kiss her.

"I'm not afraid."

"You must have been since you sought me out." His words were spoken with a bland indifference.

"I was just surprised. A deer nothing more or less. No harm." Her words were staccato like spoken quickly as if she still was robbed of air.

"Could have been a man. Someone who wished you harm," he said softly. "I would not have liked that."

"You wish to do me harm."

"Nay, I only wish to give you pleasure." *As soon as you will allow it.*

"I don't know what you're saying." She pointed down the trail where they were headed. "See, there is my home. You can leave now. You've seen me to my destination, and I thank you to go now."

"Not until I'm ready and I know there is no one dangerous inside waiting for you."

~ * ~

Earlier that afternoon, Lilly felt his insistent gaze before she saw him. When she turned her attention his way, he was sitting, his long well-muscled legs stretched out in front of him, one arm nonchalantly draped over a second chair. His eyes were the color of molten steel, his hair black as coal. The angles and planes of his face were hard and chiseled. Nay, all his body was hard, unyielding. Even sitting he was the personification of masculine grace. There was not one part of him that appeared soft. Every part of him oozed male confidence.

In one hand he held a glass of ale. His gaze riveted on her, on her lips, her breasts even as the focus of his attentions roamed down her body assessing her. In London she'd known men who were so arrogant they believed they had the God given right to anything or anyone they desired. This man appeared to be cut from the same ilk. Though he made no move toward her. A sudden unexplainable wave of fire swept through her.

Not yet.

In part that was why she fled the horrid country as well as the more horrific town, littered with vices of every kind. Every nobleman kept a mistress or made use of the whores who dotted the waterfront taverns. Few were loyal to their wives and visa versa. The stink of the town filled her with dread as well as revulsion. Even more so was the knowledge her father promised her to a man three times her age. She could not stomach the notion of lying in bed with the vile creature and allowing him to do what he wanted with her body.

Her gaze returned to the man staring at her, joined by his brother. She knew who they were, recognized the McKenna brothers by the steely purpose of their long strides and broad shoulders. They possessed the same hard gray eyes as their father. The laird warned her to stay away from his sons when he allowed her to reside in the Fraser cottage. Not because he didn't deem her worthy of knowing her sons but to keep her from getting hurt. They would only wed their mate, she understood. They loved women and never said no to a willing lady or one they could coax into their bed. Every unwed woman was fair game if they wanted a dalliance.

A woman had hurt Brady a few years back. Believing her his soul mate, he fell in love with her, offering her a place by his side through eternity, offering her everything he was. Later he discovered all she wanted was his title and wealth. The lady was no more his mate than she was. She was here with a purpose, one she meant to fulfill. She would never allow a man such as Brady McKenna to dissuade her from her good and true purpose.

Inwardly Lilly laughed. It seemed it was true of all women, even those living in the highlands. Until now, she thought it a trait of the women in London seeking to better themselves. Well, she didn't have the time or the inclination to form a relationship with anyone, let alone one of the brothers, especially not Brady McKenna. She wiped her hands on her apron, finishing with the bread dough, allowing a heavy sigh to escape her lips. It wasn't as if she disliked the work. She dreaded it because she was so bad at it. The kitchen had never been her domain. No, she was more accustomed to the parlors and sitting rooms in the elegant townhouses of the London affluent, to being served not serve.

As the evening wore on and she'd been given the ultimatum that Brady would walk her home, she dreaded the upcoming moment. She wasn't afraid of him. When he touched her, held her wrist with his long slightly calloused fingers, she knew she was afraid of her feelings for him. He wasn't gentle by any means, but she sensed he could be, suspected he could melt her heart as well as her body if given the opportunity. If she could only escape out the back door before he had a chance to know she left, she would be able to breathe a little more freely. Perhaps her heart would even stop thundering so harshly beneath her ribs. She would not have to worry that he would discover what she was about here in the highlands.

She understood the chance of escaping him was slim. He was a determined man. Had not been surprised when she spotted him leaning negligently against the doorjamb into the kitchen when she was ready to leave. She braced herself for the confrontation as well as his presence beside her while he escorted her home. She prayed her brother, Douglas, would hear them and leave the crofters hut just in case he insisted on seeing her inside. He needed to remain hidden and unobtrusive for the next few weeks so he could heal then resume their mission.

The rain began to fall, a few drops at first before turning into a deluge with gusting winds. She pulled the hood of her cloak over her head, pretending he wasn't there or perhaps more to the point wishing he would disappear. She quickened her pace, hoping to reach the cottage before she was drenched to the bone. His presence beside her unnerved her, completely terrified her. A lump caught in her throat. Her knees quaked so hard she could barely place one step in front of the other. Maybe if she stepped inside the door then slammed it shut in his face, he would understand she didn't want him to come inside.

Perhaps the world would stop turning.

A deer bounded across the path. "Oh!" she cried out, turning to him before realizing what she was doing. He pulled her close. His arms wrapped around her, warm and hard, inflexible, demanding. She had naught to give.

"'Tis nothing to be afraid of this time, Lilly Townsend. Next time the animal might be of human form," he murmured, his breath touching her face, his knuckles tenderly stroking her cheek. "Much more dangerous."

In her heart, she understood he was the most dangerous animal she would encounter.

Placing both hands on his chest, she pushed on him. He didn't move as he turned her. When she looked up, his mouth was so close to her own, intimidating, yet strangely beckoning to her. Her lips parted. She moistened them with her tongue as she struggled against her fears as well as her escalating emotions. This was not something she was accustomed to. She had never been held so close, so intimately by anyone. While she danced and was held by other men, the sensations were never like this. The threat of his hard body pressed against hers caused a strange ache as well as heat to gather inside.

"I'm not afraid." She tried to swallow, tried to look away from him. His eyes were dark, fathomless as he gazed at her, imploring her to meet him halfway, to look at him. A half smile formed on his lips as he watched her with that expression of his that accused her of lying. He knew her, understood how she felt.

"You must have been since you sought me out." His words were spoken with a bland indifference coupled with a mocking grin.

"I was just surprised. 'Twas a deer nothing more or less. No harm." Her words were staccato like spoken quickly as if her lungs still were robbed of air. Once more she pushed against him, to no avail. He would not let her go until he was ready, until...

"Could have been a man. Someone who wished you harm," he said softly. "I would not have liked that."

"You wish to do me harm." Even though she spoke the words accusingly she knew them to be false. He was experienced in the ways of sexual games between men and women, understood how to give and receive pleasure. She heard as much from her older brother when he warned her to stay away from the McKenna men. She just didn't understand what he wanted with her.

"Nay, I only wish to give you pleasure." His voice was whiskey smooth sending a telling shiver down her spine.

"I don't know what you're saying." She pointed down the trail where they were headed. "See, there is my home. You can leave now. You've seen me to my destination. I thank you to go now."

"Not until I'm ready and I know there is no one inside waiting for you."

His hands encircled her upper arms. He leaned forward as if he meant to kiss her yet he did not. Disturbed, irritated with herself for wanting just that, she trapped her lower lip beneath her teeth. She didn't desire him in her home. He would see how little she owned then he would press his case.

I want you.

Those three words reverberated in her head, her entire being crying out no, no, he could not have her as his mistress or anything else. *Stay strong.* She would have remained in London if being used by a man was her intent or even her destiny. Here, she had a purpose, a job to accomplish. That wasn't true. She could have never let her brother flee without help. His only crime was that he plead the Jacobite cause in the House of Lords. He was not a Jacobite, barely religious in any way. He had soundly fought for the English, fought for the Duke of Cumberland during the war where the Scots tried to set James on the throne. He had simply felt that two years after the last battle it was time to put the differences aside thereby living in peace with the Scots. Now all he yearned for was to find a means to help those who were persecuted.

"Shall we?" He beckoned toward her home.

She heard his voice, felt the whisper of his breath against her cheek, jerking her back to the present. "What?" She was shaking her head as he let her go. She had thought... What had she thought? That he was about to kiss her? Relief should be sweeping through her not this crazy disappointment.

"Go into your home. What did you think?" he asked as if he knew the answer before she could say.

"N-nothing. I wasn't thinking anything." At the blatant lie, she felt the flow of heat caress her cheeks.

He sent her a mocking all-knowing grin before nodding toward the door. "After you."

"Of course." She drew air into her lungs, felt the sting of the raindrops as she lifted her face away from him and his huge body no longer sheltered her. She stepped forward. At the door she paused to search his face. He was unrelenting, with only one purpose. She only wished she understood the reasons he singled her out for this torture.

Inside a small fire burned in the hearth. He gazed at the remains as well as the pot hanging over it. "Must have been a large fire you made this morning for it still to be burning. Whatever you've got cooking in that pot is most likely burned."

"I don't go to work until the afternoon, if you must know. The fire would hardly burn down to nothing."

"I will see that you work in the mornings instead. That way you won't have to walk home at night."

She laughed at him, "What? You don't intend to walk me home every night?"

"If the lass would let me stay every night in her bed, I'd be more than pleased to walk you home."

Not waiting or seeming to expect an answer, he helped her with her cloak, shaking the drops off outside the door before closing it and hanging the coat on its hook then he slipped out of his coat. Her stomach churned. The rabbit stew should have been inviting. She'd not eaten since this morning.

"Would you like some stew?" she queried, hoping for something to talk about before he pursued whatever plans he had for the evening.

"No, but don't let me stop you. Don't suppose you had a chance to eat," he said as he sat down, seemingly making himself comfortable.

"I couldn't eat a thing," she murmured, trying to look in any direction but at him. She needed to busy herself as well as her hands. "I'll clean it up and put in a container for tomorrow."

"It was nice of the laird to snare you a rabbit. Isn't something he usually does for a tenant."

She stopped surprised, as she tried to hide her emotions. She lowered her lashes. "It was," she lied.

By the look on his face, she guessed he knew. Yet his scowl told her he was thinking over something. "Why are you here?"

"I live here. Why are you here?" she shot back as she poured a glass of wine for herself and him. "I don't have tea."

"But you have wine."

She nodded. I drank the tea first. I've not been paid for my services so I can't purchase anything from the village. This is all I have," she paused for a moment. "and water of course."

"Wine is fine. Tomorrow I'll see your cupboards are stocked."

"Nay. Ye cannae."

"I can and I will."

"Why?"

"Because," he spoke slowly at first enunciating every word, "I plan on spending a great deal of time here—with you. I don't plan on being deprived of anything I want or like, beginning with you."

"I don't want you."

He rose, walking toward her, his smile firmly in place. "Let's see about that," he said softly.

"I would not like to see anything."

What an arrogant, self-centered bastard. He would do everything in his power to bend her to his will. She would do everything to prove he could not. Yet her hands were shaking, her breaths coming in tiny gulps as he pressed ever closer. His gaze was upon hers. His eyes turning to dark silver, heated to a fine sheen. He stood over her now.

"Did you realize that your fingers were moving on my chest just a few minutes ago when we stood outside in the freezing rain? You wanted me then. I'm gambling you still want me."

"They were not. You should leave now."

"In the freezing rain?"

One of his large hands wrapped around her neck, gently drawing her closer. Quickly, he undid the scarf holding her hair back. The length spilled around her shoulders. His fingers wound into her glorious hair. She felt the constant pressure at her nape. The other hand settled on her waist, stroking the curve of her hip. "No, I dinnae want this." Once more she lied.

"You will." Slowly his mouth descended, enclosing hers. He touched, stroked and nibbled across the width. His tongue moistened her lips, traced the crease between them His teeth tugged with the suggestion she open for him. Her mouth was wet and hot, swollen slightly where he caressed.

She resisted his subtle persuasion, refused to be drawn into the delicate coaxing, to the fire smoldering inside. He barely touched her and it seemed she could not draw a breath of air.

"Relax, sweetling. Give into what you are feeling. All will be as it should be." His hand stroked her back, up then down. Each pass of his hand drew her closer to the hard length of him. She felt the play of his muscles against her breasts as they began to swell and throb expectantly. She had never been kissed like this, never been unable to resist the sweet intoxication of a man's lips. The men she'd been with in London were nothing like this man.

Lilly clung to him simply because if she didn't she would crumple to the floor in a tiny ball of nothingness. Her fingers held on to his shoulders, her lips swelling under the fierce possessiveness of his mouth as he claimed her as his own. She stifled a silent whisper of expectations as he gently deepened the kiss, his tongue sweeping across her mouth finding entrance while he slowly parted her lips, his tongue delving inside, retreating then continuing the sensuous invasion. His hand stroked her back again and again then settled on her rear. As he pulled her between his legs, his hard arousal pressed against her.

"You want me," he whispered softly. "Admit it. Let me inside your sultry warmth. Melt in my arms. Let me dissolve in your fire."

Outwardly, she was still denying the feelings as well as the inferno he created within her. Inwardly, she was yearning for more, needing to feel the depth of his emotions as he enticed and lured her in ways she didn't understand to do his bidding. Refusing his insistent exploration was impossible as her hands rose higher, circling his neck. Her breasts pushed against his chest. It was everything she'd ever yearned for, to be kissed and treasured for who she was, not what she could bring to a marriage. Deep in her heart, she realized he wasn't treasuring her. He was using her for his personal needs. That fact made no difference at the moment.

This wasn't a marriage proposal, she reminded herself. If anything it was a proposal to become his mistress. She would not give in to his demands. She would resist anything more he might ask except the promise of his kisses.

She gave into his quest, opening her lips to his invasion. His tongue thrust inside then again as his lips molded to hers. He played her body as if she was created for him and him alone. Heat seared everywhere he touched then cooled when he withdrew. He nipped the corners of her mouth before stroking with his tongue and lips across her chin to her ear. He placed tiny kisses down her neck as her fingers wound into his hair in an unconscious attempt to bring him closer.

The tiny moan of pleasure rippling from her was nearly her undoing as she still tried to withhold some part of her from him. It was not to be simply because he would not allow her to hold anything back. When she tentatively touched his lips with her tongue, he sucked hers deep inside his mouth. With that simple gesture what she gave him was undeniable. His fingers clenched her body to his, tightening and squeezing her derrière until she could barely breathe, until she was pushing of her own volition against him as if she yearned to become one with him.

He pulled away as he looked down at her. Her head rested against his chest now. "Look at me," he said softly gifting her with a mocking smile that seemed to be meant to put her in her place. "Do you want me?"

She stiffened at the thought he so easily played her, toying with her. She willingly danced to the tune he set. This was just a prelude to the continuing games until he had her in his bed beneath him, her legs spread for him. She wouldn't be his plaything. Refusing his attentions in the future would not be easy. She knew she had to keep him from taking her innocence, from ruining her for a marriage.

And yet...

Lilly knew she had no prospects for a marriage, having knowingly left that part of her life behind her when she fled her betrothal and everything evil in London. The gossip surrounding her would put a stamp on her reputation that could never be erased. He would think less of her if he understood the extent of her lies and betrayals. Her father entered into the contract with good intentions.

She defied him.

Would do it again if faced with the same decision. She had no regrets. Perhaps becoming the mistress of a man such as Brady McKenna would not be so bad or humbling. Her fate could be worse. She might go through life without knowing the sweet pleasures a man could give a woman.

Brady McKenna was arrogant, a proud man who took what he wanted. He wanted her. Would that be so wrong?

"No," she told him. "No, I dinnae want you."

"Little liar, should I prove your statements are false?" he stroked her cheek, ran his fingertip along her collarbone.

She shivered in response, heat sweeping through her. Once again his mouth descended on hers, stroked and moved creating that same magical enchantment he crafted before. This time when his finger ran along her back he moved slightly. Now, his hand cupped her breast. Through the thin fabric of her gown he caressed the hard bud at the tip, torturing her with the burning need his hands and lips generated.

"If you didn't want me, you would tell me to stop," he whispered, his teeth closing over her ear, biting gently as his fingers caught her nipple, tugging. "I could take your breast into my mouth, suck it deeply and still you would not say no."

The last words angered her, bringing her back to the reality of the present. He knew what he was about. She allowed him to seduce her. "No." She pulled in a deep breath of air praying it would give her courage also. "Brady, stop. Please." Yet she heard the tone of her voice. It sounded as if she was pleading with him to continue not to cease.

He did stop then, sweeping her into his arms and striding with her to the small chair near the fireplace. Sitting down, he held her in his lap, continuing to caress her back the curve of her hip then back to her nape. It seemed to Lilly that he was trying to ease her not seduce.

"I want you, Lilly. I want you willing and begging me to kiss you, to touch you in places that only a man you care for will touch you. For now, perhaps we should sample that wine in our glasses and leave what comes next for another time."

"I won't ever beg," she told him lifting her chin, trying for an air of confidence she didn't feel. Bloody eyes but she wanted to beg him right now to kiss her again, to stroke her with his long fingers until... Determined, she would never give that kind of power over to him.

"No, Lilly, you probably will not. Perhaps beg is the wrong word to use with someone so proud." Still his fingers continued to move on her flesh, finding places that heated her as she continued to dissolve into him. Each stroke of his hand created a new fire where it burned only to turn cold when his fingers left. She tried to still the violent shivering of her body but could not.

"Please, I can take no more of this," she whispered.

"Only one thing will ease the desire you feel for me. I can do that. Ease the desire. All you need do is ask," he told her as he placed his lips on the thundering pulse at the base of her neck, lingering, touching, kissing.

"I cannae."

"Then we must wait until you want me more than you've wanted anything else your entire life. Will you want me, need me like that, Lilly?" His silken voice caressed her to her soul, made her hunger for things a lifetime of teachings had told her were wicked, sinful.

She should not, could not tell him yes.

Her brother would certainly disown her if she gave in to this man's plans. Her father had already done so. What did she care?

Her mind and body were weak.

"The rain has ceased." He swirled his tongue inside her ear.

She didn't understand his comment even now he was unfastening the front of her dress, moving the fabric aside so he could touch her, stroke her more intimately. "No!" She leapt to her feet, tugging the sides of her gown closed. "You must leave. As you said, the rain has stopped."

He smiled softly at her, his gaze moving from her breasts to the tips of her toes assessing just as he did when her hands were wrist deep in dough. "If that's what you want. A good-bye kiss first. One that will warm me through the night."

Before she could inhale again, she was in his arms, his lips touching upon hers once more, claiming them asserting himself.

Then, "I want you, Lilly. Don't ever forget that."

~ * ~

Brady left the cottage before he made the irrevocable mistake of taking Lily to bed before she would admit to wanting him. Pulling up the collar of his coat to shield his neck from the wind, he chuckled softly. She was passionate, a desirable woman as well. Her hair was as silken and soft as he thought it would be. She melted into him when he kissed her. Her breasts weren't overly large but they fit his hands to perfection. They were soft but firm, her flesh silken fire. With a little patience, he would win this game, coax her into giving all of herself to him.

Ah, but he could envision her naked in his arms.

About five minutes down the path leading to the castle, he doubled back, taking a more circuitous route to the cottage. When he mentioned the rabbit and his father's part in gifting her with the meat, she appeared genuinely surprised. The two sets of everything still bothered him. She was hiding something. Before he made love to her, he meant to discover some truths. Perhaps nothing was amiss and what she presented to him was true.

He didn't believe that.

Her home was in front of him now, the lights still shining in the main room. He hunkered down in the dark and waited. Minutes ticked by. The wind moaning around the trees surrounding him and still he waited. He shifted his weight from one foot to the other, groaning at the tightening of his muscles. Rain began to fall again. Tempted to shift, his thick cat fur would be a better barrier to the water than the coat he wore.

Perhaps he was wrong about Lilly. Maybe there wasn't a second person living with her. Quite possibly she wasn't hiding her true identity or her purpose. He heard the light tread of boots on the fallen twigs and leaves before he saw the shadow then the man. His breath caught in the back of his throat as he remained dead still. He watched. The man's fist rose to knock on the door.

"Douglas!" Lilly had thrown open the door then eagerly hurled herself into the man's arms.

"Deadly little liar," he murmured softly. His anger at her deception filled him. The question now was just who was Douglas and what did he mean to her? None of the crofters that he knew of went by that name. So, what would she tell him when he confronted her with the man?

The man kissed her on the forehead, a chaste kiss that sent his fists into tight balls. Jealousy was not an emotion he expected or ever experienced. On silent feet, he walked to one of the windows. Setting his back against the wall, he listened to the conversation between them.

"You cannot stay here any longer," Lilly told the man. "It's not safe and well you know it. You put me in danger as well as the clan. After all the McKenna has gone through to keep neutrality here, I cannot..."

"Hush now, Lilly. I would never do such a thing. Perhaps it is best I return and clear my name."

"Is such a thing possible?" she asked sounding breathless and out of sorts. When he snuck a peak at the couple, Douglas was holding her, her long slim body pressed against his. The man's hands were around her waist. A rage he'd never felt before simmered, waiting to explode.

"Perhaps not yet," he stroked her hair. "If I leave will you be safe here? This might be our last time."

"I ken it, Douglas."

I saw you with one of the sons."

"I'm sure I'll be safer than you," she told him softly. "Where will you go?"

"Farther into the highlands, north where fewer people live. I'll find a ship sailing for America. I've heard a man can live there, pursue his dreams." He kissed her again, a gentle kiss.

"I will think of you. I love you, Douglas. Where ever you go take care." She reached up, placing her palm on his cheek.

Brady's breath stopped as he digested her words, telling himself it didn't make any difference how she felt about that man. He still wanted her, the little harlot. When he first saw her, it made no difference to him how well used she was. Now he knew there had been at least one man in her life.

"If your father finds you?"

"I won't go back to London. I can't live that way nor can I marry that man father betrothed me to."

"You might not have a choice," Douglas said, smoothing her hair from her forehead. "The contract has been signed."

"You could stop it."

"Nay, not even if I could wed you myself, could this nightmare for us end. If you were to wed someone else, well, perhaps then."

"Who would want me, or want to take a chance? Lord Claymore is filled with revenge. He would kill anyone who took what he thinks is his."

"Lord Claymore cannot hold a pistol his hand shakes so bad."

"He can hire the finest assassins. You take care, little one. Don't let anyone sway you to do something you don't want to do. Don't let the McKenna—"

They both turned, searching the woods for the sound they heard. "Go," she said. "What if it's the English searching for you? For us?"

"It would be a random bit of luck on their foolish parts. No one of any position even realizes your mother was Scottish. That she lived here before she wed Lord Townsend."

Brady ducked down, moving silently behind a tree as he watched the couple from a greater distance, unwilling to give himself away.

"You will stop. Promise me you will stop."

"I cannot."

Other Books by Christine Young
Available at Rogue Phoenix Press

My Sweet Broc
Bad Boys Book One

He's a bad bad boy...

Broc Wallace is a fun-loving rake who never thought any beautiful woman could melt his heart. He lives life in the present enjoying the camaraderie of his friends and the pleasures of his mistress. When Bliss races into his life, he is ill prepared to deal with her secrets or give up the tenor of his life. When the truth is revealed, he finds himself unable to forgive and forget the betrayal.

... but she's sweet for him

Bliss MacTavish knows she's playing with fire when she refuses to tell this bad boy her name. He tempts her with sweet whispers of seduction knowing her innocent nature will be unable to refuse all he yearns to give her. Deciding to follow her heart, she finds the repercussions more than she bargains for when she gives herself to this bad boy.

Crazy for Cam
Bad Boys Book Two

He's a bad bad boy...

Lord Cam MacEwen, Viscount of Rosehill, tries his best to be proper and court the lady of his dreams in the acceptable way. The feat proves impossible when the lady in question uses every means at her disposal to tempt him. He fights his jealousy for another man as well as the need to make her his own, finally giving in to her irresistible passion.

... but she's crazy for him.

Chelsea MacTavish wants the bad boy she fell in love with and kissed just before her eighteenth birthday. With feminine wiles and irresistible allure, the sensuous lady plans to best Cam at his game of hearts and make him forget his need to court her properly.

Falling for Flynt
Bad Boys Book Three

He's a bad, bad boy...

Fascinated by Hope's loss of memory yet haunted by her sultry beauty, Flynt is irresistibly drawn to the stoic miss—and into her troubles with the sultan who wants her for himself. When he discovers she is the sister of his best friend, his pride keeps him from pursuing her and making her his.

... but she's falling for him.

Raised in a harem but now penniless, alone and without her memory, Hope must discover a way to remember all that she has lost. She finds a way to continue with her life as a servant in Flynt's home. The first sight of Flynt steals Hope's breath as well as her heart. Can she overcome her fears and give herself to the man she fell in love with.

Dancing With Donal
Bad Boys Book Four

He's a bad bad boy...

Once a bad boy always a bad boy, Donal Chamberlin's carefree ways come crashing down around him when he meets the ravishingly beautiful Daryl MacTavish, the innocent little sister of one of his best friends. He is determined to win her heart as he sets his sights on marriage and an heir. His past gets in the way of his quest when a woman he once loved threatens Daryl's life.

... but she's dancing with him.

Daryl has seen the control her sister's husbands hold over them.

She yearns for a life where she makes decisions for herself. No man will have power over her. But no man kisses her the way Donal does. No man can make her forget all her goals leaving her helpless to give up her dreams. Yet Donal is determined to dance through all the barriers she thrust in front of him, pursuing her until she says yes.

Loving Leslie

He's a bad bad boy...

Leslie Stewart, Duke of Southcliff is stoic, set in his ways, a spy who is used to having his life well ordered. He expects life to continue on in this perfectly conventional fashion. He assumes his bad boy status while keeping mamas and debutantes at arm's length. An heir is needed but Leslie has every intention of finding a woman who doesn't covet his wealth and tittle. He is irresistibly drawn to the headstrong young lady who becomes more beautiful as she develops into a woman.

...but she is loving him.

When Leslie kisses Lacie MacTavish, she knows even at the tender age of fifteen this is the man of her dreams. Forced to wait until she comes of age, Lacie withdraws into herself. Now she is eighteen and Leslie has returned from a mission for the British Government ready to claim her as his bride. She refuses him and he must find a way to seduce her and in the process create a burning passion within her, which she cannot deny.

Foolish for Piper

The pickpocket...

Piper has spent her life surviving the streets of St. Giles Parish in London, a den of iniquity and crime. Masquerading as a boy she escapes the whorehouses the young girls are sent to as they come of age. The day she encounters Brett MacLachlan begins the same as every other one. When she picks his pocket, she has no idea her life is going to change irreversibly.

... and the mark

Handsome aristocrat Brett MacLachlan has come to London for

his amusement only to find his world turned upside down by a thief and her dog. From the moment he spots her, Brett knows there is something intrinsically wrong. In his arms, Piper discovers passion and joy. Yet secrets of her past haunt her, and a scar will tell the true tale as well as her identity.

Taylor's Destiny

She traveled to another time and place to change destiny...

Enjoying a day of sailing, Taylor Maxwell never expected after a suffering a concussion she would wake up in another century. A resilient independent woman in the twenty-first century, the blond beauty is ill prepared for life in the 1800s. Her first sight of the naval captain who rescues her makes her heart stop, giving her hope for her future.

His life is transformed by a woman who appears from nowhere...

Born to a life of ease, Reid Stewart defies the dictates of those born to aristocracy and chooses a life of adventure in the navy and as a spy for the crown. When he discovers a nearly naked woman on the bow of small sailing ship, his heart warms. His love for Taylor and his need to protect her from a man who pursues her might cost him his life as well as hers.

Caitlin's Duke

She played a fiddle in an Irish pub...

Caitlin O'Shea Is the most beautiful woman Roc Leighton has ever seen. With her blue violet eyes and long black hair she captivates him. In turn he mesmerizes Caitlin. Caught in the power of his gaze as he watches her, she is wise enough to know he desires her but will never give his heart to her. Caitlin has vowed to never be any man's mistress.

And fell in love with an English Lord...

Roc knows the first time he watches her play the fiddle and dance around the pub, she will be his next mistress. Despite her protest, he will find a way to convince her that her place is with him. While Caitlin's determination to keep her vows, fate takes a cruel turn and she is forced to seek refuge with Roc.

Catching Meara
Book One in the McKenna Clan Series

Meara Thorton was a feisty, world-class computer hacker—cornered by the FBI and shockingly given the chance to be their newly acquired technical analyst. Brilliant and intuitive, yet aching with the loss of everyone she has cared about, her restless heart led her to discover a love she fought and a world she didn't know could possibly exist.

Sweet Sexy Sadie
Book Two in the McKenna Clan Series

From the first time Sadie's eyes met those of Brody McKenna in the hot Sierra Madre Mountains, theirs was a potent attraction—not gentle, slow, and easy, but hot, hard, and all-consuming. The daughter of a dysfunctional family, Sadie had dreams no man could wrench from her with hot sex and an all-consuming passion. She'd challenge this alpha male with all the strength she possessed. But her red hair, fiery temperament, and indomitable spirit obsessed Brody... and he knew he had to find a way to show her he was more than he appeared and convince her to make a life with him.

Sweet Misbehavin'
Book Three in the McKenna Clan Series

Cast adrift after fleeing the home of Jokul, the ice demon, Atantsi, a firestarter, grew to womanhood as she moved through time to keep the demon from finding her. Though stubborn and courageous, she was ill prepared to use powers she had not been taught. Her first sight of the intoxicating Carr McKenna left her breathless, and her second encounter gave her hope for a future she never thought she had.

A playboy, a second son and a shifter, a man who thought his life would be carefree, Carr McKenna was shocked to discover the woman he'd paid as an escort is a firestarter who is running for her life. He is the leader of all the McKennas around the world and that he has multiple powers. His passion for Margo and the need to defend her might cost him his life as well as hers.

Sweet Talkin' Sugar
Book Four in the McKenna Clan Series

Lyonesse McKenna, was dreaming or was she? From the instant Lyn saw Deacon McClain across a black jack table in a crowed Las Vegas casino the unmistakable attraction sent Lyn's senses flying into overdrive. Her family of shapeshifters believed in soul mates. She'd always been skeptical yet she couldn't help but question the way her heart sped when he looked at her.

When Deacon appeared in Las Vegas he knew his first job was to save Lyn from a Sea Demon, but the next order of business was to convince her he would someday mean more to her than she'd ever expected. But her stubborn nature and unbendable spirit consumed Deacon... and he had to chase away all the demons real and imagined in order to win her heart.

Sweet Surrender
Book Five in the McKenna Clan Series

Ripped from her family at the top of Infinity Cliff, Kimi McKenna finds herself thrust somewhere into the future. Dark elements threaten to destroy the earth unless Kimi can work together with the white witch to stop the destruction. Confused by her mate's role in the conspiracy, she refuses to acknowledge the connection. But amidst raging fire and attacks on the people she is coming to hold dear, she allows Maska O'keefe into her heart.

Maska O'keefe has loved the beautiful shapeshifter for years. Unable to save her life years ago, he vows to watch over her as he is given a second chance to convince her that even though he is a witch and not a shifter, they are indeed soul mates. Kimi's divided loyalties between her family and the cause she is now a part of will determine their relationship. Only the part she plays as the messiah can bring this to a conclusion in the final battle.

Dakota's Bride
The first book in the Lakota/Pinkerton Series

When Emma St. John received her brother's letter imploring her to escape her stepfather's vengeful scheme and to trust Dakota Barringer with her life, she was willing to chance it. But the handsome, brooding riverboat owner Emma found in Natchez a danger of another kind. For Emma soon found herself surrendering to an unrelenting desire.

Raised by the Sioux when his parents were killed, Dakota had been betrayed once before by a white woman. He wasn't about to trust another, especially one claiming that her stepfather, a powerful U.S. senator, had framed her as a murderess. But he couldn't let Emma's intoxicating effect on him. Now Dakota would risk his very life to protect the innocent beauty who had seduced him with her tender love.

My Angel
The second book in the Lakota/Pinkerton Series

A BEAUTY IN BUCKSKINS

When her father decided to send her to a finishing school back East, Angela Chamberlain refused to be confined to stuffy drawing rooms. Instead, the daring spitfire who could shoot like a man and ride like the wind longed for a life of adventure and romance—and she knew exactly who could give it to her. Devil Blackmoor was a hired gun with a dangerous reputation. But Angela was willing to go to the ends of the earth to capture the handsome devil's heart.

A DEVIL IN DISGUISE

He'd come to America looking for excitement, but Devil Blackmoor got more than he bargained for when he encountered a beautiful rebel who answered his kisses with a wild innocence that touched his very soul. Yet standing between them were more obstacles than either ever dreamed. For Devil had strapped on a gun for the wrong man. And that made Angela his enemy. Now he'll have to choose between his duty and the woman he loves more than life.

The Locket
The third book in the Lakota/Pinkerton Series

The year is 1894. Seeking revenge for crimes against his family, Misha Petrovich follows a path that leads straight to Ariel Cameron's boarding house in Mist Harbor, Oregon. A family heirloom in Ariel's possession leads Misha to believe she is guilty. The locket has been handed down to the oldest girl in the Petrovich family for generations. Ariel is innocent of wrong doing, but her father is not. Misha is torn by his feelings for Ariel and his need for restitution against her father. Knowing that the relationship between them is fragile, Misha does everything in his power to protect Ariel's father. His efforts are to no avail when her father is shot. Ariel comes to realize Misha's steadfast courage and determination to protect her and her father despite what has happened to his family. Ariel's love and devotion heals Misha's heart.

The Talisman
The fourth book in the Lakota/Pinkerton Series

Running from a marriage that lasted one night, Dr. Moriah McKeown discovers the land she has settled on is coveted by determined and lawless men. Yet the proud young woman who once vowed never to abandon her home has second thoughts when her adopted children are threatened. Her only recourse is to enlist the aid of a dark, dangerous gun for hire.

Haunted by the past and a betrayal he will never forgive, Ian Civanovich uses his fast gun and his reckless courage to forget the faithlessness of a woman in his past. He will trust no female—nor will he rest until the threat hovering over Moriah McKeown is put to rest.

Forever His
The fifth book in the Lakota/Pinkerton Series

Struggling to come to terms with the part she played in Jacob St. John's death, Etta Barringer resigns from Pinkerton Agency and seeks peace and solace in a Rocky Mountain Cabin.

Jacob has vowed to discover the reason Etta has betrayed him, sold him out to his enemy and left him for dead.

Isolated in their cabin, they discover their love for each other and learn to trust. But the trust is shattered when Jacob learns she is married to his sworn enemy; the man who left him in the desert to die.

Allura's Secret
Twelve Dancing Princesses Book One

Allura McClellan is horrified by her father's decision to take out an ad in the Times awarding her to the man strong enough and smart enough to win her hand and uncover her secrets. She's an intelligent young woman who takes great delight in the freedom allotted to her by her father. She's well aware that marriage would effectively curtail the adventures she's shared with her sisters and cousins.

Hunter Gray is nothing like the other men who've arrived to vie for Allura's hand in marriage and everything that goes along with it. However, he is the first to refuse to concede defeat and pursue her despite her attempts to disguise her true appearance. It's her temperament that is of more concern to him than her looks. Hunter has worked all his life with the hope of someday owning his own land. Now that it looks like there's a very real possibility that everything he's ever wanted is within reach nothing is going to deter him – including Miss Allura's disagreeable disposition.

Amorica's Wager
Twelve Dancing Princesses Book Two

Amorica Hepburn was sent to London to find a husband. Finding a man was the last item on her agenda. With her two cousins, Amorica wagers she can dissuade her suitor before the others. Despite her efforts she discovers a chemistry that cannot be denied. Suddenly she is the arrogant man's wife, pledged to a marriage neither desire. But swept off to his ancestral home above the Dover cliffs and into his strong embrace, Amorica is soon possessed by a raging passion for the husband she had vowed to despise…

Damian Andrews couldn't afford to trust the emerald-eyed spitfire who happened upon his secret. Amorica's hatred of all men of his kind only inflames the war that rages between them. Still, he can not control the intense desire his stubborn bride inspires, or make her surrender to his will until he has conquered the headstrong beauty on the battlefield of love…

Ravyn's Marriage of Inconvenience
Twelve Dancing Princesses Book Three

A REGAL BEAUTY

When the duchess decides to wed her to a wastrel and a fop, Ravyn Grahm takes matters into her own hands and declares her engagement to another man. Instead of fessing up and telling her great aunt what she has done, she goes through with the pretense. Aric Lakeland is the bastard son of an earl and has a dangerous reputation. But Ravyn is willing to do most anything to keep the duchess from discovering the lie.

A DEVIL-MAY-CARE SMUGGLER

He'd bought land in America, looking to put down roots and end his life of adventure, but Aric Lakeland got more than he bargained for when he encountered a beautiful heiress who made a promise she didn't want to keep. But the promise could not be undone and standing between them were more obstacles than either ever dreamed. Ariec had made plans to spend the rest of his life in America and that was at odds with Ravyn's plan of living in England and running her father's estate. Now, he'll have to choose between his dreams and the woman he loves more than life.

Christel's Sunrise
Twelve Dancing Princesses Book Four

He Made Her An Offer…

Life has thrown Christel McClellan some experiences that could have devastated a less determined woman. Beautiful, self-assured and fiercely independent, she is trying to forget the loss of her stillborn child. But is the child alive?

She Couldn't Deny…

Life is carefree for Ryder MacLaren who loves to see what is on the other side of the sunrise. Laird of Clan MacLaren, he is wealthy, handsome and happily unencumbered... until stunning Christel McClellan enters his life. When he hears her story, he believes the child she thought dead has been sold to a wealthy buyer.

Storm's Passion
Twelve Dancing Princesses Book Five

SHE MADE A PROPOSAL...

Life strikes Storm Graham a shattering blow when she learns her father has bartered her to a man she detests. Storm is beautiful, self–assured and fiercely independent, and refuses to be a pawn in her father's schemes, yet she can find no way out of this bargain made in hell. Going on the offensive she asks the wealthiest man on the eastern coast of England to marry her, never believing she might fall in love.

HE TRIED TO REFUSE...

For Hadden Johnston life has provided everything he ever wanted, including a sanctuary for homeless children. He is wealthy, handsome and happily unencumbered... until stunning Storm Graham marches into his life and proposes a marriage of convenience. Yet this type of marriage to a woman who inflames his senses is far from acceptable. If he's going to be tied down, he will move heaven and earth to have this woman warming his bed.

Gotta Have Fayth
Twelve Dancing Princesses Book Six

A regal beauty with raven hair and piercing blue eyes, Fayth Graham is unwilling to parade herself in front of the wealthy Lords of England during the season. Seeking a means to dissuade any man wishing to wed her, she seeks a way to ruin herself for marriage. When she unexpectedly meets a man with sparkling gray eyes and an infectious grin, she decides this is the man who will keep her from agreeing to obey.

He returned from six months at sea, looking for a few nights of pleasure with a willing lass, but Jarret Kinsley got more than he bargained for when he met a beautiful debutant who responded to his kisses with a wild innocence that touched his heart. Yet the obstacles looming between them might rip them apart. Both had vowed never to marry, so when consequences of their dalliances got in the way, Jarret would have to choose between the life he's always desired and the woman he loves more than life.

Ella's Pleasure
Twelve Dancing Princesses Book Seven

A WHISPER OF PLEASURE
Ella Hepburn was an auburn haired debutant from the harsh Scottish coastline—a wild innocent to be seduced and tamed. A spirited beauty, she captivated Drake Montgomerie's jaded heart—while succumbing to the smoldering desire she felt for her unyielding suitor.
A WHISPER OF DANGER
In Drake Montgomerie's glittering world of money and privilege, young Ella discovered passion and desire could overcome everything she'd been taught to resist—entangling Drake, the heir apparent, in a lethal coil of aristocratic family intrigue. But grave peril would only nurse the sparks of a love that knew no limits and a magnificent ecstasy that would not be denied.

Eveleen's Seduction
Twelve Dancing Princesses Book Eight

A WHISPER OF SEDUCTION
A brutal attack on Eveleen Hepburn's cherished island off the Scottish coastline leaves her shattered and bewildered. Learning a man she once trusted can kill as easily as he can breathe even though the deed saves her life, creates questions that need answers. An innocent beauty, she enchants Logan Maxwell's cynical heart—giving in to the raging passion she feels for her mysterious suitor.
A WHISPER OF INTRIGUE
In Logan's Maxwell's world of espionage and privilege, young Eveleen discovers truths about herself she never expected, and a need for passion and love can overcome all her fears if she learns to accept certain truths. She finds herself entangled in a lethal battle for land that was once

owned by French nobility, taken from them during the revolution and sold to Maxwell. But grave peril would unleash the flames of love that simmers, creating a magical union that cannot be refuted.

Tavia's Deception
Twelve Dancing Princesses Book Nine

WHISPERS OF DECEPTION

When her father decides to send her to London for her season, Tavia Hepburn resolves to see the world instead. The raven haired beauty decides to disguise herself as a lad and find employment on a ship bound for Barcelona as a cabin boy. But she never bargains on finding passion and love to a red haired sea captain who rescues her from certain death.

WHISPERS OF MURDER

For James Macmurra, the world is black and white until he meets a young debutante, who turns his world upside down. He's unable to deny Tavia's intoxicating effect on him. In a match tense with obstacles, unwillingness to divulge secrets, and unforeseen peril, irresistible desire and passion grows into undeniable love. James would risk his life to shelter and protect the innocent debutante who seduces him with her sweet love.

Larena's Fascination
Twelve Dancing Princesses Book Ten

WHISPERS OF FASCINATION

Fiery, free spirited Larena Graham never wanted to marry a duke. She is thrilled to be in love with the fourth son of an aristocrat, Gavin Broon. But when it seems Gavin ignores her, she set her sights on politics and bettering human life. Unsuspecting intrigue and a plot against her, she continues her dangerous plans despite Gavin's wishes.

WHISPERS OF TRUST

Gavin has every intention of properly courting the beautiful Larena until he must leave the city in order to put his affairs in order. Returning to London, he finds the woman he means to make his own is embroiled in political protests that could lead to a prison ship. Larena must learn to trust the handsome Scotsman whose most pressing mission is to protect her and keep her from harm.

Tira's Education
Twelve Dancing Princesses Book Eleven

WHISPERS OF EDUCATION

Learning how to build ships is Tira Hepburn's only dream until she meets Jamie Lundin and her world is turned upside down. With her raven black hair and vivid green eyes, she tempts Jamie and pushes him to defy his vows. She never bargains on finding an irrevocable love and a passion to a man who cannot fulfill her dreams despite his burning desire for her.

WHISPERS OF A BARGAIN

Arrogant and self-assured Jamie is brought up short when Tira captures his heart. All his carefully made plans are put to the test when he decides to teach her the art of ship building if she will spend a week with him alone on his ship. He is unable to deny Tira's intoxicating effect on him. When Tira leaves him behind unwilling to live with him without the benefit of marriage, he races after her. Jamie will risk everything to shelter and protect the innocent debutante who seduces him with her sweet love.

Aidan's Love
Twelve Dancing Princesses Book Twelve

Whispers of Love

Aidan McLellan has loved since she first set eyes on him as a young girl. Spontaneous, wild and eager to grow up, Aidan haunts his waking thoughts day and night, insinuating herself into his life. With her fiery red hair and sparkling sapphire eyes, she seizes Blade's heart even while he tries to resist the innocent child until she becomes a woman.

Whispers of Courage

Blade has waited what seems a lifetime to claim the woman who captures his heart as a little girl. Claiming his inheritance before his younger brother takes what is rightfully his, Blade must convince Aidan of his sincerity after years of avoidance and wed her before his father dies so he can return home, securing his rightful place. Everything is put to the test when his life as well as Aidan's is threatened by the man who once called him brother.

Twelve Days to Love

When Archer Steele shows up at Calanthe Durand's failing plantation with an alligator over his shoulder, Cali thinks she's never seen a more handsome man. During the war she had to defend herself and her servants from both union and confederate soldiers. Independent and self-sufficient, she vows to never marry.

But Archer Steele has different ideas. The first time Archer sees Cali in town, he feels an instant attraction. He decides he will do everything and anything to convince the beautiful Miss Durand he is worthy of her love. During the weeks leading up to Christmas, he gives her twelve gifts in hopes she will fall in love with him. Yet they are faced with challenges they must overcome before Cali can commit to a marriage.

Door to Heaven

Jessica Lawrence is the stepdaughter of a woman born in the twentieth century transported back in time to the year 1868. An acclaimed suffragette, she raises Jessica to believe in the equality of women. Jess Law believes everything she was taught, and when the time is right she becomes a private investigator. Courageous and impetuous, Jess finds danger in her quest to save all women from white slavery. Her passionate mission results in a wedding to Roc Newman, a man she knows can steal her heart...

Roc can't trust the sapphire-eyed spitfire who invades his home in search of secret papers and knocks him flat with her karate moves. Jessica's refusal to obey his wishes serves to inflame the war between them. Still, he cannot control the intense desire his reluctant bride inspires, or make her surrender her independence, until he has conquered the headstrong beauty on the battlefield of love...

Rebel Heart

HER REBEL SPIRIT DEFIED HIS OUTSIDERS SOUL... She was velvet and silk, eyes the color of a summer storm and amber hair. Victoria DeMontville, because of a promise and a codicil to her father's will, was forced to marry one man to protect her from another. She hated Cameron Savage with a fierce passion. But to hold on to her genetic research and find a cure for the deadly Signe virus, she must pretend to love the enemy at her door, come with weapons of fire to melt her icy heart...

HIS OUTSIDERS TOUCH IGNITED RAGING PASSIONS... He wore a mask, disguised as the Phantom, a true legend come to life. Even as war and debate over new genetic research engulfed them all, he would find his greatest adversary in the beauty who'd branded him an outsider and barbarian, the woman he was born to possess, his soul mate.

Safari Moon

Solo St. John, a wildlife photographer, is preparing for a trip to Alaska. Suddenly, Solo finds women of all sorts invading his privacy, his home and his office, all cooing nonsense words and blatantly throwing themselves at him. Solo doesn't know why, and he has no idea how to rid himself of the persistent women. He finally decides to beg a favor of his best buddy Nyssa Harrington.

In love with Solo for the past ten years and knowing he doesn't return her feelings Nyssa doesn't want to talk to Solo. She knows if she accepts his phone call, she will not be able to resist the temptation to hope again.

Straight to Heaven

Running from demons, Alexandra McMurdie stumbles into Forbidden Ground where up is down and elements of nature are contested. Though a strong independent woman in the twenty-first century' she is unprepared for life in the 1800s. Her first site of the formidable James Lawrence makes her heart skip a beat, giving her cause to reconsider her desperate need to find a way home.

Born with a silver spoon, James' life was torn apart during the War Between the States. Moving west he vows to put the life he once knew in the past. When he discovers a half-frozen woman near Gold Hill, his heart begins to thaw. His love for Alexandra and his need to keep her from a man who has pursued her through time might cost him his life as well as hers.

A Valentine's Anthology

The Lending Library-a fantasy by Christie L. Kraemer
Faeries try to fit into the human world when the forest where they make their home is destroyed by a mysterious enemy.

Chasing Rainbows-a contemporary romance by Genene Valleau
An eccentric aunt, an inventive uncle, a mother who wears poodle skirts, and a brother who wears pearls provide a hilarious backdrop for the courtship of a young woman who yearns for a "normal" family.

The Gift-an historical romance by Christine Young
A man and a woman on opposite sides of the Civil War get a second chance at love after one final battle returns soldiers to their war-torn homes to rebuild their lives.

A St. Patrick's Day Tale

Christine Young, C. L. Kraemer, Genene Valleau

Tumble through time…

…to Ireland in 1817, when tensions are high between Protestants and Catholics and fae people guide the fate of villagers. A lovely Catholic lass stumbles upon the weakly ritual fisticuffing between Irish lads. She falls into the lap of a handsome young Protestant. Family ties, grudges, and two conniving faeries threaten their budding love. But the faeries outsmart themselves when they hijack a time machine that has mysteriously appeared in their forest and are whisked to…

…Eugene, Oregon in the 20th century, amid a property feud between the local faeries and night elves. The conniving faeries from Olde

Ireland try to stir up more mischief. However, a warrior gnome convinces the magic folk to control their own destiny, and forces the intruding faeries to take refuge in the time machine again, spinning their way toward...

...A modern day castle in western Oregon. An eccentric inventor is determined to reclaim his wayward time machine and save his beloved wife from her latest misadventure. If only they can travel safely past the black hole...

a May Day Anthology
Christine Young, C. L. Kraemer, Rosemary Indra, Genene Valleau

Highland Miracle — Christine Young
HURTLED THROUGH TIME, Sean Michael Sterling, landed in the midst of a May Day celebration he didn't understand, assuming the role of Laird Sterling.

ILLIGITAMATE CHILD OF NOBILITY, Reagan Douglas searches for a way out of her half brother's house.

Defying the Odds — C.L. Kraemer
The night elves on the hill aren't happy without their magic. They concoct a plan to punish those who were involved in the act that rendered them almost human. Meanwhile, Uther, the rogue night elf, has returned to woo the Librarian to be his eternal mate.

Love in Bloom — Rosemary Indra
When childhood friends reunite it takes two fairies and a matchmaking daughter to help them admit their true love for each other.

No More Poodle Skirts — Genie Gabriel
After drifting for years in the innocent age of the 1950s, a woman struggles to join today's world by finding a career and a new love, with some help from her zany family.

Once Upon a Christmas Moon

Christine Young, C. L. Kraemer, Genene Valleau

TWELVE DAYS TO LOVE

When Archer Steele shows up at Calanthe Durand's failing plantation with an alligator over his shoulder, Cali thinks she's never seen a more handsome man. During the war she had to defend herself and her servants from both union and confederate soldiers. Independent and self-sufficient, she vows to never marry. But Archer Steele has different ideas. The first time Archer sees Cali in town, he feels an instant attraction. He decides he will do everything and anything to convince the beautiful Miss Durand he is worthy of her love. During the weeks leading up to Christmas, he gives her twelve gifts in hopes she will fall in love with him.

BOOTS AND BLADES

An ancient evil from the old country has arrived in the high desert of Oregon. Gnome children are vanishing then re-appearing, showing various stages of traumatization. Tiamoon, warrior gnome, will put her skills to use alongside Killian, a handsome warrior, also in need of a cause.

CHRISTMAS PAWSIBILITIES

With their world destroyed and their space ship malfunctioning, the dogizens of Planet Canid have little choice but to crash land on Earth. They face tortuous experiments at the hands of the Geeks in Green... or they can trust an eccentric inventor and his zany family to deliver the Canine Queen's puppies and help them celebrate new lives.